CLUB II
LIVE FREE OR DIE

WALTER GRANT
ONE OF AMERICA'S ENDURING PATRIOT AUTHORS

PO Box 221974 Anchorage, Alaska 99522-1974
books@publicationconsultants.com—www.publicationconsultants.com

ISBN 978-1-59433-656-0
eBook ISBN 978-1-59433-657-7
Library of Congress Catalog Card Number: 2016954281

—First Edition—

Manufactured in the United States of America.

This book is dedicated to
the navy recruiter who
provided me the opportunity
to escape the failure
I was destined for, opened
my eyes to new horizons,
reality vs. fantasy—the world

Other books by Walter Grant

Fulltiming,
RVing America through the Eyes of Honeybee the Cat
ISBN 978-1-59433-018-2

D.B. Cooper, Where are You
ISBN 978-1-59433-076-6

A Sound of Freedom
ISBN 978-1-59433-038-4

The Club, Revolution Continues
ISBN 978-1-59433-550-1

Special thanks to:
Jim for sharing his expertise on scotch.
Lyle, my go-to forensics specialist
Bill and Judy, my DC connection
Shelby Jean for helping with my French
Henry Norris & Associates Inc for help with Club Holly
Charlene for always being there
Pensacola Writers and Critique Group
for helping me become a better writer.

Contents

Prologue

With my debt to The Club paid in full I walked away with the loves of my life to live out my dreams in some quiet remote part of the world where the girls and I could watch from afar as America imploded—it was just a matter of time. Money was not a problem. A domestic terrorist turned traitor unknowingly helped me run a con by brokering a deal with four officials from a middle-eastern country.

They believed the X-47B prototype, an autonomous aerial platform capable of delivering a five megaton nuclear weapon, could be theirs for fifty million dollars. Anna, Rita, and I killed all five. We took their money and gave it to The Club. The director awarded each of us ten percent for services rendered.

For the next three years we lived out our fantasies in the world of *Condé Nast*. Life was perfect or so we thought. The realization came to us one afternoon while we frolicked in the surf at our villa in the Society Islands—duty and honor demanded we return home. Home was America and The Club. We could not forsake either.

The director, eager to have us return to the fold, agreed to give us a free hand in reorganizing The Club from reactionary to revolutionary. We began preparing for war: the media would soon be weighing their dishonesty in reporting the news against their personal safety.

"The press is our chief ideological weapon." —Nikita Khrushchev.

Corrupt elected officials, who lined their pockets with kickbacks and by selling the influence of their office without fear of retribution, would soon be panicked and looking over their shoulders.

"Men are moved by two levers only: fear and self interest." —Napoleon

Our third attack would be against education—university professors and the teachers union. History has been rewritten and taught to the point students believed America to be an oppressor nation rather than a model country for humanity, a nation with the greatest opportunity for individual freedom than any country to ever exist anywhere in the world.

It is imperative truth and honesty be returned to the classroom. Otherwise, guilt instilled in the minds of today's youth via misinformation, half truths, omitted facts, and out and out lies, would, as the next governing generation hand over our sovereignty to the United Nations and America, soon to be followed by all other countries, would be ruled by a one-world dictator.

"Whoever has the youth has the future." —Mein Kampf'

The Club was created and set in motion by our Founding Fathers and patriots of the revolution to save America from the fate all other countries have experienced—desolation by means of a corrupt and ever expanding central government. Will our efforts be too little too late? We don't know.

As the Continental Congress adjourned, after having framed our governing document, a woman asked Benjamin Franklin, *"What have you given us?"*

He replied, *"Madam, we have given you a republic, if you can keep it."*

The Club's mandate is to keep it.

Going Home

"When adventure's lost its meaning, I'll be homeward bound . . . ."

—Marta Keen

In French Polynesia tides rarely vary more than two feet. We could step off our lanai into the water—very convenient for a beach-bum lifestyle. Relaxing on a chaise lounge, shaded by one of the numerous palms surrounding our villa, I watched Anna and Rita riding boogie boards in the gentle surf. Unlike the girls, I was not a sun worshiper. I did, however, appreciate their disdain for swimsuits and their no-tan-lines approach to sunbathing. I sat marveling at their Venus-sculptured bodies, glistening golden in the late afternoon sun, and smiled. I had to be the luckiest guy on the face of the earth. Anna and Rita were two of the most beautiful women in the world and they were totally dedicated to me, body and soul.

Thinking back to the strange set of circumstances that had brought Anna and me together—an angel sent to protect me.

My boss had sent me on a mission to confirm his suspicions of something wrong involving a project on Sakhalin Island, Russia. There was more amiss than he'd anticipated. Anna, the daughter of a GRU defector, coordinated with my boss, half a world away, and saved my life by arranging for us to be smuggled out of Russia. Four months later she rescued me again when I was scheduled to be executed for the murder of my fiancée. A crime I did not commit. It had been a perfect frame—well thought out and faultlessly executed. She introduced me to the Club. I was accepted, signed a blood oath, and given my initiation project. Again, Anna was there for me.

With the mission completed, we took a holiday on the Italian Riviera. By the time we returned to the Club we were one—heart and soul. Rita had been one of the first people I'd met at the Club. Six months after our return from Italy, Anna invited her into our bed and the three of us were united for life.

We were multimillionaires. We could go anywhere we wanted. Do and have anything we pleased. For the last three years we had traveled extensively and played out our fantasies in resorts and ancient ruins throughout the world of *Condé Nast*. So why was I getting bored? I sensed restlessness in the girls as well.

I watched them climb the four steps to our lanai. Rita moved my feet to one side and sat down at the end of the chaise lounge. Anna remained standing while presenting me with a pose she knew I'd appreciate. Looking sexy wasn't intentional—it was impossible for her to avoid. She would look sexy in a potato sack, so would Rita. Anna was the first to speak.

"We need some action."

I knew exactly what she alluded to, but decided to have some fun by pretending I didn't have a clue. "Girls, I'm hurt; I'm doing the best I can." At that they picked me up, carried me down the steps, and threw me into the ocean. They took turns holding my head underwater until I finally sputtered, "Okay girls, I give up. What do you want?"

"Don't get cute with us. You know what we want. We want to kill somebody."

They were serious, and so was I when I answered. "I know. I've known for some time. Let's do it."

Looking at these thirty-year-old women, one would believe them to be as innocent as debutantes. In reality, they were cold-blooded killers. Rita would slit your throat while you were admiring her smile. Anna would blow your head off without a second thought. We were a team of killers dedicated to a cause.

In the beginning I had been eager to join the cause. Not just to pay my debt to the Club for saving my life, but because there were people that deserve to die—for some it was the only logical solution. It had been the same for Anna and Rita. Now, for me, and I suspected for the girls as well, the thrill was as exhilarating as the cause. Walter Eloy Goe once said, "There is no greater fulfillment than hunting a human predator equally armed with cunning and intelligence. Once you have done so, you will never care for anything less."

Over dinner we relived memories and made plans for returning to the Club. As servants were clearing the table, spreading a fresh tablecloth, and replacing our napkins and silver, our chef approached and asked our preference for dessert. "Girls: this calls for something special."

I turned to Mickael, "Do we have any Remy Martin XO?"

"*Oui monsieur*, we have a bottle of XO Excellence Special Reserve."

"Great, can you whip up some crêpe suzettes using the Remy Martin rather than Grand Marnier?"

Mickael, sporting a wide grin, replied with enthusiasm, "*Oui monsieur*!"

I figured he was excited because he intended to pinch a dram of three-hundred-dollar cognac. "We'll have the remainder of the bottle in warmed snifters."

"*Très bon, monsieur; tout de suite, monsieur*." Normally one thinks of iced drinks when in the tropics, but to sip a vintage cognac and breathe in the vapors climbing the sides of the snifter is a treat anywhere, anytime—even on a starry night in the Society Islands.

As the dessert settings were taken away, I asked Alphonse to bring my satellite phone. I checked for the Director's private number, put the phone on speaker, and touched the call banner. He answered without using names; I suspected he had me set up on a special ringtone, and my name, no doubt, popped up on his call screen.

"I expected you'd call earlier—you made me wait two years longer than I anticipated."

"Well, sir, time passes quickly when you're enjoying life, but the girls and I have had about as much fun as we can stand. We're ready to come home and get back to work, if we're still welcome."

"You and your ladies will always be welcome. You have a home for life—may it be long and rewarding. I look forward to seeing you."

"And we you, sir." When I disconnected, the girls looked at each other and giggled. For thirty-year-old women they giggled a lot. Anna, looking at Rita, arched an eyebrow and cocked her head slightly as she pushed her chair away from the table. Rita turned to look at me and said, "This calls for a celebration."

"I thought we just did that."

She responded with a sly grin as she pushed back her chair—Anna was already standing. "Oh no, we just had dessert, now we're going to celebrate; see you in the hot tub."

I smiled as I watched them walk toward the Jacuzzi, shedding clothes as they went.

Anna, being the take-charge kind of girl she was, arranged for a Bombardier Global Express with a full crew for the flight from Papeete, Tahiti to Albany, New York international. We preferred paying seventy-four thousand dollars for a chartered jet to spending between fourteen and fifteen hours on a commercial flight, while enduring hassling by TSA, and dealing with layovers, transfers, and atrocious food.

It was two in the afternoon by the time the pilot rotated and we climbed out and leveled off above a few scattered cumulus clouds. We would be airborne for twelve hours and cross six time zones. If all went well, we'd touchdown in Albany by eight the next morning. The hostess having just served us hors d'oeuvres and wine hovered nearby as we toasted our next, yet to be determined, adventure when Anna said, "This is a lot more comfortable than our first flight together—do you remember our ride into Yuzhno-Sakhalinsk and the flight to Narita Airport?"

"Of course I remember, but as for comfort—I don't know. I enjoyed the time I spent stuffed into a shipping crate with you. It was very cozy."

"You didn't like it enough to let me initiate you into the mile-high club."

"Things were different, as I'm sure you remember. Back then Emily was my only reason for living."

"I remember. I admired you for your principles but was disappointed. I've never handled rejection well. That wasn't the first or the last time you turned me down. You refused my invitation to spend the night in my quarters at our work center on Sakhalin Island. You did it again at the ANA Hotel in Tokyo and the Captain Cook in Anchorage."

"You were wearing down my resistance, but in my heart I was married to Emily."

"I know, but it was hurtful. Now, looking back, it is reassuring when I remember those times. I know nothing will ever separate the three of us—not even death. I'll come back from the other side to be with you and protect you if ever you should need me."

"You're right, we will never be separated. Does the invitation to induct me into the mile-high club still hold?" She smiled, set her wine goblet down, stood, crooked a finger and without looking back walked toward the Bombardier's master bedroom. I took another sip of wine and set the glass next to Anna's. As I stood, a soft voice from across the table asked,

"What about me?" I smiled at Rita, and nodded aft. A moment later there were three wine goblets sitting unattended on a table, two beautiful ladies, and one ecstatic gentleman leisurely walking toward the master suite in the rear of the plane.

We touched down in Albany and taxied to a stop at our assigned parking. A car was waiting to take us and our bags to customs. We cleared without incident. Outside, Mr. Wilson was waiting—besides the doctor and nurse tending me as I came out of the drug-induced coma that had simulated my execution for the murder of my fiancée, Emily Davis, Mr. Wilson was the first person I'd met at the Club. He opened the door to a limousine while his driver collected our bags. We were about to climb into the limo when a voice from inside said, "Welcome home." It was the voice of the director.

"Thank you, sir. It's good to be home. This is an unanticipated pleasure. We didn't expect to see you until dinner."

"Did you not remember me saying, 'You and your lovely young ladies take your sabbatical. Travel where you will, explore, live, enjoy, write memories and secrets on the ferrite-cores of your minds to be recalled and relived on some rainy day in the distant future. On the morning the three of you wake and are clear in your minds as to what you want to do with the rest of your lives and decide to continue with the way you are living, I wish you happiness and bliss for so long as you may live.

"'If you awake to find that you are bored and choose to rededicate your lives to the Club, I will be here to welcome you home.'"

"I remember, sir. I was genuinely moved."

"Well, I'm here, Mr. Scott. Welcome home."

Our quarters were spotless. The fridge had been restocked. Linens and towels had been refreshed. Clothes we'd left behind were clean and fresh and either hung on custom racks or lay neatly folded in drawers in our dressing room. Things were otherwise just as we'd left them. The director sensed we would return, but didn't know when.

A two-year-old edition of a DC area newspaper lay on the breakfast bar. The headline read: "After a year and a half of investigation, the deaths of a local superior court judge and her husband have been determined to be a murder-suicide. A note left by her husband alluded to his wife's affairs, and went on to accuse his wife and her lover, an attorney, of subverting the justice system for personal gain."

The story went on to say the attorney had been arraigned by a grand jury and was bound over to stand trial. A later edition of the same paper had been opened to an article stating that although the attorney had been disbarred for unethical behavior, he and his lawyer had plea-bargained the charges down to a ten-year prison term.

I made a note of his release day: I would impose the appropriate sentence at a later date. A sentence the courts should have handed down.

The headline of another edition read: "Alleged Maryland drug deal turned violent leaving five people dead." According to the article, there was no indication if the five victims were at the meeting as buyers or sellers of drugs—no drugs or money had been found. It appeared the deal had been brokered by one of the victims who'd recently purchased the property where the crime had taken place. Mohammad El, a domestic terrorist of the Woodstock generation and a recent Muslim convert, had been found at the scene with his throat cut and additional knife wounds. The other victims had been shot to death. No weapons of any kind had been found at the crime scene. A bigger mystery—a limousine registered to one of the Middle Eastern embassies in DC was the only vehicle found at the scene. The ambassador admitted the limo belonged to his embassy, but denied knowing why it was at the crime scene or how it got there. Also, he denied knowing any of the victims found at the scene although four of the dead men were carrying diplomatic passports issued by the country in question. Forensics had been unable to give law enforcement any clues as to who killed the five people or how many had been involved. After a year's investigation, authorities had been unable to identify or locate any associates of Mohammad El able to shed any light on who might have been involved in the killing. With diplomatic immunity the ambassador could not be forced to cooperate with authorities and he volunteered nothing, so all records had been moved to the cold-case file.

Reading between the lines, it appeared both cases had been put to bed and there had been nothing to connect the girls or me to the crimes.

The Bombardier's cabin crew had served us hors d'oeuvres and vintage wine, gourmet meals and vintage wine, desserts and vintage wine to the point we never wanted to see food or wine again. All the food combined with jetlag was taking its toll on our energy. We decided to skip lunch and sleep until it was time to dress for dinner. With six hours' rest we would, hopefully, be reenergized and ready for our homecoming party. Nothing had been said to indicate we would have anything other than dinner, but with my ability to read people, I knew the director had something elaborate planned.

Normally we would've entered the dining room a few minutes ahead of the director—this was tradition for all Club members. He always entered promptly at eight. Tonight the director had insisted we bestow on him the honor of escorting us into the dining room. I thought he was making a bit too much of our return.

The dress code for breakfast and lunch was casual. For dinner, coats and ties were required for gentlemen and dresses for the ladies. No one noticed me in my navy pinstripes. All eyes were on the girls. Anna, a blue-eyed, drop-dead-gorgeous blonde with her hair done up in a French twist and wearing a strapless full-length-red dress with matching five-inch heels was on my right arm. Rita in an equally stunning emerald green strapless gown and heels, with her flaming red hair in an upsweep style and a princess's braid, hung onto my left arm as we followed the director into the dining room.

From my first dinner with the director to the last, custom had demanded everyone be seated before the director's arrival. Guests at his table would stand as he approached. He dined at the center table. Tonight the three round tables with their seven chairs each had been replaced with a 30-foot oval. Two of the regular tables were situated in corners opposite the mirrored window looking into the main dining room. Curtains had been drawn to insure sound originating in our small dining room could not be heard inside the resort's public dining room. The six o'clock and ten o'clock seating had been canceled, with everyone dining at eight. Everyone stood and began cheering as we entered. The cheering continued as the director led us to three empty chairs at the head of the table. He then walked to an unclaimed chair at the opposite end, quieted the guests, and invited everyone to be seated. He remained standing. Another tradition, the director always announced his choice for dinner—he chose for everyone at his table—before delivering his monologue. Tonight was no different.

"To welcome home our prodigal son and daughters the Club will endeavor to duplicate their farewell dinner. We will feast on Lobster Thermidor and we will be serving a Grand Cru Chardonnay from the Côte d'Or district of central France. For dessert we are having crêpe suzettes and a beerenauslese from the cellars of Bernkasteler Doctor."

He waited for the usual approval of his choice for dinner. This time the guests went beyond their "good choice" and other polite compliments with applause. This, I surmised, was part of our welcome-home tribute. He then began his monologue.

"I'm sure you remember when, three and a half years ago, Mr. Scott, Miss Anna, and Miss Rita"—he addressed us with titles to show respect, as was the Club's tradition—"took down five enemies of America in a single operation and donated fifty million dollars to the Club before they departed on a three-year sabbatical. They have returned to the Club, and rededicated their lives to our cause, ready to do battle. Please join with me in welcoming them home."

There was more applause and a hearty chorus of "Hear! Hear!" followed by several individual toasts. The director picked up his monologue. "Let us enjoy dinner and then Mr. Scott and his team will lay out a plan that just might save America from the chaos of socialism and the Constitution from becoming a meaningless document. The Club, at its inception, was charged with protecting the country and the Constitution. The first name on the Club's founding document is the same as the first name on the Declaration of Independence. Consider those things as we dine and make merry, and then we will hear from Mr. Scott and his team."

I wasn't comfortable with the spotlight shining on me with such intensity. As I looked around the table I recognized all but a few and remembered their names. A few, like me, had been unjustly accused of a capital crime and rescued from the gallows. Others, due to exemplarily acts on behalf of America, had been invited into the Club. Seated next to the director was a retired judge. Most other professions were represented, as were the trades, with a scattering of doctors, accountants, truck drivers, law enforcement officers, mechanics, electricians, school teachers, computer programmers, nurses, and others—even a member of the media, a politician, and a couple of Hollywood's aging celebrities.

These dinner guests were people who, on the street or in their places of business, would appear as normal everyday Americans. Actually they were normal everyday Americans who had taken patriotism a step beyond the "Rainy-Day Patriot and Sunshine Soldier" to the level where all truly loyal Americans wanted to go, would have gone had they not lacked the courage to take one more step.

These patriots were aware of the dangers America faced, and chose to take a stand. They would accept the satisfaction of success or the consequence of failure—whatever their fate might be. Like me, they were all assassins. Five kills were required to pay your debt to the Club for rescuing you from whatever peril had befallen you. If you were someone who had caught the eye of the recruitment team because of your attitude and deeds and after an extensive investigation you were given the opportunity to apply for membership and you accepted, the price was the same, five kills.

We sometimes took extended holidays, but no one ever abandoned the Club after their debt was paid. Odds were against us, but we were confident our dedication and action would serve to preserve freedom, the Constitution, and the American Way. We, like the revolutionaries when they signed the Declaration of Independence, pledged everything when we signed the Club's blood oath. Like the revolutionaries, we dared not fail.

The table was cleared, tablecloths brushed, and we were left with a half glass of Beerenauslese. The director took an envelope from his inside breast pocket, removed the two sheets of paper, and called for quiet. "Ladies and gentlemen, I want to read to you the letter Mr. Scott and his lovely ladies left with me on the night of their farewell dinner before they departed for places unknown more than three years ago. I have discussed its contents with the directors of all other chapters of the Club. They gave their wholehearted approval to Mr. Scott's proposal. They pledged their support in whatever capacity Mr. Scott may require of them."

He paused for a few seconds as he scanned the faces of those at the table, and then began:

> To members of the media:
> I not only suggest, I beseech you to read this letter as many times as necessary to fully understand its meaning. There are one hundred names on the list accompanying this letter. You received a copy of the letter only if your name is on the list. Do not discuss the letter with anyone not on the list. The first person to mention the letter or refer to it publicly will automatically go to the top of the list. Otherwise, you will be chosen according to how you conduct yourselves during broadcasts from this day forward. You and you alone can determine your position on the list. You will move up or down the list depending on how you report the news.
>
> Should you continue to editorialize the news so as to promote a socialist agenda and undermine capitalism, liberty, and the freedom that is America, you will move up the list.

Should you begin reporting the news truthfully and in its entirety, you can move your name down the list until it drops off and is replaced with another name. Names will be added to the list regardless of how many are removed. If your network insists you continue your agenda of deceit and treachery, if they insist you continue to knowingly misinform and mislead the American people, it will behoove you to retire as of this moment.

I know what you are thinking and I know the question you're asking. Who is this nutcase? A simple answer: I am an unelected representative of the American people, a self-appointed defender of the Constitution and the American Way. If it were within my power I would arrest and deport each and every one of you for sedition. Since I do not have that power, I will remove you one by one until you decide that deceit is not in your best interest.

Now you are thinking, I'll give this letter to my boss. He'll call in the FBI and Homeland Security and they'll have this psycho before he makes his first move. I'm a network anchor, loved and respected throughout the world. No one can touch me even if they dared try. Before calling your boss you may want to review the first paragraph of this letter.

I can understand your thinking, but I have a few questions for you, if I may. When you eat at your favorite restaurant; how well do you know the chef who prepared your food? How well do you know the waiter who brings your food to the table? What about the *sommelier*? Did the glass he poured wine into for you to taste and approve have an invisible coating of polonium 210? How well do you know your doctor, your barber, your manicurist, your masseuse or masseur, your housekeeper, your chauffeur, your wife or husband, mistress or paramour, or for that matter, your friends?

Let us fast-forward. You attend the funeral of a fellow reporter who died of a heart attack. You check: yes, his name is on the list. Was his heart failure due to natural causes or was it chemically induced? You feel a prick on the neck. Was it a mosquito or was it a needle concealed in the cane of the guy standing behind you? He wasn't limping when he walked away.

A reporter you work with went on vacation and didn't return. It's been six months and no one has heard from her. Is she still alive? Is her name on the list? Again, you check. The answer is yes. A reporter from an affiliate station was killed by a drive-by shooter. Was he in the wrong place at the wrong time or was he assassinated? You check the list: yes his name is there.

You start looking over your shoulder and begin considering the best way to preserve your longevity. You reread the letter and review the first paragraph. You notice some reporters are softening their references toward capitalism and taking a harder line against socialism. They are taking a tougher stance on crime and now favor the death penalty.

You check the list. Yes, their names are there. You are talking to yourself, although not verbally. Your dreams turn to nightmares. You're asking: Should I follow suit? Should I dispense with the anti-American rhetoric? Should I start speaking out against liberal causes when I know they are wrong? Should I stop promoting statements made and statistics given by politicians as true when I know that in fact they are lies?

Perhaps I should quit my job. If I resigned, how would I eat, how would I continue living the lifestyle my seven-figure salary provides?

A natural gas leak explosion levels a fellow reporter's house. Yes, he was home and yes, he's dead. Yes he was near the top of the list. A new list arrives, names of the four dead reporters have been removed, and four new ones have been added. Your name is now closer to the top. You call your doctor and tell him you need a new prescription for Valium.

No; none of this has happened. It's merely a preview scenario of what is in store for you and your fellow conspirators. It is coming to a TV station near you. Now would be a good time to reassess the things important to you—namely your life and well-being. You may want to start hoarding Valium prescriptions.

There was complete silence as he replaced the letter inside the envelope and returned it to his pocket. No one moved or spoke and several jaws were agape. The director paused long enough to give everyone a chance to collect their thoughts before announcing, "Mr. Scott has agreed to brief you on his plan, or I should say plans. This is only the beginning of the assault he has in mind for those whose sole objective is to replace capitalism with socialism and freedom with slavery, thus destroying the most prosperous country, whose citizens enjoy more freedom and the highest standard of living to ever exist in any nation anywhere in the world past or present."

He looked at me with the same glint in his eye I'd seen when he read my letter for the first time, and said, "Mr. Scott."

"Thank you, sir." After acknowledging the director's introduction I stood without speaking for several seconds making eye contact as I scanned the faces of everyone sitting at the table. I let the suspense build. By the time I delivered my opening remark they were sitting on pins and needles, but dared not show any sign of anxiety.

"Ladies and gentlemen of the Club, I am honored to be in your company. It is indeed a privilege to speak with you tonight. It is my utmost desire to win your respect and support. Although I have been a Club member for a relatively short time I sensed the concern of the founders from the very beginning. It was for this reason I accepted the Club's invitation to join, not because the option, shall we say, would have been inconvenient.

"With my debt paid (seven assassinations sanctioned by the Club) I believed I could walk away—I could not. I asked myself: How much do I love my country? I answered: enough to make the ultimate sacrifice in her defense. I then asked two more questions: How far will I go? What are my limits? The answer for me, and it should be the same for you: I will go as far as I can and be limited only by death. By then I trust, with your help, the tide will have turned.

"The Club's founders were clairvoyant. Although the Constitution was written in such a way as to limit the growth of government and empire building within, they knew it would not be sufficient to prevent the tyrannical mind from finding a way to circumvent the intent of the governing document. They founded the Club as a counterbalance. They put their faith in the Club's members to keep their dream of an enduring free republic alive. We let them down.

"Abraham Lincoln confirmed the founders' fear of a central government to be justified when he said: 'All the armies of Europe, Asia, and

Africa combined . . . could not by force, take a drink from the Ohio, or make a track on the Blue Ridge, in a trial of a thousand years. At what point, then, is the approach of danger to be expected? If destruction be our lot, we must ourselves be its author and finisher. As a nation of freemen, we must live through all time, or die by suicide.'" I paused and once again took several seconds as I scanned the wide-eyed faces at the table before continuing.

"No informed American can deny the enemy within is entrenched throughout society. The media tell us what the enemy would have us believe. The enemy in government gives us food, housing, and money for our votes. The enemy in schools teaches our children the family nucleus restrains growth of the individual and enslaves women. The enemy in Hollywood teaches that corporations are evil. Our enemies tell us capitalism robs the poor and makes the rich richer. History paints a different picture. Prior to capitalism the only way to become wealthy was to steal from your fellow man. With the introduction of capital tools you could prosper by serving your fellow man.

"In 42 BC Marcus Tullius Cicero, a Roman orator and statesman, foresaw the same threat to the Roman Empire as President Lincoln perceived to be the weakness of America and western civilization. Cicero said, 'A nation can survive its fools, and even the ambitious. But it cannot survive treason from within. An enemy at the gates is less formidable, for he is known and carries his banner openly. But the traitor moves amongst those within the gate freely, his sly whispers rustling through the alley, heard in the very halls of government itself.

"For the traitor appears not a traitor; he speaks in accents familiar to his victims, and he wears their face and their arguments, he appeals to the baseness that lies deep in the heart of all men. He rots the soul of a nation, he works secret and unknown in the night to undermine the pillars of the city, he infects the body politic so it can no longer resist. A murderer is less to fear.'

"Our members are the most enlightened men and women in the world. If the three branches of government were suddenly populated with our members, within two years America would be humming along like the proverbial well-oiled machine. The desire to be free and have the opportunity to be the best we can be lives in the hearts of all mankind. However, in too many parts of the world that spirit has been suppressed to the point it is no longer considered possible—it is only a dream. For some the dream is dead.

"Propaganda distributed via all known instruments of communication assaults the minds of every American twenty-four seven, and manipulates their thinking and understanding of right and wrong. We face the same evil that brought down once powerful and noble civilizations—treason within the gates. The evil is repackaged and presented in a different form for each occasion and each age group. It is veiled in emotion—envy and guilt are the basic tools these saboteurs employ.

"To control the masses, you first corrupt the minds of the children. As Mrs. Marion D. Sprout, a Boston school teacher, said in 1919. 'Give us one generation of small children to train to manhood and womanhood and we will set up the Bolshevist form of the Soviet government.' In American schools our enemies teach children that work, responsibility, paying their own way, and providing for financial security in their old age are passé and irrelevant. Young people are taught they need not be concerned with responsibility since the government will provide for all their needs. By throwing off the enslaving principles of the past they will be free to indulge in whatever pleasures they find fulfilling. The director referred to the enemies' desire to replace capitalism with socialism. This is true. In my opinion, socialism vs. communism is a distinction without a difference. Karl Marx knew communism would not flourish without first destroying capitalism in America. Socialism has failed everywhere it has been tried—it failed because America remained strong. The destruction of America was designed more than one hundred years ago. It began with baby steps, now it is galloping toward the finish line.

"Our enemies began making inroads in secret and became more emboldened upon realizing our constitution could be used against us. They came out into the open when the Woodstock generation infiltrated and gained control of schools, courts, the media, and government—communists held government positions as far back as 1920. We are at war and nothing less than total defeat of our country's enemies will suffice; otherwise, in time liberty will become another meaningless word and the entrepreneurial spirit will die. When this happens, our enemies will have succeeded in their quest for a one-world government of serfs and kings—and we will then understand the meaning of the line from a Chris Kristofferson song 'Freedom's just another word for nothing left to lose.'

"Small bands with the spark of liberty and the dream of freedom from tyranny still burning in their hearts may rise up from time to time. They will be put down and systematically eliminated by the central government. The American Revolution was a one-time thing—it will never happen again. For us, it is now or never. America's fate is in our hands."
I lifted my glass, swirled the wine, held it to my nose and breathed in the bouquet, lifted it above my head, and paused for a moment.

"I invite you to join me in a toast first offered by General John Stark, a hero of the American Revolution." Again I paused and then delivered the toast with a commanding voice, "Live free or die."

Everyone at the table raised their glasses as high as they could and repeated the toast in thunderous unison, "Live free or die."

We drank our glasses empty. I thanked everyone and introduced Anna. She arose slowly and held up her hands to quiet the applause.

"We are well aware" she said, "that those we see on our television screens sitting behind tables reporting the news have little to do with what is broadcast. Owners and presidents of the networks are the ones who tell producers what they want the public to see and hear. These people will be on the list and will be included in our action. Within six months of the date we send out our first 100 letters, we will have the attention of every man and woman in the business—we will not limit our fight to television news, we will engage all media in all medians.

"Sooner or later some of our letters will be turned over to the authorities. With this in mind, we must make absolutely certain nothing is traceable back to the Club or to any member. Every precaution must be taken to insure that every letter is free of DNA and fingerprints. Copy paper will be purchased from a different store for each batch of letters. Computers used must never have been linked to the Internet or be equipped with Wi-Fi or a camera. After each batch of letters has been printed the computer and printer will be destroyed.

"For those of you willing to engage the enemy, I need you to choose a codename—use geographical references, such as Black Hills, Amsterdam, Everglades, and so on—also, give me a direct line of communications. Do not use or reference your Club name. The only other information I require is areas of expertise and dates you will be available. Please leave your information with the concierge marked Sooners. I will be the keeper of all lists. Other than me, only Mr. Scott and Miss Rita will have access to them. The lists will be coded. Without the key you will be unable to retrieve information. Access codes necessary for retrieving information will change every minute. Only Mr. Scott, Miss Rita, and I will know the formula necessary to determine the code for any particular day and time. Rest assured as the daughter of a GRU colonel, I understand codes. Not even veterans of the Black Chamber using supercomputers would, in a thousand years, break my codes."

While Anna had everyone's attention, members of the serving staff had poured a small amount of Beerenauslese into the wine glasses we'd emptied when I delivered my toast. Anna lifted her goblet and said, "We are all alive today because the Club gave us a second chance. In return we can do nothing less than to give America a second chance." She asked compellingly, "Are you with us?"

Everyone answered fervently in a single voice, "We're with you." Anna then raised her glass and repeated the toast I'd delivered, "Live free or die." Again the toast was repeated in unison and reverberated off the walls.

I stood and let the applause continue for a minute or so before I held up my hands for quiet and introduced Rita. Before anyone had a chance to applaud she bolted from her chair and began with a challenge.

"In July of 1776, fifty-six courageous men pledged their lives, their fortunes, and their sacred honor by placing their names on the most famous document ever written—the declaration of America's independence from England. Five signers were captured by the British as traitors, and tortured before they died. Twelve had their homes ransacked and burned.

"Two lost their sons serving in the Revolutionary Army; another had two sons captured. Nine of the fifty-six fought and died from wounds or hardships of the Revolutionary War. What kind of men were they?

"Twenty-four were lawyers and jurists. Eleven were merchants, nine were farmers and large plantation owners—men of means, well educated, but they signed the Declaration of Independence knowing full well that the penalty would be death if they were captured.

"Carter Braxton of Virginia, a wealthy planter and trader, saw his ships swept from the seas by the British navy. He sold his home and properties to pay his debts, and died in rags.

"Thomas McKeam was so hounded by the British that he was forced to move his family constantly. He served in the Congress without pay, and his family was kept in hiding. His possessions were taken from him, and poverty his reward.

"Vandals or soldiers looted the properties of Dillery, Hall, Clymer, Walton, Gwinnett, Heyward, Ruttledge, and Middleton. At the battle of Yorktown, Thomas Nelson, Jr., noted that the British General Cornwallis had taken over the Nelson home for his headquarters. He quietly urged General George Washington to open fire. The home was destroyed, and Nelson died bankrupt.

"Francis Lewis had his home and properties destroyed. The enemy jailed his wife, and she died within a few months.

"John Hart was driven from his wife's bedside as she lay dying. Their thirteen children fled for their lives. His fields and his gristmill were laid to waste. For more than a year he lived in forests and caves, returning home to find his wife dead and his children vanished.

"Think about these things for a moment and realize everything you are and everything you have you owe to these men and men like them. Be reminded that 'freedom isn't free,' and then ask what can I do? What do I owe these men? What would they have me do in the face of our present-day threat to liberty? What would you say to these men if they were here and asked you to pledge your lives, your fortunes, and your sacred honor?" She hesitated long enough for her question to resonate with her audience before continuing.

"We are the Club. We did pledge our lives, our fortunes, and our sacred honor when we signed in blood our loyalty to the Club and to America."

Again she hesitated for a moment and then in a voice no one could ignore said, "Our time has come!"

She held both hands above her head, palms out and asked, "Are you with us?" Every Club member at the table held up both hands and shouted, "Live free or die!"

She stood silent for a moment before turning to me. She took her seat as I stood. Everyone was applauding wildly. I held up my hand and called for silence—it didn't happen right away. After the applause died away I waited for a few seconds before saying, "My team would give up everything and make the ultimate sacrifice in a single heartbeat to honor our founders. I am convinced you would do the same. As eager as we all are to serve we must not break with the Club's tradition. Under no circumstances are we to carry out any action not sanctioned by the Club—we cannot and must not put the Club at risk. At this time it would behoove us to keep in mind a statement by Joseph Stalin: 'Any fool can commit a murder, but it takes an artist to commit a good natural death.' We will all have a chance to contribute—be patient, wait your turn."

I relinquished to the director by saying, "My team and I thank you for the welcome-home party." I paused and added, "It's good to be home."

I wasn't paying attention to what the director was saying. I was contemplating the scenario Anna, Rita, and I had laid out and set in motion. I never doubted the girl's devotion to the cause, but wondered, "Am I up to the task?"

One Traitor at a Time

"The tree of liberty must be refreshed from time to time with the blood of patriots and tyrants."

—Thomas Jefferson

I had considered we'd be slow in setting the program in motion. I was wrong. By the end of the following day everyone in our local chapter had left their information with the concierge. The director of our chapter served as the director in charge of all chapter directors—the DIC was chosen by a vote of all directors every four years. He had set the stage at the annual director's conference three years earlier shortly after I'd first proposed my plan. With my return, and after the girls and I spoke to the members of our chapter, he dispatched Club members to all chapters within the United States with our speeches recorded on thumb drives. The video and audio were to be played on each chapter's in-house-systems. The miniature hard drives were to never leave the courier's sight—copies would not be permitted. The courier's assignment was threefold: to insure our speeches were played to each chapter's general assembly, make certain the thumb drives were destroyed, and to return with the data Anna required—100 percent of the Club's membership volunteered the necessary information.

It took Anna nearly a month to encode all the data. In the meantime, Rita and I drove to Chicago. After checking into a hotel on the Magnificent Mile, we located an Office Depot and paid cash for an inkjet printer, a ream of twenty-five pound copy paper, 120 number-10 business envelopes, and a plastic bottle filled with liquid, said to be specifically designed for moistening glue on the envelope flaps. Underneath the bottle's plastic cap was a sponge stopper. At a pawn store, we found a two-year-old laptop without a camera or microphone. Again, we paid in cash. We purchased latex gloves, hairnets, a plastic sheet, and surgical masks from a pharmaceutical chain store. We weren't worried about leaving DNA or fingerprints on the printer or laptop. We were only concerned with the copy paper and envelopes and stamps.

Rita could keyboard 150 words a minute, so I left her to compose the letter and address the envelopes while I made a trip to the post office. I purchased twelve books of no-lick stamps. I was grateful when the lady serving the window put them into a little wax-paper envelope without me having to ask. I paid, thanked the lady, and left the building. Outside I dropped the stamps into a plastic produce bag, folded the bag a couple of times and placed it in my pocket.

Back at the hotel, Rita informed me she'd finished with the letter and asked me to read and approve it. I suggested two changes. As she began making the modifications, I donned a hair net, mask, and latex gloves, and then spread the rubber sheet on a coffee table in the sitting area of our suite.

While I unpackaged and laid out the copy paper, envelopes, and the bottle of moistening liquid on the sheet, Rita finished modifications to the letter. She then slipped on a hairnet and pushed her hair up underneath it, placed a mask over her mouth and nose, and pulled on a pair of gloves. We were extra careful not to touch anything other than the paper and envelopes. I loaded the printer with as many envelopes as the printer tray would hold.

We'd prepared the list of recipients from names given us by the chapter directors. Each director had submitted ten names to be considered. We completed the list before leaving home (the Catskills resort) and copied it to a flash drive and one backup drive. We'd started with the first name on each list—there were quite a few duplications. Each time we found an identical name we dropped down the page until we found a name not already on our list. We could have copied the letter onto the flash drive as well, but the letter, unlike the list of names, suggested a threat to the addressees. This could have been a problem had Rita and I been involved in an accident and the flash drive fallen into the hands of enforcement.

Rita had already plugged the flash drive into the computer. Using keystroke commands, she started printing addresses on the envelopes. Once finished with the laptop, she would need a fresh pair of gloves.

We didn't want to leave the area normally used for the return address blank, so we used the addresses for local politicians—next time, we'd use a different city and category for return addresses. I kept removing the printed envelopes and adding blank ones until they were all addressed.

Next I loaded paper onto the printer tray and Rita started printing the letters. As each letter finished printing I removed it from the receiving tray and placed it on the rubber sheet with an envelope on top. We continued the process until we had one letter and one list of names for each envelope.

I started stuffing the envelopes as Rita, wearing new gloves, used the sponge-stopped bottle of liquid to moisten the glue on each flap, seal the envelope, and then return it to the rubber sheet. When finished, we affixed two no-lick stamps to each envelope before we dropped them into one of two plastic bags. We didn't know if the combined weight of the letter, the list of names, and envelope exceeded one ounce—maximum weight for a single first-class stamp. We didn't want them returned or go into the dead-letter box for a lack of postage. Any letters being returned to the sender's address would in all likelihood be turned over to the FBI.

We figured people would be less likely to pay attention to anyone dropping a bag of letters in a mailbox during rush hour. Rita drove to a post office on Randolph Street where I shook fifty letters from one of the bags into a mailbox. I did the same with the second bag at a post office further up Randolph. It was done—now the fun would begin.

Back at the hotel, we filled the bathtub and dropped in the laptop and printer—they would never work again—we would dispose of them later. I gathered up everything we used for our project, wrapped it up in the rubber sheet and placed them in a plastic bag. Our dinner reservation at Les Nomades was five hours away, so we showered and relaxed. Relaxed—well, maybe not, but we were relaxed by the time we dressed for dinner. On our way to Les Nomades, Rita spotted a bus stop with no one waiting. I dropped the plastic bag in the trash container between two benches. A second later, we were on our way to the restaurant.

Sisters

"You know you're in love when you can't fall asleep because reality is finally better than your dreams."
—Dr. Seuss

Les Nomades, although a bit pretentious, was quiet and comfortable with attentive service—someone was always nearby. We made small talk, commenting on the savory escargot, French with a hint of Asian spice. We continued the small talk through sautéed foie gras, lobster ravioli with deep-fried soft-shell crab, and duck consommé.

This was the first time Rita and I had been alone in a romantic setting. I had been awestruck by her at the time of my first dinner with the director, when he'd introduced Rita and offered a toast to her for taking out a traitor, Michael Lewis Scoozy. How could such a beautiful young woman be a cold-blooded killer? I'd wondered. Later I would learn that blood coursing through her veins ran hot and cold, depending on the nature of her emotions.

By the time white asparagus salads with ham and sliced black truffles arrived small talk had slipped into near silence. Conversation continued in on-again off-again spurts through the combination main course—two single entrées prepared so as to produce a third taste—served on a large plate attractively decorated with harmonizing vegetables. I sensed there was something she wanted to tell me or discuss with me. Was she waiting for a signal from me? It seemed so. She had, knowingly, or perhaps unknowingly, provided me with the opportunity to open the conversation. Where it would lead, I didn't know, and wasn't sure I wanted to know, but it appeared unavoidable.

Les Nomades required coats and ties for men and dresses for ladies. Rita was a very beautiful woman. Her evening-length black-décolleté dress, pearl necklace and earrings, combined with the soft lighting gave emphasis to just how beautiful she really was. I waited until the hazelnut and passion fruit soufflés arrived before commenting on her appearance, which led up to the question I hoped would give her the lead-in she'd been waiting for. "You're looking especially pretty this evening. The pearls are lovely and perfect accents for your dress. Where did you get them?" I already knew the answer. I recognized them as the ones I'd given Anna.

"They're the ones you gave Anna when you did an overnight at the ANA in Tokyo."

"I thought she really liked them. I didn't know she'd given them away."

"She would never give them away. They are her most prized possession. You should have realized by now we're sisters, we share everything."

I almost fell out of my chair as I stammered, "You and Anna are sisters?"

"Well, not biological sisters, but we are sisters. Her father died of a heart attack when she was fourteen years old. With no other family here in America, the Russian ambassador insisted she be turned over to him to be repatriated to the Soviet Union.

"Anna and I were friends from the time she and her father arrived in America. I surmise you already know her father was a colonel in the GRU. He defected and brought his daughter with him. Her mother had died a year earlier. Then, with no ties to the Soviet Union, he took advantage of the confusion after the wall came down, and made a deal with the CIA.

"I've never known what my father did other than he worked for some agency of the federal government and I've never made an effort to find out. I'm afraid if I start digging I'll bring attention to myself, something I don't need. Be that as it may, Anna and her father were placed in our care. We lived in a large house, on a moderately secluded farm in the Shenandoah Valley. There were several other houses on the property, occupied by families of men who worked the farm, and one cozy little guest cottage—this is where Anna and her father lived. My father stayed in DC during the week, but spent the weekends with us. For the first year they lived with us Anna's father spent a lot of time with my father when he went into the District. My mother did not want Anna staying alone in the cottage when her father was away, so she had my bedroom redecorated and added twin beds for the single bed I slept on. We soon became inseparable.

"Anna and I were the same age. Since the farm was isolated and I was home-schooled, I didn't have any close friends. Anna knew no one—she left all her friends behind in Moscow. So it was only natural we would become the closest of friends. She taught me Russian and I taught her English—my mother taught her American history and all other necessities to round out her education. Also, my mother, having been born in Bordeaux, taught us French. By age twelve we were fluent in and could type in three languages. During the six years between the time she and her father moved in with us and the time he had his heart attack, our friendship took on sister status and we shared everything."

"Wait a minute. You're telling me you are of French heritage."

"Yes, my mother traced her linage back to Charles the Hammer."

"Charles the who?"

"Charles the Hammer, also, known as Charles the Ugly. His real name was Charles Martel."

"Are you royalty? Should I be bowing down to you?"

"You may bow down to me if you like—I may insist on it from time to time. Charles was a statesman and great military leader who, as duke and prince of the Franks and mayor of the Palace, was de facto ruler of Francia from 718 until his death, but he was illegitimate, so, no, I'm not royalty."

"You may not be royalty to France, but you are to me." She kissed me passionately. I pushed her away.

"Oh, so now, after learning of my ancestor's illicit past you no longer like me?"

"Oh yes, I like you. I've always liked you. I raised the question of your birthright with a follow-up in mind."

"I'm afraid to ask."

"If you are French, how is it you have red hair?" Her laugh was followed by a devilish little smile.

"Rumor has it my great-grandmother went a little too far in expressing her appreciation toward the liberation troops of World War II."

It was my turn to laugh. I asked her to finish the story. She picked up where I'd interrupted.

"When our government agreed to turn Anna over to the Russians, my parents moved to adopt her. The request was under review when, about three o'clock one morning two men broke into our house and killed my parents. The two men threatened to kill Anna and me if we did not calm down, remain quiet, and come with them. It was winter, there had been an overnight powdering of snow and the wind was icy, so the men did not think it unusual we would ask to put on heavy clothes and wear jackets. Killing my parents was proof enough they were evil men. The fact was emphasized when they watched us strip off our pajamas and pull on wool pants and sweaters. They were smiling and commenting in Russian about what they intended to do with us and to us. I guess it never occurred to them we understood Russian. They had to know Anna spoke her native tongue, perhaps they didn't care. Anna and I had learned sign language. I signaled her to take more time than she needed to dress, and to let them ogle what they wanted to see.

"There was a pretty little stream running through our farm. It was loaded with brook and rainbow trout. My father had taught Anna and me to fly-fish—we loved it. We tied our own flies and spent a lot of our spare time fishing the stream. Once a week, when my father was home, we'd feast on trout for dinner.

A Marttiini filet knife with a six-inch blade was still in my jacket pocket. I'd neglected to remove if after our last outing. It was in a sheath in the inside pocket. The two men, infatuated at the sight of a naked fourteen-year-old girl, didn't notice when I slipped a mini maglight and a fountain-pen sized taser into my pocket. I flashed Anna an okay and she finished dressing.

"The men led, mostly dragged us to a limousine parked under the trees in back of our house. They opened the doors and one quickly slipped in underneath the steering wheel. The other forced us into the back and then climbed in and sat between us. I slipped Anna the taser while the guy was closing the door. Without turning on lights, the driver eased out onto the driveway that led to a county road two miles away. A three-quarter moon and the snow made it easy to see the landscape and follow the driveway.

"We had barely started moving when the man grabbed Anna, pulled up her sweater and began fondling her. His attention was fully focused on Anna, and he was probably thinking about what he was going to do to her next. He did not see me pull the filet knife from my pocket and slip it out of its sheath. I knew exactly where to stick it into his neck. The knife was sharp. I felt very little resistance as it pierced his carotid artery. He turned and grabbed me. I still had a tight grip on the knife. The twisting action finished what I'd started. It severed the artery. Blood spurted from his neck like an artisan well, hitting me in the face, soaking my jacket, and splattered the window behind me. He had a hand on my throat trying to choke me. I stuck the knife in his eye at about the same time Anna jabbed the taser against the back of his neck. He convulsed and then went limp. He fell against Anna soaking her in blood as his heart continued pumping. All he could do was bleed out and die. He may have been conscious of his fate, and then again, maybe not. For good measure I stabbed him several more times. After every thrust of the knife I would whisper, 'That was for my mother' or, 'That was for my father.' Finally, exhausted, I leaned back in the seat, dropped the knife, and let my hands fall into my lap.

"I had forgotten about the driver. Anna had not. She opened the man's coat and removed a Russian Makarov .380 semiautomatic handgun from his shoulder holster. Besides teaching Anna and me to fly-fish, my father had taught us to shoot. We started with .22 caliber rifles and after six months he began teaching us how to use a pistol. Within another six months we could hit a bull's-eye the size of a silver dollar at thirty feet every time.

"Anna was familiar with the Makarov pistol. It had replaced the aging Tokarev service pistol. The Makarov served as the duty sidearm of the various branches of the military, as well as the police, the KGB, and all other government agencies. Her father had owned one and he'd shown her how it operated and how to take it apart and put it back together. She also knew it likely that an ambassador bodyguard—*henchman* would have more aptly described him—would be carrying one tucked into his armpit. Anna had been near panic when she thought these men were going to take her back to Russia. She recovered quickly when I punctured the guy's carotid artery. Our emotions had reversed. I was in total control and focused on only two things—avenging my parents' deaths and protecting Anna. With one of the guys now dead or dying, I was falling apart. Anna took over—she was in complete control of her emotions. She was a different person when she shook me and whispered, 'One down, one to go, let's finish it.' I think she had a flashback to some event in the Soviet Union. Be that as it may, she brought me back to reality and the present situation.

"I was now alert and thinking. Once or twice a month during the week my mother and I drove into DC and spent a couple of nights with my father. During the day we shopped and then met my father for dinner. I'm guessing he had an important job, because he would send a limo and driver to take us shopping. I remembered there was a switch to control the tinted window separating the passenger compartment from the driver.

"I used the mini maglight to locate the switch and then asked Anna if she was ready. She nodded and pointed the pistol in the driver's direction. She knew the Makarov had a rebounding hammer to make it safe to carry with a round in the chamber and the safety off. When she checked she found the hammer in the rebounded position just as she'd expected, indicating a chambered round. To make doubly sure a round was chambered, she slide back the receiver just enough to touch the bullet and then let the receiver slide back into position. Although knowing the Makarov was double action, she still thumbed back the hammer to lessen the pressure necessary for the trigger pull on the first shot.

"I manipulated the switch and the window started retracting into a partitioned area behind the driver's seat. He turned to look into the rear compartment. The first nine-millimeter slug caught him in the temple. He slumped onto the steering wheel. The second, third, and fourth went into the back of his head.

"To insure he would stay on the road while driving without headlights, the driver's speed had been no more than ten miles an hour. The limo came to a stop when it nosed into a tree alongside the driveway.

"Anna and I jumped out and ran back to the house. We woke up Mr. Horn, our farm manager and supervisor. His jaw dropped when he saw Anna and me. He took a quick look about and then pulled us inside. We told him what had happened. He got his wife out of bed and then went to check on my parents. Mrs. Horn didn't ask any questions. She tossed our blood-soaked clothes into the fireplace, punched up the fire and added a couple sticks of wood. Our clothes soon went up the chimney in smoke. She then went to my bedroom and brought us clean outfits while we took baths. The water ran pink as we scrubbed our bodies and washed our hair. Thirty minutes later Mr. Horn returned carrying a small box. He gave me the box and told us it contained cash, some gold coins, and my mother's jewelry. Said he took them from my father's safe. He told me not to worry about my parents, said he would take care of everything. He instructed us to go and pack bags. We chose the backpacks we used for camping when we'd hike into the mountains with my parents. 'Nothing but necessities,' he said. We did as we were told. We figured our Sig Sauer Mosquito Carbon Fiber .22 caliber pistols, given to us by my father for Christmas, were necessities. We tucked them, along with a second magazine and extra ammo, into a compartment not easily accessible and likely to be overlooked should someone look inside our backpacks. Before leaving I removed my belt from the first three loops on my pants and threaded the sheath holding a Fiskars Normark filet knife with a six-inch stainless-steel blade onto my belt. The sheath was designed so as to allow it to be worn inside or outside your pants. After slipping my belt back through the belt loops, I loosened my pants and adjusted the knife inside my pants so only the handle showed when my jacket was removed. I buttoned my pants, buckled my belt, and adjusted the knife's position—it lay snug against my back just behind my hip.

"It was still dark when we got into Mr. Horn's truck. The limo was no longer in the driveway. Mr. Horn had one of the farm workers move it into the barn. We reached Highway 11 and turned south. Thirty minutes later we turned onto a county road and shortly thereafter tuned into a winding graveled driveway that led to a farm similar to the one where I'd grown up. Dawn was breaking when we parked behind the house. We waited in the truck, as instructed, while Mr. Horn knocked on the back-door of the farmhouse; the door opened, he went inside and the door closed behind him. Minutes later he returned to the truck and drove us past a barn along a dirt road to another barn with various pieces of farm equipment parked outside.

"We were getting out of the truck when a gentleman, introduced to us as Mr. Roundtree, drove up on a four-wheeler. What I first thought to be a barn turned out to be a shop, similar to the one on our farm. It was used for the repair and servicing of farm equipment and other needed repairs around the farm. At the top of a set of stairs, Mr. Roundtree guided us around things one would normally find in an attic storeroom. In a back corner he unlocked a door that opened into a small room with a table and chairs, a sofa, and two beds. He gave us the key and said, 'You'll be safe here. Charles and I have been friends since we were boys. My farm has nothing to do with the safe houses here in the valley.' Anna and I looked at each other and then back at Mr. Roundtree. From the surprised look on our faces he knew we had no idea what he was talking about. 'I guess you didn't know the cottage at your farm was a safe house used by the counter-espionage division of the FBI.' I shook my head. 'Well, that's how your friend and her father came to live with you. No one was supposed to know he was a Soviet defector. He lived there incognito. Obviously, your government sold you out. It won't happen here. Charles and I owe our lives to your father and we'll give them up for you if need be. We will take care of you. Come up to the house if you need anything, but otherwise stay put until we figure out a way to get you out of Virginia and set you up with a new identity. That's another thing; destroy all identification you have with you and anything connecting you to your families or the past. Breakfast will be ready in half an hour.' I made a mental note of the time. He and Mr. Horn went down to the shop and talked for a couple of minutes, and then Mr. Roundtree went back to his house. Mr. Horn came up and told us that he needed to make some arrangements for us.

He recited an address in Coronado, California, instructions on how to find it, and what to say when we arrived. He asked us to repeat the address and the instructions. We did, and then he asked us to repeat them again. We did. Mr. Horn got into his truck and drove away, but not before leaving us with a warning, 'Keep repeating the instructions until you won't be able to forget them even if you try. Do not mention this to anyone and under no circumstances do you write them down.'

"After breakfast I opened the box Mr. Horn had given me. It contained two hundred one-hundred-dollar bills, fifty American double eagles, and two or three dozen pieces of expensive-looking jewelry. With no idea what to expect, we decided it best to hide everything. We removed the end caps on our backpack frames and dropped the jewelry into the tubes, and replaced the caps. I used my knife to make one-inch slits in the lining of our jackets near the collar. Except for three hundred dollars each, we folded the money and pushed it through the small cut one bill at a time. We kept shaking our jackets to move the money toward the bottom. Again, using my knife I made slits in the backstrap padding of our packs and pushed the gold coins down inside the padding.

Physically, we were the same fourteen-year-old girls that had been dragged out of our beds six hours earlier. Mentally, we would go to bed forty-year-old women determined to stay alive whatever the cost. Are you sure you want to hear the rest?"

"This is fascinating. I had no idea. A couple of days after I'd found Anna in my shower I asked how she'd become a Club member. She said she'd tell me if I really wanted to know. I sensed she didn't want to tell me and let it drop. I have the feeling this is only the beginning."

"It is a rather long story. Perhaps I should finish it back at the hotel."

"I agree."

We stripped naked and went to bed. Two hours later, I propped myself on a pillow. When my breathing returned to normal I pulled Rita so close we melted into one, and asked, "Are you going to finish the story?"

"Do you really want to know?"

"Well, I have wondered about your past. Especially what prompted Anna to invite you into our bed."

"During the flight from our tormentors we vowed never to let anything or anyone come between us. That included marriage. Whether you realize it or not—you are married."

"I certainly hope so. It's too beautiful to be anything other than marriage. For me it has to be both or neither—I could never choose between the two of you."

"I know."

"You were saying?"

"We decided the person we gave ourselves to would have to be kind, courageous, faithful, and agree to our lifestyles. I was excited when Anna wrote me from Sakhalin Island and told me she was in love, said she had found our husband. I was equally disappointed when she called me from Tokyo and told me you were in love with another girl. Said she had tried to corrupt you but you remained faithful to your fiancée. We were glad you were true to her. We knew if you'd cheat on her you would cheat on us. Although things took an unfortunate turn for you, it worked out for us. When I first laid eyes on you at the director's dinner and you drank a toast to me I knew that I too was in love."

"It was the same for me. I was attracted to you when I offered my toast and you answered with a smile and twinkling eyes. It was the same feeling I'd had when Anna met me at the Yushno-Sakhallinsk Airport and flashed me a smile. Enough about me, you were telling me a bedtime story, remember?"

Rita took a deep breath and began. "Just past noon we had lunch with Mr. Roundtree. He lived alone with a cook and housekeeper. The cook fixed us sandwiches and snacks for our evening meal. 'We don't eat a regular meal in the evenings,' she told us.

"Tired and with no idea what to expect next, we went to bed with the chickens. Just before daybreak we were awakened by Mr. Roundtree banging on our door. When I opened it a crack he said, 'Shake a leg girls, we're leaving right after breakfast. Come on up as soon as you're dressed.'

"As we ate what was to be our last home-cooked meal for several weeks, he explained that Mr. Horn had been arrested and held for questioning. He said, 'Charles won't tell them anything, but they'll make the connection to me sooner or later. I'd be surprised if they're not on their way here at this very moment.' We hurried through breakfast and climbed into Mr. Roundtree's SUV. At the shop we loaded our backpacks and were off. Off to where? We didn't know. 'I'll take you to Clarksburg, West Virginia. Take a bus from there to Chillicothe, Ohio. Spend a couple of nights in a good hotel in a safe neighborhood, and then take a bus to another city and do the same thing. You won't leave an easy trail to follow if you buy a ticket from one town to the next and zigzag across country until you reach San Diego. Charles tells me you have money to sustain yourselves for a year if you don't lose it and aren't foolish. So, don't let your backpacks out of your sight for one instant.' He gave us hugs and wished us good luck when he dropped us at the bus station in Clarksburg.

"It was ten o'clock in the morning, and a month later, we knocked on the door of a modest house on F Avenue near the North Island Naval Air Station in Coronado. There was no response. We waited a minute and knocked again. After knocking a third time with no answer, we gave up and turned to walk away, wondering what we would do and where we would go. It was then the door opened and an elderly gentleman, sitting in a wheelchair, bid us come inside, saying, 'I've been expecting you girls.'

"We didn't know it then, but Mr. Elmore was our first contact with the Club. The story of his life hung on the walls of his home—a decorated veteran of three wars and service in the State Department. He had not remarried after his wife of thirty-seven years passed away. His only daughter took up with the New Bohemians, moved to a commune in the redwoods. Several years later she overdosed on drugs. He had no living relatives. A cleaning lady came once a week. A catering service brought two meals a day—breakfast and dinner.

"He passed us off as granddaughters. We agreed to cook and clean in return for a place to stay and for providing us with new identities. Anna dropped some of the letters in her Russian name, Antonia Bodenikova and became Anna Borden. My mother had wanted to remind me of my French heritage and named me Aurora. In honor of my mother I kept the English translation, Dawn, and became Rita Dawn Wentworth. Our birth certificates took nearly six months. They were recorded in county seats in sparsely populated areas of northern California, and showed us to be sixteen and seventeen years old, born to an unwed mother, now diseased, with the whereabouts of our fathers unknown.

"Our academic records arrived three months later, just in time for the new school year. Our records showed us to have successfully completed grades ten and eleven from different schools in the Northwest. With out-of-state records we were required to take a grade placement exam. The exam showed us to have the equivalent of one year of college—thanks to home schooling. We were placed in the twelfth grade and allowed to graduate by taking the final exam one month later.

"Mr. Elmore hadn't complained about our intrusion into his life—I think he liked having us around—but we knew he wouldn't be around forever and we'd need to support ourselves. Since going back to claim my inheritance in the Shenandoah Valley was out of the question it was imperative we find another solution. We still had most of the money Mr. Horn had given me, plus all the coins and my mother's jewelry. We opened bank accounts in two different banks. Anna chose a bank in San Diego near where she'd applied for a position with an engineering company. I opened an account at a bank in Imperial Beach. Initially we deposited enough money to legitimize the accounts, but not enough to be automatically reported to the IRS—we added a little every two weeks. We divided the rest of the money, along with the gold coins and jewelry and locked it away in bank boxes. The plan: I would work and take care of Mr. Elmore while Anna got a degree and then we'd switch roles. It didn't work out that way.

"Shortly after my parents were killed there were a couple of blurbs in the news. It never became a major story—it should have. Now, two and a half years later, it was front page. Mr. Horn had been charged with evidence tampering. The authorities were looking for the daughter, Colette Aurora Armstrong, suspected of murdering her parents. Anna was not mentioned, probably so as to avoid an international incident. She and I powwowed with Andy (Mr. Elmore). He suggested we split up for a while. Although still pursuing degrees in accounting and computer programming at UCSD, Anna had been hired for the position she'd sought at the engineering firm. Anna's fluency in and ability to type in Russian combined with the fact the company did business in the Russian republics sealed the deal. She would remain with Andy, continue her education, and keep her job. I would quit my job with a janitorial service at North

Island, I referred to as 'Maid for a Day,' and relocate. We didn't like the idea of being separated, but reluctantly agreed to his suggestion.

"Andy pointed to a picture on his living room wall and asked me to fetch it. Two men in their early twenties stood in front of a Grumman F6F Hellcat on the wooden flight deck of a World War II aircraft carrier. He held it so I could see and pointed to one of the men. 'That's Johnny and me, you take this picture to the address on the back,' he turned it over so I could see, 'and tell them you are a friend of mine and you want to serve your country. They will take care of you.' When I asked if Johnny would be there, he told me Johnny had been shot down during the battle of the Philippine Sea. I would later learn the man I would meet, the director, was Johnny's son. Johnny had married his childhood sweetheart two weeks before he deployed to the Pacific in 1942. His son was born eight and a half months later."

"Now comes the part that blew me away. Written above the address on the picture Andy had given me were these words. 'I am in your debt. Should you ever require my help, you need only to ask.' Next to those words, I had watched Andy scribble, 'Paid in full.' I didn't inquire; I figured he'd have told me had he wanted me to know. After learning of the relationship between Johnny and the director I decided to ask—I only thought I knew the relationship.

"Andy told me Johnny had been shot down. He hadn't alluded to the obvious—he had gone down with his plane. After VJ-Day, Andy returned home to find his boyhood friend's young wife destitute—the one-time military insurance stipend was all but gone. Andy, Johnny, and Helen had grown up together. It was only natural he would marry her and adopt Johnny's young son before reporting to his next duty station. Five years later Joanne was born—on my faked birth certificate, she is listed as my mother. When Johnny's son was old enough to understand, his mother explained the trio's relationship to him. He was so grateful he made the notation on the only picture he had of his father and gave it to Andy."

"Very interesting, now I know how Anna was able to persuade the director and the board to intervene in my execution. I surmise you had a hand in that as well?"

"Of course I did. You do remember I was a board member until I resigned to help you and Anna take out Mohammad El and the Iranians."

"I do indeed. It was during the operation that my life truly came together."

"Mine too. Anna wasn't sure you would go along when she invited me to join the two of you in bed. I knew you would. The chemistry was overwhelming and would not be denied. We'd been waiting for the right moment—I couldn't wait any longer."

Conversation ceased again. An hour later as she lay quietly in my arms I asked, "Do you want to finish your story or wait for another time?"

"I'll finish now if you want to hear it. The opportunity may not come again for a long time."

"I'm anxious to have you finish it. Although it hasn't bothered me, I have wondered about the two of you for a long time. I figured there was a tie-in going way back, but didn't have a clue. To finally know will bring us even closer, if that's possible."

She kissed me, sighed, and said, "That's what I needed to hear. It means everything to me. I know it will mean just as much to Anna."

She took another deep breath and then continued.

"It was a short walk from Andy's house to work, so I hadn't bothered buying a car or getting a driver's license. Now both were necessary. With a birth certificate showing me to be eighteen I had no trouble getting a driver's license. I purchased a fifteen-year-old Ford Escort for four hundred and fifty dollars from a guy in National City who claimed he'd owned it since new. It burned oil, but seemed to run okay. I parked on Second Street around the corner from Andy's house. This was on a Saturday. On Sunday Anna and I took Mr. Elmore to the Hotel del Coronado for brunch—we used his van, the same car Anna used for getting to and from work and school at the university. It was less than a joyous occasion. Anna and I were to be separated for the first time since we'd met, and I knew it wasn't likely I'd see Andy again.

"To say the trip back east was uneventful would be an understatement, but I'll save that for another time. I kept Mr. Roundtree's words of caution in mind—'Don't leave an easy trail to follow'—and took a roundabout way and more than a month to find the address on the picture Andy had given me. To make it more difficult for anyone to follow me, I changed the way I dressed several times and took my time crossing the southwest. At a thrift store in Yuma I switched to western apparel with jeans, shirt, boots, and a Stetson. In New Orleans I took on a Gothic look. In Nashville I became country. I left the Ford, with all the paperwork in the glove box, in the Ryman auditorium parking lot in downtown Nashville, took a bus to the airport, and a taxi to the Opryland Hotel. I had not registered or titled the car, so it was still in the name of the guy I'd bought it from. After a week I took a taxi to the airport and bought a one-way ticket to Atlanta. An hour after arriving, I walked into a nearby hotel and paid for a room for three nights. When asked about my car, I said I was driving a Nissan and gave them a phony license number. Two hours later I looked like a preppie hiking in the Adirondacks when I left the room. I exited the hotel by a door that opened into their parking lot. I walked back to the airport and purchased a roundtrip ticket to Albany, New York. From there I took a bus to the town closest to my destination and spent the rest of the day walking to what I thought would be an out-of-the-way house in the mountains—you can imagine my surprise."

"Did you become a member right away?"

"Yes, I wanted to find out who ordered my parents killed and kidnapped Anna and me. No doubt whoever was behind the plot intended to send Anna back to Russia and me along with her, or they were going to dispose of me some other way—kill me or sell me into bondage as a sex slave. Either way, I wanted to kill them all. Surprisingly, the director approved and assigned two people to help me with research. Also, he agreed to invite Anna into the Club. The following spring, after finishing a second year at UCSD, she asked her employer for, and was granted, a month's vacation. She joined me and signed a blood oath.

"Anna returned to work and school. She is gifted. When applying to UCSD she had to take the SAT twice. They refused to believe she hadn't cheated. The second time she took the test with a monitor watching her 100 percent of the time she scored even higher. Two weeks later she was invited to join the Mensa Society. She declined. She earned her degree in two and a half years while continuing to work for the engineering company, and taking care of Mr. Elmore. A year later Andy became very weak, was barely able to breathe, and unable to keep food down. Anna took him to Balboa Naval Hospital. All they could do was to keep him comfortable and wait for the inevitable. I took a bus to New York City, a plane to Los Angeles and a bus to San Diego. Probably there wasn't any reason for me to take such precaution. I didn't expect anyone to be actively looking for us, but one never knows. He was weak but alert and smiled when I walked into his room. Anna and I were with him when he died a week later.

"Unbeknownst to us, a year earlier he'd made out a will leaving everything he owned to Anna and me. We were listed as his granddaughters, and our mother his only daughter. A birth certificate and death certificate were the only records of her existence. There were no other children or close relatives. His only request was to give his military records, medals, awards, and memorabilia to the National Naval Aviation Museum and to be buried in the Fort Rosecrans National Cemetery at Point Loma. We followed his requests to the letter. We didn't know he was a World War II ace until we began arranging the funeral and learned he would be buried with honors—a twenty-one-gun salute and a missing-man flyover. Anna and I were presented the flag that covered his coffin. It was the first time I'd cried since I was a little girl—at that moment I knew I'd found my calling in service with the Club. He now resides on the wall of honor at the museum. Anna and I set up a fund to pay a florist to put fresh flowers on his grave every Sunday.

"Andy's home was free and clear. He had a few dollars in the bank, several gold coins in a safe in his home, and no other assets—he lived on his navy pension and social security, which barely covered his expenses. Anna lived in his house until she quit her job when you were framed and sentenced to be executed for the murder of your fiancée. We couldn't bear to sell it, so we set up another fund to have a property-management company in Chula Vista maintain it inside and out. With the exception of the few changes we made while he was alive, it's the same as the day he left it."

"Wow, I wouldn't have guessed in a million years how your innocence was stolen from you or how you've survived since then. Your life gives meaning to the saying, live every day to the fullest, you never know about tomorrow."

"That's been my philosophy since you came into our lives. Up until then I lived to survive long enough to avenge my parents."

"Did you find out who disrupted your life and was responsible for the death of your parents?"

"Oh yes, we found out. Anna asked for a year's hiatus from work. It was granted. She was too valuable to lose. I'd already located one of the conspirators. A clerk working in the office of an FBI agent had sold Anna's location to the Russian ambassador. We lured him to a motel with a promised sexual encounter unlike anything he'd ever known. We made good on our promise—there was no sex, but it was without doubt unlike anything he'd ever known. We spiked his drink, teased, and toyed with him until he passed out. Then we tied him up, duct-taped his mouth, threw him into the trunk of our car and drove him to an abandoned farmhouse in the woods where he could scream himself hoarse without anyone hearing him. We waited until the drug wore off and then introduced him to pain. In the end we gave him a choice; he could tell us what we wanted to know and die quickly or die stripped naked with syrup poured in his ears, nose, eyes, and on other areas of his body while tied down in the vicinity of a fire ant community. We took him outside where he could view the area—there were dozens of ant hills. I thanked him for his cooperation and made sure he saw me smile as I slit his throat. They all died within a year. Each one had to be persuaded, not so gently, to give up the next in line. I can only speculate as to how deep corruption goes and who is involved in any given circumstance. I only know I will never fully trust my government ever again."

Setting the Stage

"The press is our chief ideological weapon."
—Nikita Khrushchev

With few exceptions, the Club from the time of its inception until now had been reactive. In the past the Club had eliminated, to some degree, individuals responsible for putting the nation's defenses at risk or jeopardizing the Constitution—usually after the fact. The Club had been playing defense until Anna, Rita, and I used Mohammad El's greed and radical Islamist hatred of infidels (Americans) to entrap and eliminate five terrorists and relieved them of fifty million dollars.

Treason wears many hats; evidence pointed to the necessity of an all-out offensive by the Club against enemies within our own country. If not the Club, who? If not now, when?

Too many people in America are eager to destroy freedom, capitalism, and the Constitution and replace it with Marxism, slavery, and a dictator. Some do it willingly, some without knowing they are nothing more than pawns to be used and then discarded. A majority of media are part of this faction and work hard toward this end. A dummying down of the masses into low-information individuals has been easy and unbelievably successful. These folks no longer think for themselves. Why should they when the media were willing to do it for them? This frees them up to watch sports, sitcoms, play video games, and engage in other fun, entertaining, and nonproductive activities. The media feeds us false and misleading information with just enough truth mixed in so as not to be charged with sedition. Forcing the media to report the news without editorializing, would in turn force everyone to start thinking. They would then, not only have the opportunity to weigh the facts and form their own opinion—it would be required of them. Of course, there will always be those who say, "I don't care, I'm above it all, it doesn't affect me, I can't do anything about it, I have better things to do," and so on. These people will never understand all they have to lose until it has been taken away.

"Don't it always seem to go
That you don't know what you've got
Till it's gone ... "
–Joni Mitchell

For the Club to declare war on those promoting domestic in-your-face and psychological terrorism would, I believe, loosen these domestic terrorists' stranglehold on the general population. The media are more than willing, one might say eager, to promote domestic terrorism—I intend to change their attitude.

Perhaps I should define my reference to domestic terrorism. It is the attempt to dismantle capitalism and free trade, to delegitimize the American dream. To disparage and discredit the American way of life and to make us feel guilty for our success. These domestic terrorists want us to believe America is nothing more than a colony, successful only because we colonists stole everything that has made us great from the rightful owners throughout the world. These terrorists rarely mention, other than negatively, the one thing that makes us different from every country in the world—our governing document, the Constitution.

With the media's editorial powers curtailed, the people's elected representatives would start hearing demands from their constituents not easily ignored—something new for our public servants to deal with. This, in turn, would compel the government to follow the will of the people and keep threats from abroad in check rather than supporting and propping them up. America would come first in their decision making—politicians want to remain in office, so they would follow the will of the people, as well they should. Since the formation of a central bank politicians have been able to bribe the public with counterfeit money. Doing the right thing very rarely crosses the minds of a majority of politicians. Now, with the media asking or I should say, afraid not to ask tough questions of our elected officials, citizens will begin to see things as they really are. It will not be an overnight happening, but once it begins, it will snowball—eyes will be opening and heads will be rolling.

Every member of the Club agreed with me, as I knew they would. Our chapter kicked off the program. The board was calling the shots. I was happy to let them. The first four targets were chosen. It was decided that Club members would do the legwork. Anna, Rita, and I would make the kill. Club members would gather information on targets and report to a committee formed for the purpose of collecting and charting movements and habits of the soon-to-be deceased—this was to be the modus operandi of all chapters. Their committees, once up and running, would report to those selected, the most experienced, to take out the target. Needlessly to say, targets were chosen in various parts of the country—no two in the same area, at least not at first.

It was decided the first four hits should duplicate the methods mentioned in the letter. This would leave no doubt in the minds of those on the list that these deaths were not accidents. It would be very interesting to see if, after the first four, there were any changes in the way news was presented. Would the media start presenting all the facts or would we continue to get only one side of the story—the side they wanted to give us? Would they give it to us straight or continue to editorialize? It would be especially interesting to see how those whose names moved up the revised list reacted. As more people at the top of the list died mysteriously there would be little doubt in their minds that names at the top ran a greater risk of dying than those at the bottom—or those not on the list.

When Rita and I returned from Chicago, Anna welcomed me home in ways only she could—it was a beautiful evening. Then, the following day we got back to planning our first execution. The committee had chosen a reporter from a major network—he was number two on the list. Although not a prominent network anchor, he possessed an undeniable hatred for America and the Constitution. He believed both to be illegitimate and used his position to blame America for everything wrong worldwide. He worked and resided in New York City. The *City* was less than two hundred miles from the resort. With several members living and working in the "Big Apple" it was convenient for the Club to set up and maintain surveillance. The legwork men and women of the Club had been shadowing our target for two months. They knew where he lived, where he worked, where he ate, and what he did with his spare time. They knew where he would be and what he would be doing any time of the day or night. He would be an easy target to take out; however, one would be foolish to discount the unexpected.

We met with the committee every day. Often we made suggestions in the methods of surveillance. We emphasized the necessity of remaining invisible while observing the target's habits and routines. Also, we stressed the first one would be relatively easy, since, initially, no one would take the letters seriously. This would change after a couple of people on the list had met the grim reaper, so we needed to be extra careful from the very beginning. Take school on the first assassination as well as each succeeding kill—the committee required a critique on a case-to-case basis.

The Club didn't have all the resources available to the government, but we did have members working in various laboratories scattered about the country and abroad. Our technicians had devised and tested a device based on the spray gun Bohdan Stashynsky used to assassinate Stepan Bandera in Munich in October 1959. The device used a spray of cyanide gas. It worked quickly and appeared to the medical examiner as a heart attack. We had two such weapons, disguised as cell phones, in our possession, loaded and ready to go. The phones were safe from accidental activation. Readying the weapons required using the keypad to enter the correct code followed by the pound sign. The word *armed* would appear in the numbers window after the potassium chloride and cyanide were mixed. A second safety code and the pound sign were then required before aiming the phone at the target. The word *ready* would appear. Holding down the enter button would shoot a stream of poison gas a distance of up to ten feet. Six feet would be optimum—you would be safe at half the distance unless the wind was in your face, extra precaution should be taken by filling your lungs with fresh air before dispensing the gas and then getting out of the area before taking another breath. You aimed at the victim's chest. This gave you a larger target—at five or six feet you were unlikely to miss. Upon hitting the chest a fog cloud would form around the chest and face. Ninety-nine percent of the time when hit in the chest with anything, the victim would look down, and seeing the gas would suck in their breath. Anyone breathing in one whiff of the gas would die within seconds, apparently from a heart attack.

Rita and I took up residence at the Carlyle hotel on East 76th Street—we'd become accustomed to luxury these last three years. Anna remained at the resort, where she'd have access to the Club's research center. We had satellite phones set up to bounce signals off different receiving stations and satellites, which were next to impossible to trace since the number would change each time it bounced. Anytime we needed support, information, directions, weather reports, or whatever, we called Anna. She passed daily surveillance reports to us, sometimes hourly.

Before writing the letter I had passed to the director three years earlier, I had wrestled with the question of assassinating someone who had not committed a crime. I decided treason against the United States, no matter the degree, was still a crime, and for me, treason was enough. Those undermining the country with words were just as guilty as Mohammad El—words and deeds were interchangeable or as I saw it, one and the same.

If recon was correct this would be quick and easy, providing nothing unexpected popped up at a critical time. It seemed the guy wasn't as clean as one might expect of a person of his standing. We knew lying was considered a virtue for news anchors. There were different ways to lie—omission of the facts worked well for the media. Our target used the omission technique, but often went well beyond deceitfulness by creating facts and statistics out of thin air—it was said 85 percent of statistics used by the media were made up on the spot. He served as a panelist on a late-night news show and occasionally reported on a particular situation on the street—usually a protest or rally for some liberal cause. After participating in his discussion with the other panelists one would think he'd be anxious to get home, but no. He liked to make the rounds of midtown strip clubs. Once or twice a week he'd leave one of the clubs with a girl on his arm—money talks, virtue walks. Most interesting of his habits was a stroll in Central Park every Sunday evening. He appeared to walk around aimlessly, but always ended up on the same bench near the Alice in Wonderland statue. He waited ten to sometimes thirty minutes for a guy to come and sit beside him. They would talk for a few minutes and then, before leaving, the man would pass him an envelope. Our target waited another five to ten minutes before leaving the park and returning to his high-rise apartment on the Upper East Side.

Our recon team had observed the man with the envelope leaving the Office of Trade Representation for the Russian Federation on Lexington Avenue. He always took the same route to the park. Seventy-five years before he'd have taken a different route every time. Unlike in the days of Alger Hiss, Elizabeth Bentley, and Whittaker Chambers, very few operations were clandestine, everyone operated in the open without fear of reprisal. The only thing left over from back then was the walking.

The man with the envelope would walk along Ninety-Second Street to Fifth Avenue and then along Fifth Avenue to Seventy-Ninth Street, where he entered the park. Once in the park, he took less-traveled trails on his way to meet our media guy. This worked well for me—the fewer people the better.

Rita and I reserved our room for fifteen nights. This gave us a week to learn the lay of the land and have one rehearsal. The practice run went just as planned. We refined our strategy and walked it through every evening. The day of reckoning for Mr. Media was dark and dreary with a threat of rain. Not many people in the park. Things were working out better than I'd hoped. The fewer people the better. Mr. Envelope followed his usual route. I was close behind when he entered a poorly lighted area on the trail. He didn't feel anything for several minutes after I tapped his temple with a spring-loaded leather-covered blackjack. He would, no doubt, have a headache when he regained his senses. By then I would be long gone with the envelope safely in my pocket. The blackjack would go into the first pond I passed and the surgical gloves would go into the first trash can.

Rita was sitting on a bench near where Mr. Media waited for the guy he would never see. In less than a minute he would never see anything again outside of hell. When she read my text, it contained a single word, "Done." A minute later I received a one-word text, "Finished."

Back at the Carlyle we showered and dressed quickly. We'd estimated the time we would finish with business and made dinner reservations accordingly. In case there was a question we wanted to be seen at the restaurant as soon after the event as possible. Three hours later we were preparing to retire when I removed the envelope from my jogging suit. I'd figured the guy from the Russian Federation wouldn't report anything to the police. What could he tell them—he was mugged? After opening the envelope I realized he would've had a legitimate complaint had he reported the robbery. Inside were ten thousand dollars and two single-spaced typed pages of instructions. These days we hear such instructions referred to as talking points.

Number one on the list: keep pushing for laws to take guns from citizens. A lengthy paragraph cited an upcoming event where a gunman would shoot several students and then commit suicide. The shooter had volunteered to die for "our cause" (his words) and to get his name in the news and history books. He quoted the shooter as saying "I want to take my video-game skills to the next level."

The paragraph listed statistics he could cite. Other parts of the letter suggested how to keep race relations stirred up by citing white-on-black crime. It was made clear he was never to mention black-on-white crime or black-on-black crime.

He was to push for same-sex marriage and open homosexuality in the military. Refer to those opposed as homophobes wanting a return to the fifties.

I would never ever again have second thoughts about assassinating a liberal reporter.

I was so wound up after reading the letter I would probably have stayed awake all night had it not been for Rita. She made me forget everything outside the room.

Our old landlord in Georgetown remembered us from the time when we'd stayed with him three years earlier.

"Mr. Taylor, so good to see you and Miss Jennifer! Will you be in the district long? Do you need a place to live while you're here? How was your trip to the Orient?"

"Our trip was great. We do indeed need a place to live for a few days. Do you have anything for us, Frank?"

"Always for you, Mr. Taylor. However, I'm embarrassed to offer you the only unit I have available at the moment. A small one-bedroom with an efficiency kitchen, it will be pretty cramped for the three of you. I will be able to move you into something more appropriate at the end of the month."

"We'll take whatever you have. We will be here for only a few days visiting old friends. Small won't be a problem, Rachel isn't with us. She's in France looking for a place to live. We're going to be living in Europe for a while."

"My, my, you three sure like to travel. Do you think you'll ever become less restless and pick a place to settle down?"

"Probably one day we'll move into a place with a nice green lawn and a shiny marker that reads 'home at last, rest in peace.'"

"Mr. Taylor, you shouldn't joke about things like that."

"Yeah, you're right. Let's see this little place you're ashamed to show us." We made a deal with Frank. We'd take it for two weeks with the understanding we could be leaving at any given moment—without a refund, of course. Frank was a good guy and I felt a tinge of guilt using him for an alibi, should the need arise. We'd leave him with the understanding we were on our way to France, just as we'd left him believing we were on our way to the Orient when we took out El and the Iranians. If the question ever arose, he would honestly, without knowing, give confusing information to any investigator checking into our whereabouts. Frank didn't know we had already checked into a motel on the district's fringe. We'd check out with Frank three days before we sprang our trap, just as we had done last time.

We waited until everything was in place before calling Anna and informing her we were ready to play.

The telephone rang. "Hello, this is Frank."

"Hi, Frank. This is Rachel. I haven't been able to reach Warren or Jennifer, could you give them a message for me, please?"

"Oh sure, no problem, Miss Rachel. Mr. Taylor tells me you are going to be living in France."

"For a while. Tell them I've found a beautiful place in Nice. Ask Warren to give me a call, would you please?"

"No problem, I'll tell them the moment I see them."

"Thanks, Frank. Good talking with you."

"You're welcome, Miss Rachel. Enjoy your new place in Europe."

"Thanks, we will."

A Washington-based columnist carried in several major newspapers was about to depart on vacation at a five-star resort in Cancun. The bon-voyage party was breaking up with our target on her way to the limo that would take her to Ronald Reagan National Airport. I received a one-word text from Rita, "Rolling." On the way to the airport she kept a couple of cars between her and the limo. A porter opened the doors of the limousine when it stopped at the curb. Rita took a parking spot, immediately after it was vacated, two spaces forward of the limo. The columnist exited and dug through her Hermes Birkin handbag, removed a sheet of copy paper and handed it, along with a ten-spot to the porter. He nodded, thanked her, and took her bags to the scales—obviously; she had checked in online and already had a boarding pass. I approached her as she headed for security to be cleared to the boarding area.

"Excuse me, ma'am." I showed her my FBI badge and credentials, which were authentic. She was a smart cookie. She reached into her fourteen-thousand-dollar handbag, pulled out a cell phone and called the Bureau—she had their number in her contact list. She asked to speak with the name on the ID card, Agent Shurberte, and cited the badge number. She was put on hold. The Club was more powerful than I realized. It was then I remembered the director's words at our first dinner. He wanted me to understand that he knew all about me as he ticked off a list of events in my life. I don't remember my comment about the Club's efficiency, but I remember his, "Mr. Scott, there is no segment of society or government we cannot reach into and extract information." Obviously, he could extract more than information.

A few seconds later Agent Shurberte's cell phone rang—it was in my pocket. I answered on the second ring, "This is Agent Shurberte."

"Agent Shurberte, would you mind telling me where you are at this particular moment?"

"I'm standing in front of a very pretty lady about to board an airplane bound for Cancun. I'm trying to warn her about a threat on her life and explain to her that she is in grave danger." Her eyes popped open to the size of saucers, she dropped her phone, and I thought she might faint. I recovered her phone and took her by the arm.

"Don't be alarmed ma'am, the FBI has everything under control. We'll make sure you are safe and you can depart on your vacation without concern. We know about the death-threat letter and the list. You are, no doubt, aware of the reporter dying of a heart attack in New York's Central Park. You may not know forensics found traces of cyanide in his blood. It was a chemically induced heart attack—in other words, murder." Her knees sagged and her complexion was a ghostly white. Had I not been holding her arm, she might have collapsed.

"I'm telling you this not to alarm you, but to ensure you we have everything, including your safety, under control. There are two individuals involved. We have one in custody. He made a deal with us. To save his worthless skin he agreed to give up his accomplice. His accomplice is, at this moment, in the terminal waiting for you. We have several FBI agents in the terminal with one masquerading as you. We need to get you out of the terminal so your lookalike can take your place. We will spring our trap when he makes a move on your impersonator.

"You will not miss your departure time. I will escort you through a service entrance and make sure you are safely on your flight. Just in case the guy evades capture—I assure you he won't—there will be a federal marshal on board to take care of you."

Natural color returned to her face and she was able to walk unassisted as I guided her toward Agent Shurberte standing outside by Rita's SUV. "I need to inform my team captain you are fully cooperating."

While talking with Agent Shurberte, I slipped him his ID and cell phone—he would replace the faked ID with my picture for his authentic ID at the first opportunity. Shurberte opened the rear door of the SUV. I helped her inside and closed the door. When the columnist saw Rita, whose hair was dyed and cut to match her color and style sitting beside her, she did a double take. I slid underneath the steering wheel. From outside the SUV it was impossible to see anyone inside. As I pulled away from the curb, Rita slipped a needle into the columnist's arm and emptied the syringe. The succinylcholine worked super fast; she was completely helpless in a matter of seconds. The drug affected the lungs, so when the paralyzing drug took effect Rita secured a bag-valve-mask attached to a medical oxygen bottle over her nose and mouth to maintain oxygen flow—we didn't want to kill her just yet. It was difficult to undress a dead person—she was unable to resist, even helpful, as Rita removed her dress, jacket, and shoes.

As I followed the flow of traffic out and then back into the terminal, Rita quickly donned the columnist's clothes and climbed into the front passenger's seat. The Christina Dior dress and jacket hung slightly loose on Rita, but noticeable only to someone scrutinizing beautiful women—the columnist carried a few more pounds than Rita. The shoes matching the handbag were manageable. While she familiarized herself with the contents of the Hermes Birkin Togo leather purse to make sure the boarding pass was there and her passport in order, a cell phone signaled an incoming text message.

Rita read the message and exclaimed, "Well, isn't this just peachy. Now we know why she didn't take her husband along on vacation. Little Miss Goody Two Shoes Bleeding Heart has a paramour waiting in her suite."

I stopped at a crosswalk in between lobby entrances. Rita cast a concerned eye toward the gathering clouds as a few drops of rain landed on the windshield, grabbed her carry-on bag, gave me a quick kiss, opened the door, and departed. She had used a temporary rinse to color her hair—getting caught in a heavy rainstorm could be a problem.

I drove away and headed for a parking area at the George Washington Masonic National Memorial. I pulled in beside a red Ford Taurus. The doors opened as I came to a stop. Two men (Club members) exited the Taurus—I'd met only one. The drug was wearing off. The woman was beginning to breathe on her own and struggling to remove the oxygen mask. I hit a switch to unlock the doors. One of the men, carrying a satchel doctors sometime carry on house calls, got into the back seat with her. She was trying to form words, or perhaps scream when he slapped a piece of duct tape over her mouth. I was barely out of the SUV when the other man took my place behind the wheel. The doors closed and they drove away. Not one word was exchanged. They were headed to a privately owned airport in St. Charles County, Maryland. From there Miss Spousal Cheating Goody Two Shoes Bleeding Heart would receive a free extended vacation, including a lesson in skydiving without a parachute, in the badlands of New Mexico.

I drove back to the airport and returned the Taurus to the rental car agency. A driver for the agency dropped me at the curb by a lobby entrance to the terminal. Rita had passed through security without problems and boarded her flight before I reached the airport. She would arrive in Miami in two hours. After a short layover passengers would board a different flight and continue to Cancun. Rita would not be on the flight. At the Miami airport in the privately operated lounge at terminal J she would pay for a shower, wash the rinse out of her hair, change into clothes she had in her carry-on bag, and board a red-eye to Boston. Her reservations had been made by a Club member in Miami after she'd learned everything was going down as planned. The Club member had been waiting for Rita to deplane. Recognition was made signals were exchanged and understood. The Miami Club member followed Rita and waited in the vicinity of the lounge for her to shower and change clothes. In a nearby restroom she handed the ticket and boarding pass for the flight to Boston to Rita, took the carry-on bag containing everything belonging to the columnist, and walked out of the terminal. You were practically stripped naked when entering the boarding area, but no one checked you as you left.

Before giving birth to this project—referred to as *Chimney Sweep*—I was doubtful it could succeed. Now, having witnessed the long-reaching tentacles of the Club and the efficiency, dedication, and loyalty of its members, I was beginning to believe we had a better than average shot at saving America from her detractors.

I took a taxi to a restaurant in nearby Old Town Alexandria, ate an early dinner, and then took another taxi to our motel. Got into Anna's Windstar—Rita and I had already checked out and loaded everything we'd brought with us into the van—and drove away. Six hours later I entered our residence at the resort in the Catskills. Anna was in my arms before I closed the door. Rita arrived the following afternoon.

Making a Difference

"No great idea in its beginning can ever be within the law."

—Emma Goldman

After the dinner, the cheers, the toasts, and the speeches, the three of us left for the Esperanza in Cabo. This served a double purpose. It gave us time to unwind and rejuvenate our minds and bodies, while our west-coast chapter stepped up their surveillance and finalized their report.

Our counterpart on the *left* coast had chosen for their target a San Francisco primetime panelist for a major network. By his own admission in a novella-length, self-serving, narcissistic autobiography he told of watching television in 1964 and seeing *flower children* in Golden Gate Park. They were smoking marijuana, singing protest songs with Buffy Sainte-Marie, Joan Baez, Pete Seeger, Bob Dylan, and others, promoting free love, and having a good time. He was stuck with a controlling, prudish—his words, not mine—upper-middle-class family and not having fun. He'd just graduated from junior high and his father had insisted he spend the summer mowing lawns or doing some other menial work. To prepare for the real world, his father had said. Well, he'd seen the real world and it was in San Francisco.

On a Monday after his father had gone to work and his mother was grocery shopping, he took most of her jewelry, anything he considered valuable enough to pawn, what money he could find, and started hitchhiking to California.

On the road he learned quickly it was better to pretend to be broke than to have money in your pocket—fortunately he'd put most of the money from the sale of his mother's jewelry under the insoles of his shoes. He hadn't shaved or had a haircut since he left home. By the time he arrived in San Francisco three months later he was ragged, with long hair and with enough fuzz on his face to pass for a beard. He was a quick study and fit in almost overnight. Your cause was his cause as long as it was antiestablishment—anti anything American.

He joined organized demonstrations and was active in helping start spontaneous, on-the-spot disturbances. At Berkeley he joined the free-speech movement. Later he was singing the praises of Mao Tse-tung while selling the "Little Red Book" of quotes in what became known as Peoples Park. Although his rhetoric today was toned down, his communist ideology had expanded far beyond what it had been back then. Now he more eloquently reinforced the convictions of those of the same ilk worshiping at the elitists' altar and injected his vitriol into the minds of the young eager to find their own rebellious niche.

One had to wonder how his résumé read when he applied for a job with the network. Perhaps letters following your name were not required for reporting the news if your attitude fit the producer's agenda. Possibly he'd returned to school and despite or with the help of hallucinogenic drugs obtained a degree. Nevertheless, he was considered an authority on all things social, from roots and causes to effects and remedies. He tied all solutions to Marxism, free love with no restriction to gender, women's "right to choose," and legalized marijuana—a typical representative of the city's lifestyle.

From his first day of exposure to San Francisco he took to the hippie lifestyle like a duck to water. Life was far more exciting than mowing lawns in suburban Detroit and beyond anything he'd seen on TV or could imagine. He was welcomed into a commune in the counterculture enclave of North Beach where marijuana, psychedelic drugs, wine, and free love were mixed and served as the adhesive to the antiestablishment rebellion. The summer of love in Haight-Ashbury was the last hurrah of the counterculture. The shooting at Kent State marked an end to the movement. Most young people had engaged in the sixties experiment out of boredom, the need to be recognized for their own rebellious identity, the lure of drugs, free love, and a no-rules lifestyle. By the end of the decade the majority began looking toward their future—a career, a wife or husband and family, and financial security—only a few hangers-on remained. Unfortunately, too many of the most rebellious of the Marxist-loving, communists-endorsing, anticapitalist, anti-free-market socialists continued their revolution through infiltration of the media, schools and universities, the Justice Department, Hollywood, and the very government sworn to protect the Constitution and defend the country against foreign interference. Whether planned or not, it had brought America to the brink of desolation. As Abraham Lincoln put it, it would come from within. "... If destruction be our lot, we must ourselves be its author and finisher."

Although the communes were gone and North Beach more or less had been gentrified, remnants of the revolutionaries remain. Our target was among those dregs of the Woodstock generation. He remained true to his philosophy and practiced what he preached. You might see him dining along the Embarcadero, in the financial district, or Chinatown. Sometimes with a woman on his arm and at other times holding hands with another man. Since he was still an advocate of free and unrestricted love, he never married. His housemates came and went without schedule, or as best as could be determined, a preference to gender.

We knew our holiday would be over way too soon and were determined to make the most of it. We didn't leave our room until evening of the second day. We tired of room service and reserved a table for dinner at Cocina del Mar. As was normal whenever we made a public appearance, men at nearby tables cast glances at Anna and Rita to the chagrin of their wives, girlfriends, mistresses, or whatever category their escorts might fit into. The reason was obvious— two exceedingly beautiful women with an undistinguished-looking guy. I knew what they were thinking and whispering—I smiled.

We were finishing a seafood tortilla soup when I asked Anna if she'd considered upgrading her Windstar to a Lexus LX570 of perhaps a Porsche Cheyenne. She responded in a tone somewhere between hurt and offended.

"No. I like my Windstar and I'm not getting rid of it."

"I was just thinking, since it's almost fifteen years old, you might want something a bit more comfortable and reliable."

"It's very reliable and comfortable enough for me. It's my first car. Andy gave it to me and I'm keeping it."

I shrugged an okay and moved on. "Now that I know you are sisters, I'm sure Rita told you about answering a lot of unasked questions, while we were in Chicago—"

She cut me off, gave me an eye-twinkling smile and Rita a wink.

"Oh yes, she told me, said you two had a really good time in Chicago."

"Well, I can't speak for Rita, but I enjoyed it."

"I'm sure you did and I assure you she enjoyed it just as much."

"I certainly hope so—"

She cut me off again.

"And now you want to know what I did between the time I went back to work in San Diego and when I met you at the airport on Sakhalin Island."

I shrugged, "Only if you want to tell me."

"We haven't had much playtime together since we departed French Polynesia, so how about we enjoy ourselves while we have the opportunity and I'll tell you in San Francisco?" She gave me another big smile and Rita another wink and added, "Besides, my sister promised me equal time."

I shrugged again and with a smile said, "Works for me."

We spent another two hours eating while the girls smiled, winked, teased, giggled, and spoke in a language only they understood—a language developed during their preteen years. By now, men at adjacent tables were salivating, while their escort's eyes were shooting daggers.

As the saying goes, time flies when you're having fun. Now it was time to get back to work. We flew into Lindbergh Field in San Diego, bought tickets on another airline to LAX. There we parted ways. I needed a shooter for this one. Since Anna could shoot the wings off a housefly at a hundred yards, she was the logical choice. Rita reserved a seat on yet another airline to Albany to take over the command center. Anna and I rented a car and drove to San Francisco. We each had multiple IDs and passports and it wasn't likely anyone could trace our movements. Nevertheless, should anyone try, we made it as difficult for them as we could. Anna and I hadn't eaten since breakfast at Esperanza and were beginning to run out of steam. A hundred miles before we exited Interstate 5 and headed into "The City" we stopped at Pea Soup Anderson's for dinner and a highway break. Four hours later we turned in the rental car at the airport, took a shuttle to the Fairmont, walked to the Mark Hopkins, checked in—our reservation had been made two weeks earlier—and went straight to bed. A kiss goodnight and ten minutes later we were asleep—it had been a long day.

We awoke early and began our day as we had so many times before. Two hours later we got out of bed, showered, dressed and went to breakfast. We ate slowly, enjoying small talk and a great view from Top of the Mark. This was our first time in San Francisco, so for a week we became tourists, familiarizing ourselves with the City. We mixed fun and business as we toured and ferreted out our target's haunts. We left the Mark

Hopkins and climbed onto a trolley. Hopped off near Pier 41 and took a ferry to Tiburon for lunch. The trip gave us a tour of San Francisco Bay, but made for another long day. We caught the trolley back up to Nob Hill, had a light dinner at Top of the Mark, went to bed, and enjoyed another good night's sleep.

Again we awoke early and started our morning as we had the day before. Except this morning we ordered coffee, fruit, bagels with lox and cream cheese from room service. After breakfast we went back to bed. At noon we met our Club-member contact for lunch at John's Grill.

I thought it ironic we were lunching clandestinely in the restaurant featured in *The Maltese Falcon* where Kasper Gutman slipped a knockout drug into Sam Spade's drink. Lunch served two reasons besides the obvious. First: have our contact tell us about our target and his routine. Second: to get a good look at the target—he was sitting two tables away, facing us. We were told the man and woman with him were local politicians.

It appeared they were discussing whatever was on the sheet of copy paper he held in his hand—probably talking points for his next on-air discussion. There was a lot of pointing at whatever was on the paper and tongue wagging. I only needed one look. He would be recognizable in any crowd—a skinny little guy with a weasel face. I guessed him to be twice my age. The woman passed him an envelope as she and the other politician pushed their chairs away from the table. There was no shaking of hands when they departed. They left him to pay the bill—I had the feeling they owned him. He ordered another drink and threw it down as the waiter tallied his bill. The waiter picked up the money he slapped down on the table, counted it, and gave him the finger as he walked out the door—apparently he was a cheapskate.

Our contact drove us past some of the little guy's hangouts, through his neighborhood and by his residence. I was surprised to learn North Beach was not a beach community nor near a beach—there may have been a beach before the Embarcadero was built a hundred or so years ago. I learned San Francisco was made up of districts often named for ethnic groups such as Russian Hill, Chinatown, Japantown, Haight-Ashbury, Nob Hill, Castro, Twin Peaks, Upper Market, and at least twenty others.

North Beach was and still is Little Italy, but also known as the city's red-light district. At night it becomes the bustling neon home to strip joints, bars, cafes, and Italian restaurants. This was where our target spent most of his leisure time—close to home. The one thing interesting me most was his weekly meeting with a pusher—once a druggie always a druggie. Just like the pizza man, his supplier delivered. I couldn't have asked for a better setup.

A New Bohemian commune of the fifties having survived the flower children of the sixties and hippies of the seventies stood two doors up and across the street. It had been spruced up enough to satisfy the housing codes and presently used as a rooming house. An upper street-side unit had been leased three months earlier when the SF chapter's choice of targets had been approved. It had been used for surveillance—no one questioned those entering or leaving as long as they had a key to the building, the rent was paid, and the police didn't come calling.

Our target owned an older compact car. Most of the time during the day, he left it parked on the street and used public transportation walking to and from a nearby bus stop. Now and then he took a taxi, and occasionally got a lift from an acquaintance or associate. Only after 7 p.m., when the city-operated busses stopped running did he use his car—shutting down public transportation ensured tourists had to shell out money for taxis. The Club kept an accurate log of his comings and goings. He didn't appear to be on any schedule except when he left for the studio and on Thursday evenings when he was always home to meet with his supplier—weekend parties demanded a buffet of drugs.

We spent several hours over a ten-day span familiarizing ourselves with his daily routine and the flow of traffic. Apparently considerably fewer people owned cars in San Francisco than one might imagine. The greater part of daytime traffic consisted of people driving into the city to their jobs. During the day residents were out and about, but most stayed home after hours. If they ventured out in the evening they walked to their favorite neighborhood bar, club, or restaurant. By 6 p.m. traffic was sparse in most residential areas. People walked and utilized public transportation and taxis more than one might expect—even the pusher. This was shaping up as a twofer.

From the rooming-house advantage on our Thursday-evening recon we watched the soon-to-be-deceased network panelist arrive, unlock his front door, and enter his residence. This was just before 6 p.m. Twenty minutes later his supplier turned the corner, walked up the street, and knocked on his door. Our target opened the door and was visible for five seconds before he backed up to allow the dope-delivery guy to enter. Timing would have to be perfect—a very small window with no room for error.

We'd done our homework and thought it time to relax and enjoy the City. The Club would continue to monitor and report. Anna, still the take-charge kind of girl she was, had made reservations for the 10 p.m. seating at Fleur De Lys on Sutter Street. We opted for a four-course dinner with wine pairings. While waiting for escargot and truffles I kept looking at Anna and smiling, I couldn't help it—did I mention I smile a lot? She was smiling back and her eyes twinkled when she asked, "What?"

"Oh, just thinking how lucky I was to have had my boss assign me to check up on the operation at Sakhalin Island."

"It wasn't Lady Luck that brought us together—it was destiny. So, when are you going to ask me?"

"Ask you what?"

"Ask about my life in Coronado before I was assigned to the job in Russia."

"I figured if you wanted to tell me, you would, otherwise it's none of my business. I'm curious, but I don't need to know."

"Just the same I need to know there are no unanswered questions about me lurking in the back of your mind. I want you to know everything about me there is to know."

"Fair enough, you already know everything there is to know about me."

"True. Like Emily—I mention her name not to renew your hurt, only to make a point. She was innocent of everything outside her music. She wanted to experience love and discover things outside her safe little world. She was fortunate—she met you. Unlike Emily, Rita and I didn't get a chance to make decisions about our future. Long before we had a chance to grow to womanhood, taste love or learn anything about the world outside, we were ripped from our safe haven in the Shenandoah Valley and became fugitives running for our lives.

"After Rita joined the Club I was left alone. If not for Andy I would probably have gone crazy. He was the only one I knew or trusted. He became my father. I sought his counsel and trusted him to advise me on all matters, those serious as well as the not so serious. Going to school, working a job demanding extensive research where accuracy was critical in my every decision, cooking for Andy, as well as for myself, and keeping the house clean left little time for extracurricular activity. Still, at age twenty, I was curious about life outside work and school.

"It was after Andy's passing I finally ventured out into the real world. A world far more complicated than I'd imagined. I quickly discovered it was a 'me' world with everyone in it for what they could get out of it with little if any thought for others. Complicating things even more, I could torture and kill a man, but couldn't talk to one about anything personal or express my feeling, expectations, or desires.

"Another problem: most women had little or no respect for themselves and therefore didn't demand any. They just wanted to be one of the boys, get drunk, tell dirty jokes, and do whatever felt good at the moment. I had various offers, some borderline vulgar. I finally accepted a dinner date with a guy I worked with. He seemed nice enough. I had never tasted an alcoholic drink, but since most everyone appeared to be having before-dinner drinks I accepted his offer of a cocktail. It tasted sweet and creamy. When I asked what it was, he told me it was a panty remover. Call me naive, but it wasn't until after dinner and a few more drinks at the bar, when he took me home and invited himself inside, that I realized what he had alluded to."

"Are you telling me you had never heard the term and didn't know what he was talking about?"

"I had no idea. Surely you didn't forget Rita and I lived very sheltered lives up until the night her parents were murdered."

"What did you do?"

"I killed him."

My jaw dropped and I asked,

"You what?"

She laughed and said, "Just kidding, I managed to escape with my dignity and virginity intact." She laughed again, hesitated, then smiled.

"I'm betting he still remembers our first date."

"How did the second date go?"

"There was no second date. There were no more dates, ever." My mouth was open, but no words came out. Finally I managed to ask, "No more dates, ever, how—" she cut me off with a statement and a smile.

"I was dispatched to pick up someone at an airport and you got off the airplane." My mouth was still open. Before my mind could form the obvious question she smiled, her eyes twinkled, and she said, "Yes, Rita too."

We spent an hour looking into each other's eyes, smiling, and making small talk as we dined on rye-crusted salmon combined with a Fleur De Lys vegetable feast. Anna's playfulness continued as dessert and a wine pairing were served. I had just taken my first bite of Amaretto soufflé when she gave me another eye-tinkling smile and teasingly said, "I just realized, counting Emily and Tracy, you must hold some sort of record for deflowering young women." Her smile turned into soft-mocking laughter as she hooked her foot behind my leg and moved it up and down my calf while my face turned red.

It was well after midnight before we fell asleep and almost noon before we got out of bed. We lunched at the Japanese Tea House in Golden Gate Park and spent part of the afternoon wandering through the gardens. The week went by quickly as we rode the trolley and walked through California history with tourists.

We'd arranged for a late checkout, settled our account, and spent the afternoon relaxing in our room. At 4 p.m. I called our local contact and informed him we would be leaving the hotel in thirty minutes. One of the fogs San Francisco is famous for was rolling in—this was a perfect evening for taking care of business. The moment we stepped outside, a cabbie opened the door of his taxi. He closed the door immediately after we climbed inside and then loaded our luggage into the trunk. There was no conversation, nor did we give the cabbie instructions. A few minutes later he pulled into a parking lot in Pioneer Park near Coit Tower and stopped behind a five-year-old Chevy Malibu—a car not too new or fancy to attract attention. A woman, perhaps twenty-five years old, dressed in a running suit, complete with headband, exited the driver's seat as we approached and jogged off into the fog without looking back. The taxi driver drove away within seconds after we exited, again without statements or questions from anyone.

"I'm beginning to like having the Club do all the heavy lifting while we get to have all the fun."

"I have mixed emotions. I enjoyed the sleuthing, planning, and follow-through on the judge and El. Without those operations I wouldn't have had a chance to introduce you to Rita, the Rita you didn't know but wanted to know."

All I could do was smile and whisper "Touché" as I kissed her.

My plan had been to do an actual drive-by shooting. With Anna in the backseat using a Browning SA-22 semi auto .22LR takedown rifle, the low decibel report from the .22 caliber weapon would hardly be noticeable. She rejected my plan as too chancy and ticked-off a list of things that could go wrong. I didn't like her up-close and personal approach, but since she was the shooter I figured she had a right to make the call.

I found a parking spot a hundred feet down the street from the front door of a guy with at most an hour to live. Anna was all business as she sat in the backseat getting ready for her cameo performance—teasing, small talk, and reminiscing were over. She pulled on a pair of latex surgical gloves and a plastic charcoal-colored slicker with a hood. The slicker would not appear unusual for outerwear in heavy fog. She removed the Sig Sauer Mosquito Carbon Fiber .22 caliber semiautomatic pistol from its case—the exact model Rita's father had given her and Rita for Christmas when they were twelve years old. Having run hundreds of rounds through her personal weapon as a little girl, she was as familiar with the Sig Sauer as she was with her own magnificent body. She ejected the magazine, checked to make sure it was fully loaded, reinserted it, worked the slide to chamber a round, and put the little handgun on safety. She checked the extra magazine to make sure it was full and slipped it into her pocket. The pistol went into the waistband of her designer jeans.

We didn't have long to wait. The delivery man turned the corner and started walking up the street. He was within a few feet of the car when Anna opened the door and got out. I rolled down my window. She stepped up to the open window when the guy was two paces away, and gave me a big kiss. As he drew even with us she said, "See you Monday." She turned to walk away and then, just as he passed, she asked, "You want me to bring you anything?"

This had been planned and rehearsed, all for his convenience, we wanted to make sure he heard our conversation and witnessed our interaction, meant to lead him to believe we had an open relationship. This would become apparent during their following conversation.

I answered, "You can bring me a bag of *sopers*." A junkie or anyone dealing drugs would know I was referring to Quaaludes. Using the term would serve to help alleviate any questions about Anna's appearance at an inopportune time.

Anna maintained a distance of ten feet behind the delivery guy. He didn't see her pull the pistol from underneath the slicker and thumb the safety off. She held it behind her right buttock as they walked up the street. The carbon fiber construction very nearly matched the color of the slicker. Without knowing what you were looking for it was unlikely, even while looking at her shapely bottom, you would have spotted the little handgun. She made sure he'd knocked on the door before she approached and stood beside him.

"You must be the candy man."

"Do I know you?"

"No, you staying the weekend?"

"How long have you known *my man*?"

"I've known *your man*"—she said it mockingly—"since I was a teenager."

"Yeah, well tell me something I don't know about him."

"He's AC-DC."

"I know that, everybody knows that."

"Well, he's an slimeball."

He laughed, "I guess you know him pretty well." If he'd had earlier misgivings he now appeared at ease with Anna's presence.

The door opened and her target was framed in the doorway. Half a second later a small-dark hole appeared just above the bridge of his nose and both eyes disappeared in a bloody mess as three Teflon-coated twenty-two-caliber slugs entered his brain. For good measure she put two bullets in his heart. He was dead where he stood. Before gravity had taken control of his body, she turned her attention to the drug dealer and administered the same justice for his crimes against humanity. Anna was already walking away when she heard their bodies hit the floor.

She was five feet away when I stopped in front of her and opened the passenger's door. She slipped into the seat and closed the door as I drove away. Anna was still all business as she climbed into the backseat and put the pistol and extra magazine back inside its case and placed the case in the bottom of a black plastic bag. She stripped off the slicker and shoved it into the bag and then peeled of the latex gloves, dropped them in the bag and pulled the yellow handles tight. When she climbed back into the front seat she was all giggles as she leaned over, gave me a peck on the cheek and whispered, "That felt good. Didn't realize how much I'd missed it. There's nothing like the smell of cordite to turn a girl on." She let her hand fall to my lap and tried lying across the center console. She smiled and said, "I hate bucket seats."

I adjusted the steering column up as far as it would go. With considerable effort and no doubt some discomfort she achieved a position that made me smile. Have I mentioned that I smile a lot?

Leveling the Playing Field

"If we do not maintain justice, justice will not maintain us."

—Sir Frances Bacon

What should have been an easy two-hour drive to Sacramento turned into a long, white-knuckle, three hours—everyone slowed down for the fog. As I pulled into a parking place in front of the California State Military Museum in Old Town *Sac* the same girl I'd watched jog away in Pioneer Park stepped out of the shadows. When we exited the Malibu she slipped in behind the wheel, backed out of the parking place and drove away.

We walked across the street to the Firehouse. We were ten minutes late for our reservation. We were seated immediately. We'd finished the first course of Firehouse oysters, the second course of Dungeness crab and tomato bisque, and were enjoying the third course, *Frutti di Mare,* when the manager approached and addressed me. "Mr. Hanson." We'd used the name Alfred and Joann Richardson while in San Francisco. For the next couple of weeks we would present ourselves as Alan and Kristine Hanson.

"Yes sir."

He handed me an envelope and asked, "Does everything meet with your approval, sir?"

"Yes sir, food prepared to perfection and the service exceptional."

"Thank you, enjoy your dinner and come see us again."

"We'll do that, thank you."

"The pleasure is mine, sir."

He knew I wasn't referring to the food and table service. I was telling him the Club members were on top of everything, that I couldn't have asked for more cooperation or received better assistance.

The envelope contained sleeper-car tickets on the midnight Amtrak to San Diego and a key to a locker at the train station.

At 11:45 we removed our luggage from the locker and boarded the train. Although Amtrak was strictly for passengers, in the days when trains pulled freight cars and passenger cars in the same drag this would have been labeled a *milk train.* It took about the same time as it would have had we driven from Sacramento to San Diego, but it was a lot less stressful. We arrived just before noon and took a taxi to the Grant Hotel on West Broadway.

Although we'd eaten a full meal in Sacramento twelve hours earlier and had the Firehouse pack us some snacks for the train, we were running low on energy. After checking in, the bell captain had dispatched someone to take our luggage to the suite we'd reserved on an upper floor; we walked into the Grant Grill and approached the *maître d'hôtel.*

We'd managed to sleep in fits and starts on the train, but now, after eating more than we should have, we needed a siesta. We napped all afternoon, ordered dinner from room service, and finally fell asleep around 10 p.m. By morning we were back into our normal routine. Awoke early, showered and dressed by nine, and went to breakfast. At ten thirty we stopped by the front desk and had the valet bring around a rental car the hotel had reserved for us, which had been delivered sometime after midnight.

Anna wanted to visit Andy in Rosecrans. She took flowers. As she laid the flowers on his grave I saw a tear pearl down her cheek. The only other time I'd seen her cry was the first time she visited me while I was in jail waiting to be tried for Emily's murder. She wanted to show me where she'd gone to school and worked. I was a little uneasy about checking out her workplace since Geoff Jepson had been well known to some of the executives. We drove past Andy's house. The outside was sporting fresh paint and the lawn and shrubs were neatly trimmed. Apparently the management company had been doing their job. She said Rita had suggested they set up a trust to allow destitute retired navy fliers to live there—she'd agreed. They wanted to set up the trust in a manner so as to provide this service ad infinitum.

With a long day ahead of us we asked the concierge at our hotel to make early dinner reservations at the Prince of Wales outside dining room in the

Hotel del Coronado. Anna wanted to show me the crown room where she and Rita had taken Andy to brunch before Rita departed for the Catskills.

"This is beautiful, did you eat here often?"

"Good grief, no. We had no idea what the future would hold and we were saving every nickel we could, which wasn't much with me going to school. We ate at home, at Andy's, we considered it home. Rita did most of the cooking. I packed a lunch for school and we both brown-bagged it at work."

"Well, you can afford it now, so how about we do brunch here tomorrow?"

"Thank you, but no. Since this was where Rita and I had our last meal with Andy, we vowed to never eat in the crown room again."

"You girls really liked him."

"He kept us alive, guided us through very trying times—from the nightmares of the night Rita's parents were murdered, through growing pains of our teenage years—outside of our parents he was the only father we knew or would ever know."

Next morning we ate brunch at the Grant and then drove to Los Angeles. Our target lived on a Beneteau Oceanis at Marina Del Rey. Until six months ago he'd lived in an impressive 8,000-square-foot house just off Mulholland Drive. A year prior to his divorce he was indicted for taking money from a lobbyist for promoting her position on a bill slated to go before Congress. His wife did her duty and stood beside him giving cover as she stated that his opinions were his own and he would never take money or favors from anyone regardless of the cause, and further stating, "He is a man beyond reproach."

Although claiming the charges were false and without merit he cut a deal requiring him to pay a small fine and perform 1,000 hours of public service. As it turned out, he was taking more than money from the lobbyist. Six months later when it became known he was sleeping with her, his previously dutiful wife filed for divorce. The lobbyist found it more profitable to sleep with him in exchange for his cooperation than to make monetary payoffs. By sleeping with him she not only got help with lawmakers due to his influence with the low-information voters, the flow of money reversed. Now it was flowing from his wallet into her purse—he would have been better off had he continued to take just the money. Obviously it never occurred to him the proper thing to have done would be to refuse both the money and her sexual favors. Again, he made a deal to keep the reason for his divorce from the public eye. She got the house along with all the furnishings, her LS 460 Lexus, and a nice alimony payment to cover house payments, taxes and upkeep along with enough to keep her living without suffering a diminished lifestyle. He got the *Rainy Daze,* a sixty-foot sailboat—an appropriate name considering his situation.

The divorce left him financially unable to keep his mistress in the luxury she'd become accustomed to, so she promptly found another sugar daddy and put him on the street or more accurately, on the boat.

Neither his wife nor the mistress had been attracted to him because he was a good-looking guy with a great personality and oozing masculinity. His wife was attracted to his seven-figure salary. His mistress was attracted to his media position and used him to promote whatever she was peddling to Congress at any given time. He was the type of man you could dress in a six-thousand-dollar Tom James custom-made suit and he would still look like a bum. His personality made the wicked witch of the east appear angelic. Killing him was going to be a pleasure.

We knocked on the door of a house in the Venice Canal district where our Los Angeles contact, a distinguished-looking gentleman of sixty, perhaps sixty-five, was waiting. I never asked who owned the three-million-dollar house. We viewed pictures, activity logs, and videos of our target. He no longer lived the high life he had grown accustomed to before justice caught up with him—I was going to administer the final justice he would receive from mortals. He ate at fast-food restaurants, but still frequented his favorite bar with the hopes of picking up women—it wasn't working. Without money to throw around he had little appeal to women when there were handsome and personable men with the means to show them a good time. For most women, sleeping on a sailboat and riding to Taco Bell in a ten-year-old minivan didn't compare with a chauffeured limousine to Larry's, the Belvedere, or Ruth's Chris for drinks and dinner before retiring in a luxurious suite at the Ritz Carlton, the Jamaica Bay Inn, or the Beverley Hilton, and perhaps a nightcap at Trader Vic's. This was going to be easy. No man, especially an obnoxious little has-been that hadn't been getting any, could resist Anna when she turned on the charm—I know I couldn't.

His weekly after-work routine was pretty much the same. He pinched his pennies during the week by eating junk food and then hitting the bar on Fridays and Saturdays. He timed his arrival to coincide with the beginning of happy hour. He'd buy a beer and load up on hot wings, fried calamari, potato skins, and whatever was on the buffet bar. He'd nurse his beer through a second and third turn at the buffet while keeping an eye out for unescorted women.

There were more women than one might expect playing the bar scene, and just as their male counterparts were looking for single women or ones with a telltale tan line on their ring finger, they were looking for unaccompanied men. These women not only knew what they were looking for and what the men were looking for, they knew the score. The limo provided for more than transportation. It provided the opportunity for them to make a down payment on their dream weekend while on the way to a restaurant, or wherever.

Plump, unattractive women stuck with neighborhood bars where they knew the clientele and what to expect. These women were just as desirous of a fun weekend, but were aware of their limitations and set their sights lower. I wouldn't rate this particular bar as high-end, but because of its location it drew big spenders and attractive, suggestively, seductively dressed, women. They weren't interested in men without money to spend. Guys without money should be in the neighborhood bars with the fat, ugly women. It was only rare that our target could engage a woman in conversation for longer than five minutes, let alone talk her into going back to his sailboat.

We explained the plan to our contact, gave him a list of what was needed, and the assistance required to make it work. He assured us there would be no problems and that working with us would be a pleasure and an honor.

We drove back to our hotel in San Diego and took the following day off. At 10 a.m. on Tuesday, using our satellite phone, I checked in with Rita. She said there appeared to be nervousness in some of the panelists during discussions on news shows. Some had even been questioned by other panelists about their change in attitude toward discussions involving specific current events and politicians' comments when discussing these events. She believed operation *Chimney Sweep* was already having an effect. Said no one had alluded to a letter, but it was obviously a concern for those possessing one.

I brought her up to date and promised to check in with her after we'd reconnoitered the bar and the *Rainy Daze,* and then handed the phone to Anna. The two of them spent the next ten minutes engaged in girl talk. Since they still used their secret code, a code they had developed as young girls, I couldn't understand a thing they were saying. I suspected some of their conversation was about me. My suspicions were confirmed when Anna smiled at me and winked.

Driving from San Diego to LA and back again was inconvenient. We could be staying at a hotel practically next door to the bar or living at the canal house, but I figured no one would connect the crime with a couple residing at the Grant, two to three hours away—drive time depended on traffic and the time of day.

The door opened a few seconds after I knocked. Inside the house was the man we had met on our first visit, a woman, and a second man. I estimated the couple to be in their forties. The props were laid out for us to inspect and approve. I reiterated the part Anna and I would play in the plan—the older man had heard it from me already. The couple were already familiar with all the details of what was going down and to prove it, they explained their part, how it would work, and how timing was of the essence. When Anna and I were satisfied everyone knew their part, the four of us donned dry suits—in California, the eastern Pacific at its warmest is sixty-five degrees. The older gentleman escorted the four of us outside and across the backyard to a canal behind his house. A couple of two-man kayaks lay upside down on the lawn. The man and woman carried them down steps to the water—no motors were allowed in the canals. The woman held the kayak tight against the canal wall and suggested I squeeze into the front cockpit and adjust the spray skirt. Anna followed suit while the man stabilized their kayak.

As we paddled along the canals I learned a bit of history. It seems some guy decided he was going to build an exact replica of Venice, Italy in California, thus the name Venice. He built sixteen miles of canals with the idea of selling lots along the canals for houses and businesses. Unfortunately for the builder, the automobile came along and people preferred riding home in a horseless carriage to paddling a boat home. Most of the canals were filled in and the area became, shall we say, an area less desirable than other neighborhoods—an area to be avoided. Fifty years later, with the movie industry flourishing and hippies abounding, Venice began to grow. By the end of the twentieth century it had experienced a rebirth and the canals became a neighborhood where multi-million-dollar homes were built, and in conjunction with Marina del Rey with its high-end condominiums, where million-dollar yachts were kept, a very exclusive area.

During the history lesson our attention was directed to several landmarks we would need to recognize in order to find our way back to our starting point. Today's starting point would be our destination once we finished doing business with our target—a treasonous news show panelist passing himself off as a fair-minded reporter. Recognizing the landmarks would be more difficult at night. The canals would appear different in the dark even where lighting was provided. We paddled along the canals until we reached the channel leading to Big Lagoon. A small opening underneath the street opened into a deep, wide channel. To the left was the marina. To the right lay the Pacific Ocean. My tour guide warned me of possible problems.

"Finding the entrance to Big Lagoon can be tricky in the dark. If the surge gate is closed you will have to portage."

We then paddled out beyond the breakwater. This, according to my guide, was important for two reasons: one was to introduce Anna and me to the rough water outside the marina, and to make sure we would know what to watch for when looking for the entrance. We went out past the breakers before turning around.

Back in the marina we paddled past the *Rainy Daze.* She was sleek, a nice boat, virtually the same motor-sailer we spent a year on while cruising and spending time in port towns on the Mediterranean, Ionian, Adriatic, and Aegean Seas. She was a bit larger and a few years younger than the one we had sailed, but she was likely to handle the same, perhaps a little easier and more smoothly. We already knew the slip and pier and we'd studied an aerial view, so I wouldn't have any problems locating it on foot.

My guide insisted I find my way home, or I should say, to where our contact would be waiting. I missed one turn, but quickly realized I was on the wrong canal. She turned us around and we paddled back to the marina before starting over. This time I got it right and we ended up where we'd started our tour. A half hour after we'd gone inside and removed our dry suits Anna and her guide came inside and shed their suits. Her guide had insisted she find her way home, just as I'd done and waited to start her from the marina until after I'd arrived at our safe house. We hadn't flipped the kayak, but took a lot of spray from the breakers. Our dry suits would be hung up to dry and then stored in bags to be delivered to the *Rainy Daze* on the night we'd need them. We went over the plan one last time before Anna and I departed for the bar.

The moochers were already there waiting for the buffet to open. Anna ordered an Irish cream, I had a light beer—low-alcoholic drinks. We let the crowd have at the buffet and wandered around to familiarize ourselves with the bar's layout—we didn't want any surprises on opening night. When action at the buffet slowed down we took our turn. I took some fried clams, Greek olives, and celery sticks. Anna took vegetables only. It was no surprise Anna was already getting some not-so-casual glances from guys with beer and plates loaded with nachos. She was out of their class and they knew it, but that wouldn't keep them from making a play if opportunity presented itself. The high rollers wouldn't be there for another couple of hours. The classy women—I use the term rather loosely—would show up even later.

We'd seen enough. I dropped a sawbuck next to our glasses for the bartender as we were leaving. By the time we got back to our hotel we were both famished. I asked the desk clerk to make reservations at the Grant Grill. Informed him we would freshen up and be down in forty-five minutes. He made the call and ten seconds later, told us our reservation was confirmed.

Tomorrow was payday and play day—payday for him, play day for us. It was imperative we get a good night's rest. After dinner we showered and went straight to bed—an hour later we were asleep. We slept late and awoke rested. We resisted the urge to play house and went to lunch—time for breakfast had come and gone.

We loaded up on carbs and protein. It was going to be a long day and we didn't want to run out of energy when we'd need it most. We went back to bed and slept another two hours. I woke first and dressed in black pants, black turtleneck, running shoes, and a Harris Tweed jacket. Normally I would wear running shoes for only one reason, running. Running was exactly what I would be doing. While Anna was dressing I talked with Rita. Told her we had everything lined out and didn't see any problems. She finished with thirty seconds of sweet talk before I gave the phone to Anna. I'm sure my eyes popped out of my head at least an inch when she reached for the phone. Her dress wasn't sheer enough to be considered transparent, but you didn't need much imagination to know what was underneath and none whatsoever to realize she wasn't wearing a bra—Venus in five-inch heels.

She and Rita engaged in their secret code-speak while I double-checked to make sure I had everything I would need for show and tell. She disconnected the call, handed me the phone, then pressed against me and asked teasingly, "Do you think he'll notice me?"

She knew by my voice inflection, I didn't think it was all that funny. "You will have the moochers fighting to get in line even before we go into our act, and there's a good chance you'll be raped after I leave."

"You know I can take care of myself. All the money I spent for martial art classes didn't go to waste."

"I know, but I like to think all the things those jerks are going to be ogling are for my eyes only."

"They are, darling. I'm just baiting the trap."

"Yeah, I know. Actually, I feel sorry for those poor suckers. Our target will never know what hit him and I mean that literally."

She pulled on a lightweight knee-length coat and held it closed and asked, "Is this better?" I just smiled and kissed her.

As I pulled up in front of the canal house the garage door opened and I pulled inside—except for the walk-in entrance, the garage occupied the entire front. Our contact was there to escort us from the spic-and-span Saltillo tiled garage floor into the house.

Everything was still laid out on a long table in what appeared to be a media room. A girl, I guessed to be in her late teens, sat at a desk at the far end of the room with her eyes glued to a TV monitor.

I would later learn she was a nineteen-year-old Russian, the victim of an illegal immigration scam. Pretty young girls, often as young as twelve, were promised American citizenship and careers in modeling by unscrupulous recruiters for crime families. These girls paid to be smuggled into America. If they had money they paid up front; if not, they signed an agreement to pay with money earned from their modeling—either way, once they arrived in America they were sold into the sex-slave trade. The dream job and citizenship were the hook, neither was ever going to happen. These girls were introduced to drugs and remained sex-slave prisoners until they were no longer useful to the mob and then disposed of by various means.

Lidiya was fifteen when her parents, against their better judgment, paid five thousand dollars up front for what she believed and her parents were told, was a golden opportunity. Upon arrival in Los Angeles she learned the horrifying truth when she was taken to a house in a rundown part of town, stripped naked, raped, and then locked inside a closet. The man she'd thought to be a friend slipped Rohypnol into a soft drink after they deplaned. The date-rape drug had rendered her helpless.

While waiting in the locked closet to learn her fate, the drug began to wear off. She was desperate and scared, but still able to think. She found the pull cord for a dim overhead light. Boxes of junk were stacked against the wall at one end of the small closet. One box yielded some useful items: a letter opener with the words Hollywood, California on the handle, which she placed on a shelf by the door, a cigarette lighter that worked, and a can of lighter fluid. She placed the lighter by the letter opener.

In another box she found a collection of demitasse cups with names of different states on them—people seemed to have the need to display junk from places they had visited. By squeezing the lighter fluid tin, she was able to transfer the volatile liquid to the largest cup she could find. She placed the cup alongside the lighter and letter opener and waited.

She lost track of time and was half asleep when she heard someone rattle the hasp on the door as they slipped a key slip into the lock. She was wide awake in a heartbeat. When her captor opened the door and reached for her she doused him with the cup of lighter fluid and touched the flame of the lighter to his shirt. As he started to back away from the closet door she stabbed him in the throat with the letter opener. She had no idea what blood vessel she hit, but he began bleeding profusely. She slipped past her captor while he was tearing off his shirt. When she tried the front door, it wouldn't open. She found the deadbolt, twisted the knob, and opened the door just as the guy swung his fist at her head. She ducked underneath the blow and escaped from the house.

With no idea what to do or where to go, she ran down the first street she came to. She was looking over her shoulder and did not see the car making a right turn at an intersection and slammed into the passenger's door. Addled by the collision she fell to the pavement and was unable to move for a couple of seconds.

The driver lowered the passenger-side window and looked at the naked girl trying to stand. She hung onto the door, looked across the empty seat and said to the driver, in perfect English, "I'm in trouble and I need help." Fortunately for Lidiya, the driver was a Club member of the Los Angeles chapter. She accepted the Club's offer without thinking twice and had been a loyal member ever since.

On the monitor was a tight shot of the *Rainy Daze.* Without looking in our direction, she announced, "He's still inside."

Now it would be a waiting game.

A call came in and was answered on the second ring by the girl monitoring the TV screen with just three words, "This is Shirley." She listened intently for perhaps fifteen seconds and then said, "Roger that, nothing yet, I'll get back to you. Thanks." She turned to our contact, "Al and Lorie are in place and awaiting instructions." She was a girl of few words.

The older gentleman running the show was apparently on top of logistics. He nodded his approval to the girl.

Our host had cold shrimp, cracked crab, and salad with various condiments, iced tea and bottled water spread on a bar at the end of the room opposite the girl. Since we didn't know when we'd eat again, and with nothing to do but cool our heels, we took advantage of his generosity.

According to the bar's schedule, the buffet had opened forty-five minutes ago. I was beginning to think our quarry might live another day. Just then the girl announced, "He's on the move." She made a phone call and said, "Game on." she repeated the process a second time. I didn't try to second-guess her, I had no doubt she knew her part in our three-act tragedy.

When I checked the monitor the picture had changed. She was obviously tied into the marina's security cameras. She was either an IT specialist or had one on her team. A wide-angle shot showed our target walking along the pier toward a pedestrian gate.

Our kayak tour guides pulled on coveralls sporting a scuba-diving supply company logo and loaded all the stuff on the table into a van with the same logo as the one on their coveralls.

It was no more than a five-minute walk from the *Rainy Daze* to the bar. We waited. A few minutes passed before the phone rang.

"This is Shirley. A few seconds later she gave a one-word reply, "Thanks."

She turned and reported, "He's inside."

The couple cranked up the van and left. We waited.

Twenty minutes later, another phone call, "This is Shirley."

She listened for no more than ten seconds before saying, "Thanks."

She looked at me and said, "All your gear is on board."

It was my turn; I smiled and nodded, "Thanks."

We could have eliminated this little excuse for a man without such elaborate plans, but the idea was to follow the first four predictions mentioned in the letter. This was needed to assure the recipients of the letters these were executions, not accidents, and directly connected to the letter. After tonight there would be no need for further demonstrations. Anyone having received a letter would know, without doubt, if their name was on the letter they could be next.

There were no predictions for how the fifth death or any subsequent assassinations would occur, so we could keep it simple after this one. However, should they get cocky and pretend these deaths had no connection to their dishonesty when reporting the news or try to dismiss them as accidental we might remind them we were for real by telling them exactly how the next one was going down.

A third reason was to get all chapters of the Club involved, and to give them some hands-on experience. From what I'd seen it appeared there wouldn't be any problems with recon and preparation. For the next round I'd find out if they were up to taking it all the way—doing the deed.

Our host pulled into the parking lot to one side of the bar and killed the ignition. Anna and I exited and headed for the front entrance. Our guy was easy to spot. He was sitting at the bar gazing into the mirror—his eyes darting back and forth from one woman to another. When we walked behind him he locked in on Anna and continued to stare as she took the stool beside him. Stools on either side had been empty. Obviously, he didn't have a lot of admirers. If the empty stools were an indicator, he didn't have any.

We knew from our recon when you ordered any beer other than tap you got the bottle and no glass. We ordered a popular, and ridiculously expensive, light beer. Anna took a good pull on hers immediately—I left mine on the bar. I was standing behind and slightly to her left. She'd unbuttoned her coat before we entered. When she turned to face me, her assets, except for what little the dress hid, were fully exposed to the little twerp. He didn't even try to disguise his stare by casually looking away from time to time and watching her out of the corner of his eye. It was hard to resist punching him in the face.

I leaned over and whispered in her ear. She bit her lip to keep from laughing. The idea was to make her angry and upset. I shouldn't have cracked a joke about her and ogle-eye. She recovered and when I whispered again, the fight was on. There were daggers in her eyes when she looked at me. A few more whispers and then she started in on me with some uncomplimentary language referencing my manhood. The argument quickly progressed to its climax—the hook. It would be up to Anna to set it and I had no doubt she would.

The fight ended when I called her a slut. Spectators no doubt concluded my comment had elevated her to high dudgeon when she slapped me and snapped, "Don't ever call me a slut."

I pushed her to one side, picked up my beer, drank half and slammed the bottle down on the bar, grabbed her by the hair, pulled her head back and spat the words into her face, "Well, screw you, lady."

I let go her hair and turned to walk away when she said, condescendingly, "Somebody will, but it won't be you." She flipped me the bird as I walked away.

I knew it wouldn't be long before she would leave the bar with our target on a leash. Our contact was waiting and started his car when he saw me. I removed my jacket, crawled into the backseat, and exchanged my pants for sweats. He dropped me a hundred yards from the gate that opened onto the pier where the *Rainy Daze* was tied up. Pretending I was just finishing my evening run, I jogged to the gate and then, with my hand on the key hanging around my neck underneath the turtleneck, snapped the cord and inserted the key in the lock. The Club was very resourceful and efficient. The key fit perfectly and the gate opened smoothly. I pulled it closed behind me and made my way to the sailboat. I didn't need to check the name, but I did, and then climbed aboard.

Inside, I found all the gear I'd inspected at the canal house laid out on the bed—the cabin was forward of the saloon and out of sight to anyone climbing down the ladder. There was no need to check it again. I found a comfortable chair and waited, it wasn't a long wait. I recognized Anna's voice even before they climbed onboard. From her statements it appeared she was having to fight off the slimy little guy. I suspected she wanted to kill him then and there, but she kept her cool. Her voice was musical. "Now behave, you're too impatient."

I was anxious myself and could hardly wait to deck the little jerk. She was laughing, but not for the reason he thought, when she said, "Slow down. You're going to spoil everything."

He slithered down the ladder into the saloon and then, clearly salivating, turned to watch Anna descend the steps into the saloon. He never had the pleasure. "Hey bozo, how's your date working out? You sure know how to pick 'em. She's hot, much too hot for you."

He turned to look at me with saucer-sized eyes. His mouth was moving, trying to form words—slobber was the only thing coming out. I gave him a hard right fist to the face. The one I'd held in reserve since the moment he started ogling Anna at the bar. He was already folding up when I follow the straight right with a left hook to the temple. He crumpled to the deck. I could have taken him out with a couple of classic martial art moves without bruising my knuckles, but he brought something primitive out in me. Something requiring a less than civilized solution. A crushed trachea, a broken clavicle, and ruptured spleen weren't enough. There's something about good old-fashioned street-style brawling that provides greater satisfaction.

Anna was in my arms before I could move. "I need a bath to wash off all this sewage. I've never met anyone as filthy as this slimeball. You have to let me kill him."

I gave her a hug. "You got it, but let's finish this the way we planned."

She gave me a peck on the cheek. "Okay, I'm back, I'm focused, let's get it on."

A waterproof bag on the bed contained everything we would need during the time we would be on board the sailboat. She changed into sweats and running shoes she'd removed from the bag, while I bound and anchored our guest, perhaps I should say our host, to the ladder with the type of plastic ties police use for handcuffs. He would be out until we were well out of the marina, but just in case I slapped a piece of duct tape over his mouth. From there I moved to the wheelhouse and checked battery power and fuel capacity. I turned on the ignition and waited for the glow plugs to heat up, switched on the fuel pump, checked the pressure, and hit *start*. The VW diesel engine turned over a couple of times, caught and idled smoothly. Anna was already on the pier and had disconnected all services other than shore power. When the engine caught I checked generator output, turned on the running lights and gave her a thumbs up. She made the final disconnect and signaled okay. I pushed the gear lever forward to make the forward lines slack. She threw off the two lines. We repeated the process for the aft lines. She stepped aboard, pulled in and stored the lines, and then joined me in the wheelhouse.

The *Rainy Daze* had everything you would want in electronics. It no doubt had chart readers and at least a few local charts—you could spend tens of thousands of dollars on charts. We had no need of charts since we'd studied a map of the marina and knew how to get to the main channel. From there on, buoy lights would show us the way to the ocean. It wasn't like we were off on a long voyage. Ten miles out Al and Lorie were waiting. We cleared the marina entrance and were about a mile out when

Anna switched on a low-power radio beacon—part of the gear delivered on board by our kayak guides. This was not an emergency beacon. It was especially designed to transmit on a commercial AM radio station not used locally. No one would suspect anything unusual since AM radio is very susceptible to electronic inference. This would allow them to home in on us. The sun had set ten minutes before we cleared the marina. It was a moonless night—they would not have a visual on us since I turned off the running lights fifteen minutes outside the marina entrance. The 140-horse diesel would move us along much faster than the speed I was running, but I didn't want to hit a log or some other hazard hard enough to punch a hole in the hull. I could have turned up the radar, but someone, the Coast Guard perhaps, might pick up our transmissions and check to see why we weren't showing running lights.

Sinking the boat along with our friend would have taken care of part of the problem. The letter had promised the media something a little more spectacular, however—I wanted to make sure our little show lived up to their expectations.

With the lights of Venice well behind us Anna called in to the girl in charge of communications. She had the satellite cell phone on speaker. The now familiar voice answered, "This is Shirley."

"Kristine here, we're two miles offshore. The parrot is singing. All is well."

"Al and Lorie are listening to your music. We'll talk later." She signed off with her standard, "Thanks."

I turned the helm over to Anna and went below and located the fuel lines leading to the engine. Both fuel tanks, the primary in the engine room, and the secondary hidden away in the galley had pumps inside them—similar to the gas tank in your car. The two lines terminated at a manifold with a single line to the engine. It would be simple enough to disconnect the two supply lines from the manifold. When the pumps were turned on the engine room would flood with diesel fuel within minutes. With the engine and all electronics off there would be nothing to accidentally start a fire or cause an explosion. I checked the tool closet for the proper wrench, found it, laid it aside, and then climbed out of the engine room and relieved Anna in the wheelhouse.

She descended the ladder to the saloon, went to the forward cabin and removed two satellite phones from the WP (wet proof) bag—I was a little concerned the phones could somehow be traced back to the seller and thus the purchaser. I was uneasy for no reason—they were never going to be found. We could have used throwaway phones, but cell service is sometimes unreliable a few miles offshore. She placed one on the deck in the cabin and the other on the saloon deck, using duct tape to keep them from moving about as the sailboat pitched and rolled. Next she removed two small devices containing LC circuits, plugged them into specially designed jacks on the phones, and secured them with duct tape. One was enough—but why take the chance?

The devices were simple. As the phone rang—actually, they wouldn't ring—current normally used to provide a ringtone would build on the capacitor and at a certain level would discharge through the coil across an air gap and produce a spark. Similar to the one on a gas range that ignites the burner, but producing a much hotter spark, more like the spark used to ignite fuel in an internal-combustion engine. The air gap would keep arcing until the call was disconnected or . . .

Finished with her chores, Anna donned her dry suit and came topside. We left everything we'd brought with us in the salon except my cell phone and a few items that would go inside my dry suit before we abandoned ship. There was no need to be concerned about fingerprints or DNA. Anything the fire or ocean didn't completely destroy would be useless to forensics.

It was thirty minutes later the phone in my pocket vibrated. I checked the number and then answered, "Alan here."

"Al and Lorie are 100 yards off your starboard beam. What are your instructions?"

"Wait ten minutes, and then send over a skiff."

"Thanks."

After killing the ignition, turning off the fuel pumps, and all electronics, I climbed back down into the engine compartment.

The connectors were tight, but since the *Rainy Daze* was a fairly new boat, they were not frozen. With the lines disconnected from the manifold I turned off the engine-compartment lights—the twenty-four-volt lights ran off four twelve-volt batteries. Two batteries were connected in series providing a twenty-four-volt service. The other two, also connected in series, provided a backup system. This system would provide power to the fuel pumps. Switching on the pumps would be the last thing I would do before we abandoned ship.

As we were no longer under power the *Rainy Daze* was at the mercy of the ocean, she pitched and rolled with the waves—the sea was running higher than I would have preferred. I descended the ladder to the saloon. After switching the phone's power to *on*, I moved to the cabin and switched on power to the second phone. I removed my dry suit from the WP bag, donned it and slipped a couple of items inside my suit before securing it. The two duel-tank scuba rigs were still on the bed where they had been placed by our assistants. Upon opening the first of four valves, garlic, used to insure it was impossible to be unaware of a propane leak, reached my nostrils immediately. The compartments were watertight. I'd turned off the forced-air ventilation system. Once I climbed the ladder and closed the hatch the compartments would be airtight as well as watertight. The tanks would empty within five minutes, leaving the compartments filled with highly volatile gas.

Our host was conscious now and jerking at his bindings. The only thing he would accomplish would be to rub his wrists raw. His eyes were still the size of saucers. He was trying to talk or perhaps scream. The duct tape would crease and then pull tight as he tried to open his mouth. I patted him on the head and said, "If you believe in God, now would be a good time to start praying." I considered turning off lights in the cabin and saloon, but then thought better of it. No sense taking a chance the switch would arc when the contacts were broken and set off the propane bomb thus blowing us sky high. I ascended the ladder and closed the hatch sealing the compartments shut.

Only one thing left before we jumped ship. A four-man Zodiac was hanging ten yards away on our windward side. Battery power was still on. I flipped the fuel pump switches and heard the pumps start. They would pump twenty to thirty gallons a minute into the engine room. I'd already disabled the bilge pumps, so diesel fuel would spread throughout the bilges, finding its way into every nook and cranny of the lowest level. Fumes from the diesel fuel would provide for a secondary explosion.

Making sure we were all on the same page, I called Shirley. When she came on I reported. "We are abandoning ship and need a pickup."

"Roger that. Stand by, please." Ten seconds later she came back on line, "You're good to go. Thanks"

I sealed the phone in a small watertight container, dropped it inside my dry suit, resealed my suit, turned to Anna, and asked. "You ready?"

"As ready as I'll ever be. Did you forget anything?"

"I don't think so, but if I did, how would I know?" She laughed, kissed me, activated the light stick attached to her dry suit and jumped into the ocean. I cracked my light stick and followed her.

Showing Panic

"Reality is merely an illusion, albeit a very persistent one."

—Albert Einstein

The *Rainy Daze* presented a much larger surface to the wind than a couple of heads bobbing up and down and soon drifted away. The electric motor was barely audible as Al maneuvered the Zodiac alongside us. I caught a tote handle, and flipped into the boat. I extended my hand. Anna grabbed it and swung over the gunwale.

A modified cigarette boat, without running lights, sat low in the water. When I spotted it we were only fifty feet away. I'd heard the engine purring before I spotted the boat. Once on board the speedboat we disconnected the light sticks from our dry suits and dropped them into the ocean. The cigar boat, as it was previously known, had become famous during the rum-running days of prohibition. In the last couple of decades it had been upgraded, thanks to newer materials and advanced technology and used for smuggling narcotics and tax-free cigarettes—thus *cigarette boat.*

Al used the bow line attached to the Zodiac, walked it aft, and then pulled it onto the cigarette boat's stern. We wouldn't be running at a high speed, so it would ride without a problem. With the Zodiac secured, Al turned on the boat's radar—not standard equipment for *Go-Fast* boats—

engaged the transmission, and opened the throttle. Seconds later only the props and control surfaces were touching the water.

Lorie reported to Shirley, "We had a clean recovery and we're on *the step*." At the moment, two things were important: to get as far away from the *Rainy Daze* in the next ten minutes as we could and to be close enough to shore for Anna and me to climb back into the Zodiac and safely reach the marina. We would use the battery-powered motor until we entered the canals—then we would paddle.

Al knew the waters off Venice and had reliable radar. Twice, when an alarm sounded he turned to port for a few seconds before turning back on course. We were running at forty-five knots, nowhere near top speed. We were covering three and a half miles every four minutes. When he cut power and the boat settled back into the water we were a quarter mile offshore. While Al untied the zodiac's bow line and pushed it off the stern and then walked it around to the starboard side, I took our satellite phone out of its waterproof compartment and offered it to Anna. She took it and punched in the number of one of the two phones on the *Rainy Daze*. Nothing happened. Five seconds passed and she was about to call the second number when just short of the horizon, the sky lit up like the Fourth of July. A big smile was on her lips and her eyes twinkled as she handed me the phone. I returned the phone to its WP container and dropped it down inside my dry suit.

We climbed into the Zodiac. I switched the electric motor power switch to three forward. We had barely cleared the cigarette boat when Al was off and running. Two minutes later the only sound we heard was the wave action slapping against the Zodiac and surf breaking on the beach. I pointed our little boat toward the light atop the breakwater at the marina's entrance and increased the little electric motor to maximum RPMs.

Now the seas were running higher than when we abandoned the *Rainy Daze* and I found myself wishing our little boat was a bit more stable—the Zodiac would not sink, but the wind had picked up and I feared we might capsize in the chop outside the entrance. Once inside the marina we were free of the chop, but the swells still affected our little boat. There was not a problem finding the entrance to the canals. The problem—we'd been warned it could happen—the surge gate had been lowered into place.

The Zodiac was a small boat and considerably lighter than wood or fiberglass even with the marine battery and electric motor, but it was still more than I wanted to portage up a rocky embankment, across a street, and down the other side. It was doable, but might pique the interest of some law enforcement agent driving by or living nearby or perhaps a concerned civilian who would call it in to 911.

I discussed the situation with Anna and we agreed a better plan would be to exit the marina, motor out beyond the chop, and then proceed up the beach to an area where the State of California, using eminent domain, had forced an easement across private property. We would abandon the Zodiac on the beach and use the easement, bridges, and walkways along the canals to reach our safe house. In all likelihood forensics would conclude the owner of the *Rainy Daze* was murdered and the explosion rigged to destroy prints and DNA left behind by the culprit or culprits responsible. We weren't concerned the Zodiac would be associated with the *Rainy Daze*. Even if the connection was made, it wouldn't yield evidence to lead them to the killers. There were no markings to connect it with Al and Lorie. We'd worn dry suits, which made it highly unlikely they could lift anything useful from the little boat. The items we carried inside our dry suits could easily be explained away should we be stopped by any law-enforcement-type.

Getting past the breakwater on the way out was more hazardous than getting into the marina. The Santa Ana wind was in our favor, but the tide and surge were against us. Cold air falling down the Sierra Nevada slopes as the ocean and San Joaquin Valley cooled—a normal evening and nighttime occurrence—increased the problem of chop when outbound. Several boats were leaving the marina, adding to the hazard we faced. Apparently several boat owners had been alerted to the fireworks show and were headed out to the area, probably with the idea of rescuing survivors. Without running lights we were a hazard to the outbound boats as well as to ourselves. We kept just outside the northern channel markers. I was concerned someone might spot us and call the Coast Guard and report a boat in violation of the ordinance requiring all boats to have running lights at night. Once outside the rough water I headed north. We no longer had to deal with the chop, but swells beyond the area where they become the type of breakers surfers revel in, were five to six feet. This required turning into the swell to ride over it and then running in the trough paralleling the beach until I had to deal with the next swell.

Once inside the breakwater I'd run at half power, but after leaving the marina I'd been running the little electric motor at its highest setting. Now, turns on the propeller had begun to fall off. Whereas flashlight batteries just keep getting weaker and weaker until the light is useless, deep-cycle marine batteries are designed to give you max power until they are totally spent. If we didn't get to shore quickly we would be dead in the water and the Santa Ana wind would blow us out to sea. If this happened and we were swept past the Channel Islands we'd be in big trouble. Either way we'd be in trouble. Keeping the power on the max setting, I pointed the Zodiac toward the beach. Fortunately, we got to the point where waves were just beginning to break before the battery was completely discharged. We broke out the paddles and made an all-out effort to catch the first breaker. Had we missed, it was likely the wind would have taken us out to sea. Once the wave ran out of energy we lost the progress we'd made as the wind took us out again—we were unable to hold our own, let alone make any headway with the paddles. Fortunately the wind didn't take us out past where the waves were breaking. We caught the next breaker only to have the same thing happen. After the third try I knew we were in trouble.

Originally, I'd planned to beach the Zodiac. I wasn't concerned about it falling into the hands of law enforcement. Most likely it would have been inside someone's garage before sunup. Considering our situation we decided to abandon the little boat and body-surf to the beach. Three breakers later we were in knee-deep water walking on a sandy bottom. Lights from the fishing pier at the end of Washington Street were visible a hundred yards farther up the beach. No need to break out the laminated map and waterproofed LED light I carried inside my dry suit. From here I knew exactly how to get back to the canal house and so did Anna—we'd walked through it in our recon.

Adventures can be exciting, but there's nothing like returning to the Catskills and being welcomed home by Rita. Two days later, rested and relaxed, the three of us met with the principal committee, headed up by the director. After the committee analyzed and followed up on data submitted by subcommittees, it would either sanction or reject projects submitted for consideration.

There were now several subcommittees—all overwhelmed by requests, from other chapters, for permission to proceed with a project. It was obvious, the Club had been waiting for someone to inspire and move it to action. Genesis was the catalyst Club members had needed. Now they were ready and eager for action.

I feared there would be members of the Club too eager to get involved who would initiate projects on their own. Proceeding without supervision, a chain of command, and guidelines for committees and individuals would invite disaster. Subcommittee chairs had to know their limits. Everything had to be spelled out. At the moment nothing was spelled out as to how information flowed or how subcommittees were to respond—this had to change. The entire system of subcommittees had to change. Of necessity, a shakeup was in the immediate future. I asked for a special meeting to discuss my concerns.

One subgroup had been assigned to follow media reaction and report any obvious or perceived changed or altered attitude of media members whose names were on the list. This committee also analyzed how the demise of their four comrades had been reported. They watched for any mention of attempted media intimidation. When and if anything was revealed it would, no doubt, be couched in the language of "a conservative lunatic's effort to bully reporters and their associates." Liberals and the media equated bullying to rape and murder and viewed all conservatives as lunatics, therefore anything traditional, like standing up for the Constitution, was the act of a bully (a conservative lunatic). So far, no one had mentioned threats or the letter. We weren't so naive as to not consider it likely the FBI had a copy of the letter in their possession, but then again one never knew. What if they did? How could they keep all 100 people on the list under surveillance at all times? They couldn't. With fewer than 14,000 agents, it would take 5% of their force to keep a two-man team with eyes-on their assigned subject twenty-four-hour a day for those on the list. Even then, their chances of thwarting an assassination wasn't likely—they could react only after the fact. We could tie up even more agents by doubling the number of people on our list.

This was exactly what we would be doing when we extended our attention to the Department of Health, Education, and Welfare. Our first priority for this bureaucracy would be education. Our focus would be on historical revisionists from kindergarten teachers to seditionist university presidents—names for the list were already being compiled.

The next group would be politicians—a wide-open field. Somewhere, down through the years, someone had cited the First Amendment to the Constitution as protection for politicians who knowingly articulated terminological inexactness during campaigns. Then First Amendment protection was interpreted to also cover lies after they were elected to office. The Justice Department had been and still was, as were the media, a willing accomplice—this had to stop. How long would it take? I didn't know, but I had no doubt whatsoever, when the consequence for lying to the citizens became unacceptable for those guilty of what has become a socially acceptable disease, the practice would stop. These things were already working their way through the planning stage, but first things first—we were still in the training stage and working with a single list.

Training was exactly what I had in mind. What I'd seen of the Club's members while working with them on the first four executions had convinced me local chapters were up to the task of taking subsequent operations all the way to completion. My concerns involved organization, a chain of command, and certainty that everyone, especially those in charge of a specific operation, knew when to pull back. There could be no second-guessing at this juncture.

In the planning stage, every detail would be scrutinized and evaluated with an eye to what could go awry. In any action a hundred things could go wrong. If you could think of half of them, you were a genius. Having backup plans was crucial. There was no way of knowing when switching to a secondary plan would be required to insure the operation would be successful or to insure your escape. If in doubt, walk away—there would always be another opportunity.

The girls and I met with the director and requested a general assembly of members in our local chapter—we knew it would be granted. It was set for the following evening.

Everything was arranged as it had been for our homecoming. The large dinner table had been rolled out again. Two of the regular tables were situated in corners opposite the mirrored window looking into the main dining room. Curtains had been drawn to insure sound originating in our small dining room could not be heard inside the larger dining room. The six o'clock and ten o'clock seating had been canceled with everyone dining at eight.

The director, as was traditional, announced his choice for dinner—when dining at the director's table he always preordered and you ate whatever he ate. We gave him the appropriate commentary remarks, "Good choice," and so on. After announcing his dinner selection he went into a short monologue promising an exciting evening, but first we would enjoy our meal. As dinner was served there was a gentle yet audible murmur as diners were trying to guess what the director had meant by the term "an exciting evening." As dinner wound down and the tables were cleared, the director stood. Everyone was paying close attention as he began.

"As you know, for the past six months we have been engaged in operation *Chimney Sweep*. A strategy conceived, designed, and implemented by Mr. Scott, Miss Anna, and Miss Rita. Each chapter of the Club will, in time, form and employ groups from their membership to plan and carry out their own particularized actions against our mutual enemy.

"In order to avoid the use of member's names, we will use a letter from the Greek alphabet to identify each group. Members of these groups will be known only by committee members of their related chapters and Mr. Scott, Miss Anna, and Miss Rita. From this moment on you will not hear those three names associated with operation *Chimney Sweep*. For several days I pondered and searched my mind for an applicable name. I didn't consider a Greek letter since their name needed to set them apart from the rest and show them to be the creator of operation *Chimney Sweep*. At first I'd thought 'the A team' would work, but that's too cliché. Finally, last night as I prepared for bed and picked up the bible for my evening reading, the name flashed through my subconsciousness like a bolt of lightning shooting across a summer's night sky."

The director looked across the table at us for several seconds before he raised his glass and said,

"Ladies and gentlemen, I give you *Genesis*."

Amid wild applause and "Hear! Hear!" I turned my head back and forth looking at the girls. They were all smiles with their sparkling eyes fixed on me. Several seconds passed before I took their hands in mine and lifted them out of their chairs as I stood. The applause continued with everyone now on their feet. Still holding the girl's hands, I lifted them above our heads. Several seconds later I let go of their hands and they sat down. I waited a few more seconds and then held up my hands for quiet. As the applause died away I thanked the director and Club members for their support and display of respect, and then continued.

"I'm reminded of a song, popular when I was growing up. The last line of the first stanza declared, '*and we've only just begun*.' This is indeed the beginning. Whether America stands or falls depends on each and every member of the Club. It requires an all-out effort. We are all chess pieces on the board of reality. Most of us are pawns. As pawns we have limitations, but an army of pawns can be overwhelming. To survive, we must overwhelm our enemies. The director gives me too much credit. Like you, I am a pawn. Admittedly, I have two beautiful queens at my side," I gestured as

I looked at Anna and Rita, "to protect and guide me. Whatever accolades you have reserved for me belong to them. Please treat them accordingly.

"Since launching *Chimney Sweep* we have successfully completed four projects with several more in progress. My team and I have been privileged to work with Club members in New York City, Washington DC, San Francisco, and Venice, California. Each member has shown the utmost in professionalism. They were thorough in their research, showed up at precisely the right time, knew what was expected of them, and carried out their assignments to the letter. In my past existence, I worked with members of a governmental law enforcement agency who were far less professional and dependable. If these four operations are indicators, and I believe they are, by the time we expand to include all phases of our plan, the Club will be the most efficient and professional law enforcement agency in the land. We were appointed and sanctioned by the founding fathers. This in my opinion, makes us a legitimate branch of government—an army at large, Minute Men of the twenty-first century.

"I thank you for the opportunity to serve you and with you as we all strive to serve our country."

There was more applause. Before sitting down, I looked across the table and said, "Mr. Director."

The director stood. When the applause died away, he announced. "The next segment will be long, so we will take a fifteen-minute recess. When you return it will be your pleasure to hear from the brainy and beautiful members of Genesis. Afterwards, there will be the opportunity for questions and answers."

Members returned as libations were refreshed. When the last returning members took their seats the director tapped on his glass. Murmurs and soft undertones were hushed immediately. He lifted his hand and extended it in our direction. All eyes were on Rita as she rose from her chair. She began without pomp or ceremony.

"Our goal is to expose sedition and dishonesty in the media, education, courts, government, and Hollywood.

"There are always skeptics. Paul Dickson, in a *Saturday Review* article, stated '*It'll Never Fly, Orville.*' Admittedly, formulating an idea is easier than implementing your plan—strategy, when applied, does not always guarantee success.

"With pride I stand before you and jubilantly report: with a mere 1 percent of our stratagem deployed we have evidence it is working—we will hear from a committee chair later. And yes, we've only just begun.

"This brings us to an agenda item. We realize some of you spend all of your time making sure the resort operates smoothly, which is no small feat—we thank you. Others have positions demanding part of your time must be dedicated to the resort—we thank you as well. We all are required in one way or another to insure the resort continues successfully. Many of you are no longer obligated to the Club—your debt has been paid, as it is with Genesis. We could walk away, no questions asked. You could walk away. Yet we are still here. You are still here. We are here because the Club is our calling—it is no longer an obligation. I believe it is the same for you.

"With this in mind, we need volunteers for committees and chairmanships. All chapter directors are responsible to our director since he is the director over all chapters. For this reason and the fact that Genesis is based with this chapter, we will consider committees at other chapters to be subcommittees. The chain of command will be a two-way street. Information and requests from subcommittees will flow up to their counterpart (committee) here at *Chimney Sweep* central. Committee chairs will report to Genesis. Genesis is responsible to the director. Information, directives and counterdirectives will flow back down the chain. Everything moving up and down the chain will be in code and will require authenticators. Also, these messages will have action indicators, such as routine, operation immediate, and emergency.

"Committees and subcommittees will be charged with monitoring a specific segment of society we are at war with and reporting obvious changes in attitude and behavior. Although we are concerned only with the media at this time, we will soon focus on education, courts, government, and Hollywood. Besides monitoring we will have training and planning committees. As we expand our war your jobs will become more difficult and time consuming. The chairman of subcommittees—your counterparts in other chapters—will report to you. You will compare, analyze, and evaluate their findings, and in return, your chairman will report to Genesis.

"Other committees will be needed to monitor progress by the police, FBI, and forensics. These are friends—we cannot fault them for doing their job—in time they may come to realize we are their friends as well. It may become necessary to feed them false information at times. At other times we may need to drop a clue or a person's name. Whenever it is possible, we need to know what they know.

"We need experienced personnel in all areas I've mentioned, as well as areas I haven't gotten around to yet. We are most interested in your expertise, whatever it may be. A committee for scheduling training will be the next committee to organize. If you have something to offer in these areas please contact Genesis.

"When we were inducted into the service of our country we all signed the Club's code of conduct by pricking our thumbs and attaching our fingerprint in blood to the recruiting documents. We all know the consequences of breaking the oath. With this in mind we understand why it is imperative to always follow the chain of command. Only in the direst of situations should it be broken. The chain of command starts with the individual. The individual will pass ideas as well as rumors—sometimes rumors are facts—and concerns in the general population to a subcommittee. Subcommittees report to committees, the committee chair will report to Genesis. We are responsible to the director. Instructions and requests will travel back down the chain of command until they reach the level responsible for implementing a specific directive. This is not a superhighway of communications, but it will serve our purpose. The nature of a communication chain requires accuracy and promptness and it must for all times remain secret. If it appears I am repeating myself in areas of committees and the chain of command, I do so because it's of the utmost importance and cannot be repeated too often—no detail is insignificant. To quote Benjamin Franklin:

> *'For the want of a nail the shoe was lost,*
> *For the want of a shoe the horse was lost,*
> *For the want of a horse the rider was lost,*
> *For the want of a rider the battle was lost,*
> *For the want of a battle the kingdom was lost,*
> *And all for the want of a horseshoe nail.'*

"We are on the threshold of greatness. We have, at last, engaged the enemy. We are answering our call to duty. There are exciting times ahead of us. Will you answer the call?"

There was a resounding yes. She sat down amid the applause. Anna rose immediately and called for quiet. She began as had Rita, without formal procedure.

"Our enemies have been eroding the Constitution and the American Dream for a hundred years. We cannot undo the damage in a year, ten years, or a hundred years. It will be necessary to continue this war for our lifetime and beyond. Our enemies began in secret, just as we are doing. Now they operate openly using emotion to snare the innocent and uninformed. We will never have the advantage of publicly declaring our quest. Logic and reality are no match for emotion and promised utopia. We must work in secret, just as we have in the past. You will never be honored with a trip to the White House, given the key to a city, or throw out the first pitch at a World Series game, or have people ask to shake your hand at a dinner in your name. You will never receive the Nobel Peace Prize or the Distinguished Civilian Service Award—your adornments must be worn on your soul, not your lapel.

"We will not attempt to take out a target without having considered every detail and every possibility. Nothing will be left to chance. Any indication something is amiss at anytime during an operation, the field commander not only has the option of pulling back—he or she is expected to do so. Regardless, every war, even with the best intelligence, reconnaissance, planning, and execution, has casualties. I do not need to remind anyone what our code of conduct expects and requires of us in any given situation.

"Some things are known about Genesis, some are not. I tell you this so you will know I am speaking from experience, not just theory: Mr. Scott, Miss Rita, and I have taken out a total of nineteen of our enemies—all, except for the last four, we did without assistance. It was time consuming and took a lot of work, but we didn't take chances. Everything went as planned and without fallout. With the help of Club members from the New York, DC, San Francisco, and Los Angeles chapters, the last four went down as smooth as silk. We expect nothing less for future operations. With training and experience we will, as Mr. Scott said earlier, 'become the most efficient and professional law-enforcement agency in the land.'

"The key for reading, composing, and passing commands and information will change every minute of every day. You will be given passwords good for a single operation according to how you are involved. After a target has been sufficiently dealt with the password and all details of the operation will be deleted—zero information will be retained. It will be as if it never happened.

"Most pressing at the moment is the need to form committees—I need volunteers to make it happen. I know you are eager to be a part of *Chimney Sweep*. You may think serving on a committee is limiting and you are eager to serve in the field. You want in on the action. Nothing is more important than serving on committees—this is where the important work takes place. Without committees nothing goes forward—who, what, when, where, and how are all products of committee work. When your time comes to serve in the field, you will not be second-guessing your assignment. You will know every action has been planned and researched to the nth degree.

"The way we did it when you gave me your preferred codename worked perfectly. Use your codename, tell me on what committee you prefer to serve, and give me your expertise. Mark your envelopes Beowulf and leave them with the concierge. Our present need is in the areas of monitoring, planning, and training. At the moment we want to focus on training. This, more than other committees, will require working directly with other chapters—if this is your choice, be ready to travel.

"At this time I call on the chairlady charged with monitoring the media's reaction to recent events unleashed against four of its members. We considered these four to be among the top 2 percent of those exhibiting and teaching sedition to the general public.

"Miss Laura has a doctorate in behavioral psychology with twenty years experience as a behavioral psychologist and fifteen years teaching behavioral science. Miss Laura."

A lady looking young for someone in her midsixties stood to brief applause.

"Thank you. I will keep this short and to the point. Without explaining how I interpret reactions of those I observe. I will give you my findings to this point of those on the list of one hundred.

"The New York City execution didn't make a single ripple as far as I could tell—it appears everyone bought into the heart attack theory. It isn't likely anyone checked their list for that one. However, I suspect after the DC columnist failed to return from Cancun and after it was confirmed she never checked into her hotel, everyone checked the list and reread the letter. There appeared to be a general nervousness among those on the list I was able to observe—some more than others. After the reporter, a primetime panelist, was shot pointblank and killed alongside a known drug dealer in San Francisco there was a noted change in attitude in most everyone on the list. Now there was bickering between panelists as some were turning against their ideology of six months earlier. After the sailboat blew up ten miles off Venice, California I detected near panic in a couple of reporters topping the list.

"No one mentioned the letter or the list outright, but a few speculated something was strange about the deaths of four prominent people of the media in such a short time frame. One added, 'Someone must have it in for us.'

"I suspect it will be only a matter of time before someone mentions the letter, perhaps not the list just yet, but they will mention the letter. When it happens, I suggest you take the person out immediately. It will send two messages. One: it will drive home the meaning of the first paragraph in the letter, and two: all doubt will be erased from the minds of those on the list. They must change their ways or risk dying."

At that she sat down and Anna rose while members were trying to digest Miss Laura's last statement.

"The director mentioned a question and answer session. This would be a good time for you to ask any questions you may have."

She looked around the room waiting. It was a full minute before a middle-aged gentleman stood. "Miss Anna, I recently retired from an agency whose mission is code breaking. We don't advertise or deny it when confronted, but we can hack into just about any computer in the world. I am fully aware of your expertise in writing codes. I have yet to get past your first firewall. I don't think anyone can get into any of your programs. My question is this: If for some unknown reason your computer falls into the hands of the government, given enough time they will break your codes. What precautions have you taken to prevent this from happening?"

"Yes, Mr. Hughes, I detected your probing right after I collected code names from the members. You haven't found the cookies or bombs I left on your computer, have you?"

"Uh, no, I haven't. How did you get past my security?"

"It wasn't much of a challenge, sir. I considered melting your hard drive, but I thought I'd wait to find out if you were a friend or foe. Which are you, sir, friend or foe?"

"It may be difficult for you to trust me after you caught me trying to hack into your computer, but I swear to you, I am a friend."

"I believe you, sir. If I called on you to assist me from time to time, would you be agreeable?"

"Absolutely, I would be honored."

"Now, to answer your question, just how secure is the information I have about you. I'm sure you aren't the only one with questions about my security. Thank you for the question and for being up front about your attempted hacking.

"You are wondering what will happen if my computer falls into the wrong hands. You should be concerned; it could mean death or prison to many members and perhaps an end to the Club. Rest assured I have covered everything you can think of and perhaps more. If this appears about to happen, I can write a command that will detonate three acid bombs inside the computer. All hard drives as well as every program and everything inside the computer will be destroyed and leave nothing retrievable—I can do this at my keyboard or remotely. This can be achieved by any member of Genesis—I say any member of Genesis because it will one day become necessary to replace the leaders of *Chimney Sweep*. There are younger Club members who, in time, will become very capable leaders—I already have one in mind. I met her on our last operation. She is intelligent, capable of great things, and loyal to the core—she will never forget she owes the Club more than she can ever repay. The Club is fortunate to have her as a member—all things in due time.

"Back to security, all committee and subcommittee chairs will have a laptop. These laptops will have access to information required by the chair and nothing more. I can destroy any or all laptops at any given time and there is nothing anyone can do to prevent it. The beauty of the system of laptops is the fact that no data are retained in the laptops. When these laptops are booted, several passwords are required. If the passwords are correct and entered correctly the appropriate data for the laptop will be downloaded from my computer. As they work a project the data will be stored on my computer, not their laptop. When they shut down the laptop there will not be a trace of data on their hard drive.

"I know what you're thinking. Most of you are aware when a document is deleted from a computer it is still on your hard drive. All you have done with the delete command is to remove the link to the document. It will remain on the hard drive until it has been written over. No, not even an advanced Grace Commission armed with today's technology would be able to find anything in a hundred years, because there is nothing there. I hope this puts everyone's mind at ease as far as security of their personal information is concerned.

"Another question? Anyone?"

A young man, at one of the corner tables, of perhaps twenty-two or twenty-three started to stand, but had second thoughts and settled back into his chair. Anna waited a few seconds and then said, "Mr. Hightower, do you have a question?"

He was a bit unsteady when he rose from his chair. "Yes, Miss Anna. The Club is all I have and I desire nothing more. I've signed the oath, but after ten months I have yet to be assigned an initiation project. Although I will never leave the Club of my own free will, I want to pay my debt. I have much to offer. I will serve in any capacity. Can you help me?"

"I am aware of your situation Mr. Hightower. I believe you have great things ahead of you and will serve the Club well. However, initiation projects are chosen and approved by the board. I cannot help you."

"I will take any project no matter how dangerous. I am willing to risk it all. I just want a chance to prove myself worthy."

"I know. May I suggest, perhaps you are too eager, too willing to take risks. When you take risks, you put everyone in danger. The board will find something for you, be patient, and wait your turn."

Anna looked around the room, "Another question? Anyone? Okay. Thank you."

She turned to me before settling into her chair. "Mr. Scott."

I arose quickly and began before the applause could build—it died away within a couple of seconds. I repeated my first sentence to insure I had everyone's full attention.

"Miss Anna, Miss Rita and I were christened Genesis this evening. The director expressed his desire we no longer use our Club names in conjunction with *Chimney Sweep*. In keeping with his wishes: when Genesis' sabbatical ended and you were presented with our plan, you gave it your overwhelming approval. Some of you wanted to go all out from the beginning. To do so without having infrastructure in place could doom the Club and its members and in turn, doom America. We should never put the Club at risk or America at risk. I truly believe the Club is the last remaining force standing between capitalism and communism, between freedom and slavery, between the constitution and a dictator. America is the world's only chance—we are America's last chance.

"In my opinion we are off to an exceptional beginning. This is because we are all in the game. I know you agree with me: to fail means the end to the America we know, love, and respect. We dare not fail. It will be at least two years, perhaps longer, before we are fully organized and can implement our overall plan. We will continue at our present pace for the moment. We'll kick up the tempo as we go along. The earlier we get the committees in place and our programs installed, the sooner we can launch our all-out offensive against America's enemies. So, get those letters marked Beowulf to the concierge and let's get started."

I turned the meeting back to the director. His remarks were short. He closed by announcing another full-membership dinner to report on progress and answer questions would be scheduled—the date would be announced at the appropriate time. Full-membership meetings were difficult since it left the resort short of decision makers—only general (nonmember) employees were available to care for guests and handle complaints during a full-membership assembly. These employees knew nothing of the Club's existence. Our dining room and quarters were serviced by Club members. Most Club members took a turn for varying periods during their internship as servants within the set-aside confines. Although they were privileged to discussions within the Club's dining room and private areas, nothing overheard would ever reach the ears of the general staff.

Training

"Before you exploit this country, serve it."
—Marcus Luttrell

Genesis met with each committee as they formed and explained how to encode and decode, how action codes were to be used, and how authenticators were determined. Taught them how to retrieve their personal passwords—a new one was required for each project and changed every time data flowed on the communication highway. We may have been overcautious, but Genesis didn't think so, and neither did the director.

Within two months the committees were set and raring to launch a full-scale attack. Everyone knew we were just getting started and it would be a year or so before we were ready, but enthusiasm ran high and we found it necessary to remind them patience would pay huge dividends.

Miss Laura was the obvious choice to head up a group for monitoring media reaction. Considering the mind to be a creative force and along with Christian morals the foundation of society, and this being the first committee formed, her code name was *Alpha*—subcommittees reporting to her would be known as *Alpha* plus two English letters designating a particular chapter—to keep up with what chapter was reporting she would, at first, need a cheat sheet.

All subcommittees would be identified accordingly: a Greek letter followed by two English letters identifying their respective chapters.

My old friend—"old friend" relative to my induction into the Club—Mr. Wilson would chair training. He would have the largest group. Members of the training committee would spend a week with their counterparts in each of the different chapters and would return for retraining when requested or required. Mr. Wilson had several very talented individuals—a retired marine drill sergeant, an ex navy Seal, a retired member of the counterintelligence division of the FBI, and a defector from the *Spetsnaz.* Since training was an unpleasant necessity his committee was designated *Nu.*

Mr. Bartow, a historian, was chairman of education. His team would sort out teachers and professors spreading sedition and submit the names of those in need of an attitude adjustment. Since he was dealing with enlightening of the masses, which began with the scientific teaching of the first four elements, fire, air, water, and earth, his committee was designated *Delta.*

Mr. Ainge, columnist and retired editor of a Midwestern newspaper had been charged with sorting through politicians and cabinet appointees. He would list, and separate those who used their position to subvert the Constitution and fill their pockets with no-bid contract kickbacks at the taxpayer's expense from those wanting and trying to do what was right for the country and her citizens. Since he would be tasked with finding a balance between what is right and what is necessary, his committee would be known as *Eta.*

Planning was chaired by Miss Karla, a retired comptroller and enrolled retirement agent for a major trucking firm. She had been charged with setting up operational guidelines for operations and requirements for the chain of command. Her guidelines, if followed, would guarantee a successful conclusion; therefore her committee would be known as *Omega.*

Monitoring and following up on law enforcement and forensics progress would be headed up by Miss Marie, a former crime reporter. She would be assisted by Mr. Bratton, retired FBI. This committee focused on those sworn to protect us from the common criminal and would be known as *Mu.*

Courts would be monitored by Mr. Dixon, a retired circuit court judge, and Mr. Carver, an ex lieutenant governor. Their duty was to compile a list of attorneys and judges for special attention. As the courts had the authority to decide who lives and who dies; this committee would be known as *Gamma.*

Miss Alana had been chosen as chairwoman for actions against the Hollywood community. *Xei* was the obvious choice for this committee.

Except for training, operations and acquisitions, one of the more important committees and involving more personnel than the others, was the last to be formed. Mr. Whitehall, a former instructor of operational warfare, was eager to get back into the art of coordinating minute details of tactics with the overarching goals of strategy. Since it was a stroke of bad luck for whomever the chairman focused his attention on and in the end meant death was inevitable, operations was christened *Kappa*.

Miss Eleanor was my recommendation to head up communications. However, her full-time position as the Club's research analyst left her with too little time to give the committee the proper attention to the program, but she agreed to serve as chairlady provided she had a capable apprentice. We checked with the Los Angeles chapter and found that the girl coordinating our Venice operation, whose Russian name was Lidiya and we knew as Shirley, had no ties to LA except for her Club benefactor, Miss Angie. With Angie's encouragement she readily agreed to join us in the Catskills as Miss Eleanor's protégée. We learned her Club name was Miss Mindy Patterson. As communication flowed from satellite to earth to satellite and repeated several times, it was coded and difficult to define, so it had to be known as *Ypsilon*.

When we started setting up committees—only *Alpha* existed—information and instructions as to how subcommittees would be involved were hand-delivered to other chapters. Three months later they were all up and running. Committees worked with their chapter counterparts to plan and carry out mock executions. A member of Genesis was on hand to observe and evaluate the team at critical junctures of the operation. At the conclusion of a practice operation each team was critiqued. Only two chapters were directed to plan and simulate another takedown.

Genesis now dined once or twice a week with the director—necessary to keep him current on *Chimney Sweep*. It was at one of these dinners that he expressed his desire to have another meeting with our members, report our progress, and take questions. I suggested rather than convening with just members of our chapter, we also assemble the subcommittee chairs, introduce them to Genesis, explain the thinking behind *Chimney Sweep*, and provide a progress report.

"I like your suggestion, Mr. Scott, but we do not have the space to accommodate a gathering of this magnitude. Perhaps we would all be better served if Genesis visited each chapter and explained to their membership the intent of *Chimney Sweep*, followed by questions and answers."

So it was agreed. I should say settled. Without having all the facts and solid logic in your favor it was unwise to challenge the director. Although he was not inflexible, you should make sure you were on solid ground and had all your ducks in a row before you considered testing him.

Four months later Genesis finished its tour and reported to the director. He was pleased with our assessment of members' acceptance of *Chimney Sweep* and their eagerness to participate.

"How many active projects do you have?"

"Two are in their final stage, one in New York and one in DC. Recon teams are setting up on four other targets: one in Seattle, one in Philadelphia, and two in Chicago—a member of Genesis will observe the takedown. If these all go as planned I believe it safe to say *Omega* and *Nu* have performed well. At which time they can limit their involvement to critiquing projects and providing assistance only when requested.

"All active projects are limited to media. Next on our agenda is to mail out an updated list of targets after the projects in process are completed and to decide on which group we take on next."

"Which faction do you prefer?"

"Personally, I'd like to go after politicians, but I don't think it's their time yet. Leaving them 'til last, I believe is a more practical and logical approach. By the time we send them notices and accompanying lists, they no doubt will already be aware of letters sent to others. I suspect by then they will be scared out of their minds and will change their ways with very little persuasion. If we want to get a little more ambitious and at the same time make it a bit more difficult for law enforcement when it comes to light there is a letter accompanied by a death list, we could take on education and Hollywood at the same time."

"Do you think it wise to expand so quickly? Are you not acting a bit too hasty in expanding the game at this stage of development?"

"As I see it, there are two things to consider. The more slowly we proceed the more time authorities have to try and figure out our next move. By increasing the number of targets and expanding our sphere of interest we will make it more difficult for them to second-guess us. Also, it is likely to create contention within the ranks of precinct commanders and FBI agents on the question of how they should proceed."

"Good points, I will leave these decisions up to Genesis."

"Thank you, sir."

"I wonder if you could do me a favor." he continued without waiting for a response. "Would you mind taking Mr. Hightower under your wing, or I should say wings?"

He waited for my response as I glanced at the girls. Without commenting they shrugged a, "How can you say no to the director?"

"Certainly, sir. What would you have us do?"

"I'm sure you know part of the story. He is a very angry young man, and in my opinion he has the right. His tragedy in some ways parallels the heartbreak and injustice you experienced. Like you he wants revenge. Mr. Scott, you are still waiting. While your lovely teammates extracted their pound of flesh, I'm sure they will tell you, it wasn't enough. It's never enough. The only other thing he wants is to serve the Club and be respected by the membership. He wants to pay the Club more than he owes. I know you can help him find his way. He's a good kid. His life was interrupted by evil people, as is the case for several of our members."

"We know part of the story, I'm sure it would help if we knew everything."

"He was born into poverty, as many are. He never complained or asked for handouts. He believed in and sought the American Dream. By working hard and getting an education he landed a good job in accounting for a local firm. He'd waited until he saved enough money to make the down payment on a small two-bedroom house before marrying his childhood sweetheart.

"His wife worked six hours a day at the high school cafeteria—her workday ended at three in the afternoon. They saved every penny and looked toward the day he would start his own accounting firm. On the afternoon that changed his life forever, three seniors followed her home—they had only one car, so she walked. When she unlocked her front door they rushed up and pushed her inside. Mr. Hightower arrived home to find they had torn off her clothes and were taking turns raping her while the other two held her down. He was overpowered, tied up and forced to watch as they continued taking turns with his young wife. When they tired of her one of the three shot her several times and killed her. He then turned the gun on Mr. Hightower and shot him in the head and again in the chest. They left the house thinking he was dead.

"The shooter's aim wasn't as accurate as he'd thought it to be. The round to his chest missed all vital organs while the bullet from the small caliber pistol ricocheted off Mr. Hightower's skull, leaving him unconscious but still alive.

"The trio was arrested the same evening. They made bail two hours later. Since all three were seventeen years old they were tried in juvenile court. They were found guilty and sentenced to jail until their eighteenth birthday. Although not a small town, it was small enough to where well-known families have influence. Probably being high school football stars played a part as well. Be that as it may, their attorney cut a deal with the court to have their jail time reduced to time served, a total of two hours, in exchange for probation until their twenty-first birthdays.

"The afternoon he was released from the hospital, Mr. Hightower went home, got his shotgun, walked onto the football field during practice, and shot them dead. From there he drove to the lawyer's office and killed him. He then stopped at a liquor store, purchased a six-pack of beer, went home, left his shotgun on the front porch by the open front door, and waited for the sheriff. He had plenty of time to get drunk for the first and only time in his life—the sheriff had figured his next stop would be the judge's house and had waited there for more than three hours. After a deputy had been dispatched to check Lester's house and found him home he was taken into custody without a problem.

"How he became a member of the Club is irrelevant; what he needs now is our help. His grief is overwhelming him. It is known he has considered suicide. He is not unlike you in his thinking. You considered there was nothing worth living for and elected to die at the hands of the state. There is no doubt in my mind that today you are happier than you could have ever imagined.

"Mr. Scott, I know you can help this young man save himself from his anger and desolation. I have no doubt you will help him look to the future with purpose and dreams, and to become a responsible Club member. Any questions?"

"Only one, how do you suggest I approach him?"

"I leave that entirely up to you."

"Can you arrange to have him dine with Genesis and Miss Mindy with no other guests at the table for a week, starting tomorrow evening?"

"Certainly, which seating do you prefer?"

"I think ten o'clock will work best." I looked at the girls. They nodded their approval.

"No problem. What do you have in mind?"

"Nature, sir. There is nothing created by God or man anywhere in the universe capable of making a young man forget his troubles more quickly and completely than a beautiful young woman. We have a couple of young people with similar tragic pasts—deception, heartbreak, and murder." I looked at the girls again. They were smiling.

"I see where you're going. How will you get them involved?"

"Genesis will discuss events in our lives. We'll talk about how hopeless things appeared to be at the low points in our past, how wonderful they are now, and how beautiful the transition from then to now has been and how it grows every day. Sooner or later one of them will ask a question. Then, eventually, they will talk with each other about whatever and wherever. Subsequently nature will take over and we can slowly withdraw and leave them to mend with each other's help."

The girls and I arrived early so as to force our guests to sit next to each other—two chairs had been removed leaving only five. The director had sent out memorandums explaining why it was necessary to rearrange dining times and seating schedules—there was no schedule for breakfast and lunch, but members were assigned tables and seating times for dinner.

We were perusing the menus when our first guest arrived. "Mr. Hightower, I remember you from the full-membership meeting, and I've seen you around, but we haven't been properly introduced. I'm Maxwell Scott; these lovely ladies are my teammates, Miss Anna Borden and Miss Rita Wentworth." He and the girls exchange proper expressions of recognition.

I stood as Mindy approached—Mr. Hightower quickly followed my lead. "Good evening Miss Mindy, I'm delighted to see you again."

"The pleasure is all mine, sir." She curtsied slightly.

"Thank you. You know Miss Anna, Miss Rita is the other half of my team." She curtsied again, "So nice to meet you."

Rita returned the compliment. She turned back toward me. "And this is Mr. Hightower." She nodded, "Good evening." Lester bowed slightly, "Good evening, Miss Mindy."

Lester was seated next to Rita. I stepped behind and around Anna to pull the chair out for Mindy. She sat down and then lifted slightly so I could push the chair closer to the table. Lester appeared embarrassed when he realized he should have helped Mindy with her chair.

After the waiter took our order and disappeared I proposed a toast to Mindy, welcoming her to the Catskills and commended her professionalism in handling communications and coordinating our operation in Venice. She thanked me and then we were silent for a few seconds before Anna, looking at Mindy, asked, "Where did you go to school?"

"Cadet Boarding School No. 9."

Anna acted as though she was astounded. I didn't think she was acting. I think she was genuinely surprised.

"I'm impressed. Cadet boarding schools take only the prettiest and brightest young ladies. Why did you leave school? How did you end up in America and a member of the Club?"

She thanked Anna for the compliment and then related her story, adding parts we didn't know and then asked, "How do you know about cadet boarding schools?"

"I spent my childhood in Moscow."

Anna's answer opened the door to conversation lasting through dinner. We'd just finished the main course when I was handed an envelope. Inside was a sheet of paper with a note scribbled, "Here is your excuse."

I showed the note to Anna and Rita and then looked at Mindy and Lester, "I apologize, I'm afraid we are going to have to skip dessert. We have an emergency demanding an immediate response."

I pushed back from the table and helped Anna and Rita with their chairs. I looked across the table, "Again, I apologize this is a hazard Genesis often encounters."

We made a hasty exit without looking back. The girls were stifling giggles as the dining-room door closed behind us.

"Girls, I think we should launch a dating service, what do you suggest we call it?" Still giggling, they answered in unison, "Lost and found!"

Operation "Lost and Found" as we dubbed it, appeared to be going well. As we approached the dining table on the fourth evening Lester and Mindy were already seated and talking softly and smiling. They fell silent as we approached. Lester stood and helped Rita with her chair as I assisted Anna. We made our choices for dinner and then conversation picked up where it had left off the night before with the three girls speaking Russian. After a few minutes, inflexions and sideways glances were a dead giveaway.

"Mr. Hightower, I do believe we are the focus of their conversation."

This triggered a symphony of giggles. I used the following lull to move the dialogue to an area of interest to me. Anna had left Moscow at age eight and I was curious as to what might have been in store for her, the daughter of a GRU colonel, had she remained in Russia.

"Miss Mindy, you are a remarkable young lady. You're not just another pretty girl, you're refined, elegant, graceful, and learned beyond your years. Tell me about your education at the Cadet Boarding School. How old were you when you entered the boarding school?

"Girls are sworn in at age eleven."

"Sworn in?"

"Yes, it is a military academy. We enter as little girls and are treated as such. I slept with a teddy bear—yes, we call them teddy bears. My days were full. After our morning rituals, we started with the grades—math, science, history and so on as well as English and one other foreign language of our choice. Also, we learned about the military—drilling, and the use of weapons, as well as first aid, martial art, and federal law. In the afternoon, we were taught to be proper young ladies, wives, and mothers. We were schooled in ballet, cooking, and everything ladies need to know—swearing, alcohol, and drugs are strictly forbidden. In the evenings, we had an hour of free time to call our parents or just do fun things. Sometimes we dressed up for socials when boys from one of the military academies were invited."

"What martial art discipline did you learn?"

"We were taught the Spetsnaz system of hand-to-hand combat by students of Vadim Starov."

"Very interesting. I had a brown belt in karate when I joined the Club. Mr. Wilson works with me once or twice a month—I'm still a step away from a black belt. Perhaps I should give you the opportunity to humiliate me sometime."

"I haven't worked out since becoming a Club member." She then gave me her little-girl smile and added. "You will lose."

"Who taught you ballet?" Anna asked.

"We were schooled by the Vaganova Ballet Academy."

"I wish our schools were run like your boarding school. Why did you leave?"

"On a Saturday during my fifteenth summer, I was browsing at GUM (Glavny Universalny Magazin) just off Red Square, when I was approached by a very official looking gentleman. I would not learn until I reached America he was no gentleman—he was Russian mafia. He was very businesslike when handing me an impressively designed card announcing him to me as an agent for a prestigious modeling school and placement agency in New York City. He asked if I would recite a few lines for him while he took a video to send to the placement agency. I was reluctant, but he was very convincing and I was intrigued by the idea of going to America and becoming a model. He gave me half a dozen cards with lines I studied and memorized. We went to the upper rows, an imposing area of

GUM, where he directed me in posing, walking, and laughing and teasing while he asked questions and I recited lines from the cards. Then we did it all over while he recorded the video. It all seemed very professional. He asked me to call in two weeks. By then, he said, he would have an answer from his agency.

"Two weeks passed, I called, we met, he gave me a copy of the video and told me he'd heard from the placement agency, and they were anxious to meet with me to discuss a contract. Having heard stories about what can happen to young girls traveling alone my parents were concerned for my safety and were reluctant to give their permission. He assured them nothing would happen to me since he would be my escort all the way to the school in New York. There the school would provide room and board and training until the agency arranged for a signed contract with a clothing or cosmetic line.

"Again, they were leery when he asked for five thousand dollars. He took money from my parents under false pretenses. They were told it would be used to pay for my airfare, passport, visa and other expenses. He said they would be reimbursed from the up-front money when I signed the contract. Another carrot he dangled in front of my parents was that a year after I received my American citizenship, they could join me and become American citizens. My passport and travel papers were all faked. He bribed an official to clear me at Sheremetyevo onto Aeroflot, and you already know the rest of the story."

"Do you miss your home? Have you ever considered going back?"

"Yes and no. This is my country now and the Club is my home. I do miss my friends, my parents, and the culture, but I could never go back to Russia, even if I wanted to. The government would consider me a traitor and send me back to America to face a murder warrant. Because of the rape my parents would consider me damaged goods and disown me. So no, I will never go back."

"Miss Mindy, you are not damaged goods and I don't want to hear you reference yourself in such terms ever again. You are a remarkable young lady and I would be proud to have you as my daughter. I will adopt you anytime you say."

I saw a tear glisten as she gave me a weak smile and said, "Thank you."

Rita touched her hand and said, "That goes double for me." Anna was quick to make it unanimous.

Another smile, another tear, and another thank you. Melancholy was hanging heavy over the table. In an effort to elevate the mood I asked, "Miss Mindy, you said, at the boarding school you were required to learn English and had a choice of another language. What did you choose?"

"French."

I knew I'd made a mistake in asking. I also knew it served what I had in mind better than I'd hoped. Rita engaged her immediately in French, Anna joined in at the first opportunity. I turned to Lester and said, "Looks like we've been cut out of the conversation again."

He laughed, "I'm used to it. My grandparents on my father's side emigrated from Poland in the late fifties. Although very young, they remembered the great purges of the Soviet Union and suspected it was about to happen in Poland—it happened ten years later. My father was four years old at the time, his sisters were two and three. My grandparents arrived with only the clothes on their backs and a few gold coins. My grandfather found work in the coal mines of Appalachia. When my father was eighteen he met and married my mother. He found work as a carpenter in a larger town and was able to escape life in the mines. During my second year in high school my grandparents came to live with us. Mining was becoming mechanized and my grandfather was in poor health and unable to find other work. I tell you this so you'll understand when I say I'm used to not understanding conversations conducted in foreign languages. My grandparents learned a little English, but when talking with each other spoke only Polish. They tried to teach me their native language, but I was never interested enough to learn—wish I had."

"I guess your friends called you 'Ski' and you suffered the Polack jokes."

"He laughed, hundreds of them, there was a new one every day. The first thing I heard every morning when I arrived at school was, 'Hey Ski, did you hear about the Polack . . .' but I didn't let it get to me. As far as friends, I didn't have any; I was pretty much a loner."

"Do you have a job to keep you busy and your mind occupied?"

"I assist Miss Rebecca in accounting, but I don't think I'm earning my keep. I'd like something more important and I guess you could say, more exciting."

"Miss Rebecca does a great service for the Club. Besides accounting she arranges for all the documents we need for traveling and doing our jobs when in the field."

"That's where I want to be, in the field."

"Don't be too anxious. I'm sure you've heard, 'Rome wasn't built in a day.'"

"No sir, never heard it."

"I guess school isn't what it used to be. Take my word for it. One day you'll wish you could go back to those easy and less stressful days working for Miss Rebecca."

Using my limited Russian I interrupted the threesome's conversation. "Mr. Hightower and I are feeling left out. We know you are talking about us and probably saying unflattering things."

Pretending to be hurt, Rita declared. "We would never say mean things about you."

This triggered another chorus of giggles. We were all pleased with the way things appeared to be going between Lester and Mindy. I turned to them and trying to look embarrassed said, "I married a couple of teenagers who have yet to grow up, please excuse them."

It would be impossible to describe the look on their faces when Rita said, "Yes, and we don't intend to grow up."

When Anna chimed in with, "So, you'd better get used to it," they looked at us and then at each other wide-eyed and back at us.

Lester stumbled over his words as he said, "The three of you are married?"

"It's not all that simple—the rule involved here is, you marry one sister and you have to take the other one." I knew the follow-up question. I just didn't know who would be asking. It was Anna.

"Oh, and just which one of us did you have to take?" Looking at Lester, I said, as though the girls hadn't uttered a word, "I should have said, if you marry one sister you get the other sister for free." There was more snickering. Mindy and Lester seemed more perplexed than ever. Finally he smiled at me and said, "They don't look like sisters. I think you are just having fun with us."

Anna looked at him and said, "It's a long story, one you probably wouldn't believe, but we are sisters."

Rita quickly added, "You may not believe this either, but we are married." She then put both hands on my arm, leaned close and whispered to me, but loud enough for them to hear, "Married for life."

I took Anna's hand as I replied, "And I wouldn't have it any other way."

This ended all conversation. I pushed back, stood, and pulled the girl's chairs away from the table as they rose. We said goodnight and left Lester and Mindy as we'd found them, sitting together. Only now they weren't talking as they had been when we arrived. They were too stunned to talk at the moment. We knew there would be lots of talking after we departed.

Completely relaxed from late-night activities, I slept late. When I climbed out of bed the girls were nowhere to be found. I'd finished my shower and was making a cup of coffee when the girls waltzed in with a breakfast tray for me.

"Guess who we saw having breakfast together?" they giggled. They really did act like teenagers sometimes. It was a beautiful thing to watch. I figured they were trying to live, in bits and pieces, their teenage years, years they never had.

"Lester and Mindy."

"Yes!" replied Anna. Rita followed up with, "I think Lost and Found is destined for success."

"Perhaps we should take Lester with us to New York when we observe and critique the takedown? Give him a taste of what he's been craving."

Rita was quick to reply, "Good idea, it will help with Lost and Found as well—absence makes the heart grow fonder."

Anna agreed but added, "We should help him polish his table manners unless you plan to eat at McDonald's."

I was more or less thinking out loud when I said, "I'm sure Mindy will be pleased to handle that little chore."

Rita was quick to reply. "I don't know. We need to be careful. We don't want him becoming defensive toward her."

"True," said Anna, "but I've watched her at dinner and I think, having a cultured heritage and the epitome of a prim and proper young lady, she's put off by his lack of etiquette. I think Mindy would welcome a chance to elevate Lester to a higher level of social grace. So yes, we do need to interfere, but in a way so as not to insult or embarrass either."

"We'll work out the details. He won't suspect a thing. We'll spring it at dinner tonight."

Dinner started the same as it had the night before with Lester and Mindy already seated and engaged in conversation. Talking ceased and Lester stood as we approached. He helped Rita with her chair as I assisted Anna. We made our choice for dinner and before we started fumbling around trying to find a subject for small talk, I got down to our plan straight away.

"Mr. Hightower, Miss Rita and I are going into the Big Apple to observe the takedown of a target. More than once, you've indicated you'd like to find out what it's like in the field. Would you be interested in coming with us?"

"Absolutely. Do you think Miss Rebecca will give me time off?"

"She's very understanding; I think I can arrange some time off for you."

Before he could respond Mindy asked, "May I come with you?" This was working out better than I'd anticipated. With Mindy practically begging to come with us Lost and Found would have more time together and would give Genesis a chance to observe them together and see how they reacted toward each other.

"You understand this is not going to be a shopping tour? We have vermin to kill, or more accurately stated—to observe vermin receiving their just rewards."

"Whatever business you have to take care of is fine with me. I've heard about New York for most of my life. I'd like to see it just once. I promise to not get in your way and I follow instructions well."

I looked at Rita and asked, "What do you think? I'll leave it up to you."

"As a young girl I was fascinated with the idea of seeing New York City. I think it would be good for her. I don't see it as a problem." She turned to Mindy and said, "There are neat things in New York, but there are too many people. Getting around is next to impossible even when you know were you're going. Taken as a whole it is likely to be a disappointment."

"That's okay. At worst I can scratch off one of the places on my wish-to-see list."

"Okay, you may come with us if you will help me with a little problem."

"Yes ma'am."

"When it comes to social skills, Mr. Scott is lacking in several areas. He is occasionally an embarrassment. When it comes to etiquette he thinks Miss Anna and I pick on him. He doesn't become defensive, but often tends to dismiss us. I've watched you these past few evenings—you could write the handbook on table manners. Would you consider giving Mr. Scott a refresher course and just point out a few things as we enjoy our dinner this evening?"

Rita had put her in an awkward position and it was only natural she would be apprehensive. She remained poised, but chose her words carefully. "You flatter me. It would be my pleasure to honor your request, but it wouldn't be proper for me to suggest Mr. Scott might be less than fully schooled in etiquette. I wouldn't want him to become upset with me."

"He won't get upset with you, he barks but never bites. How could he become upset with a lovely young lady he referred to as 'refined, elegant, and graceful and someone I would be proud to have for my daughter?'"

Mindy smiled her relief and then asked, "What would you have me do?"

"Just point out where he needs improvement as we work our way through dinner. When there are people present you can work out a signal no one other than Mr. Scott will notice or whisper in his ear if you are close enough."

Anna was quick to add, "Just whisper, don't breathe in his ear."

Mindy blushed, to relieve her embarrassment I quipped, "What a stick in the mud you are." Everyone laughed; everyone but Lester. He was already jealous of her. A good sign, hopefully he wouldn't become too clingy.

"Am I to understand I should begin now?"

"Anytime you're ready."

She apologized and asked me if it was okay. I assured her I welcomed her assistance, "Miss Mindy, I'll do whatever it takes to keep my wives happy, I'm sure you've heard the old axiom 'If the wives are happy everyone is happy, when the wives aren't happy no one is happy.'"

She smiled and said, "Your version is a little different than the one I remember. If you are sure about this, I suggest you remove your elbows from the table."

I made a display of following her instructions to give Lester a chance to ease his elbows off the table. We continued through dinner as I purposely displayed faux pas I'd notice Lester making during previous dinners. Each time she calmly and respectfully reminded me of the "do not" and the proper "do" Lester would follow suit. At no time during her comments did either of us look at him. She taught me the signal no one would ever pick up on when I should watch for her to indicate a correction I should make. She showed me how to place my silver when I was finished and ready for the waiter to take my plate, and what a lady would do when she was ready for me to help her with her chair. Lester listened to each and every word as he observed her movements.

We all were standing and about to leave when she moved close to me and said, "Please don't think I was chastising you. I was only doing what Miss Rita asked of me."

"I know and I'm grateful. I'm lacking in many ways, so keep reminding me."

At that she stepped forward, touched her lips to my check ever so gently for just a moment as she whispered, "I know what you are doing. Thank you."

There was no need for me to comment. She knew I understood.

"We need to work out several things in the morning, so how about you two stopping by our quarters after lunch, say, one o'clock." I got a couple of yes sirs and they hurried off—to do what, I didn't know. Excitement and anticipation would probably keep them from a good night's sleep.

After breakfast I called on the director to update him on Chimney Sweep. He asked if, in my opinion Lost and Found looked promising. He seemed pleased with the details and my assessment. He asked when Genesis planned to expand to the next level. I told him I wanted to monitor and critique three more takedowns by other chapters, before adding education and historians to the mix. He nodded his approval, but I had the feeling he'd like to step up the timetable.

I spent a few minutes with Miss Rebecca arranging for passports and other necessary identification for Lester and Mindy. She asked me to bring them by before 2 p.m. for pictures. Although undetectable by even an expert eye, the documents would be forged.

Rita and I spent the rest of the morning going over the plan and recon data. The plan appeared sound. However, we always prepared for the unexpected. Backup plans were necessities. It was lunchtime when we finished screening the operation for glitches—we didn't see anything disturbing. Anna had our transportation and accommodation in the "City" lined out, so we left for the dining room.

While cruising the buffet we spotted Lester and Mindy sitting together—we joined them. After seating Anna and Rita, Lester-assisted, I sat down and plopped an elbow on the table. Mindy gave me the signal and looked at my elbow. I visually expressed embarrassment and moved it at once. She flashed me a smile. I returned it with a wink. Later, she tactfully informed me I was dragging my shirt cuff in my plate. Lester immediately elevated his elbow to the level of his fork as he lifted a bite of crab cake.

"So you two are ready for the Big Apple?" They replied simultaneously. "Yes sir."

"Okay, knock on our door at 1 p.m. this afternoon. We have a lot to discuss. Oh yes, you might want to primp before you come calling and dress as though you were applying for a position in management and will be interviewed by the company's CEO—you're having your pictures taken."

The rap on the door came at one o'clock sharp. Rita let the couple into a foyer that served as an open hallway and led to the kitchen and dining area some twenty feet away. I didn't know how they were quartered, but obviously their accommodations didn't compare to ours. I suspected they each had a modest sitting area with a desk, TV, breakfast bar with an efficiency kitchen all in one room and a fairly small bedroom suite like the accommodations I'd seen of other members. Member's quarters varied according to seniority and how much they contributed to the Club. Lester stood with his mouth open, while Mindy looked around admiringly. On one side of the hallway was a library with barrister bookcases along three walls. With a table and ten chairs it served as a conference room. Across the hall and equal in size to the library was a media room. Comfortable lounge chairs fanned out in front of a projection-television screen. A computer monitor and keyboard sat on a large desk at the opposite end of the room. Beyond the kitchen and dining area double doors opened into the bedroom suite.

I was at the conference table studying pictures, on a laptop, of the area where the execution would take place. Rita seated them on the opposite side of the table and then sat next to me.

"You passed your first test. Punctuality is crucial in this game in which we find ourselves engaged—nothing less can be tolerated. Also, you scored pretty high on following directions. You are dressed as I instructed. Miss Mindy, you were in charge of communications for our Venice operation. You understand it is crucial to have a solid plan and the necessity of walking through the plan. It is equally essential to have a backup plan as well as a fallback position when things appear to be going south. Am I right?"

"Yes sir."

"You also know the importance of following the chain of command. In the field it is critical. To take the time to second-guess or question could cost a life."

"Yes sir."

"Mr. Hightower, this will be your first time in the field. Aside from your required studies I don't know how much you know about what happens once a target has been selected. This little foray is to give you an eyes-on—we are going to New York simply to observe an assassination. Some will say there's nothing simple about killing a human being, be it your enemy or not. This is for God to decide, not you or me. Since this will be your first time in the field there are several things to consider. We will not get to participate unless it becomes absolutely necessary—there is always that possibility. With involvement comes risk. Considering Miss Mindy has experience and having seen her in action I'd have to say she runs a first-class operation. With this in mind, even though she is younger than you, should there come a time when the two of you are alone, she will be in charge. If circumstances demand a decision be made, whatever she decides is to be followed without question. Is that understood?"

"Yes sir."

Considering the possibility he might feel his male ego bruised. I considered telling him about how my boss put Anna, a younger woman, in charge when we were fleeing Russia, but decided against it. Better for him to face reality now rather than later. He might grow into a Bonaparte, but for now, Mindy was superior to him in every way. Thinking it might help him to understand her qualifications, I asked,

"Miss Mindy, how long would it take you to fieldstrip an AK47?" I knew this was part of the curriculum in Russia's cadet boarding schools.

"Fewer than six seconds."

"Six seconds?"

"Yes sir, blindfolded."

"How long for a Makarov .380?"

"About the same."

"What is your rating on the range?"

"I haven't had much practice lately, although I'm confident I can still shoot expert."

"Where did you learn about weapons?"

"At cadet boarding school."

"What is your school's motto?"

"Always ready to respond."

I turned and asked, "Any questions Mr. Hightower?"

"No sir."

"I suggest you never do anything to upset her." To keep him from possible embarrassment, I continued before he could answer. "Let's move over to the media room and I'll explain the setup and show you pictures of the area we'll be watching."

Using sign language the girls had taught me I conveyed a request to Rita. She disappeared momentarily and returned with five bottles of water—one for Anna working with the computer at the opposite end of the room. I showed them a picture taken from the window where we'd observe the takedown and pictures of the players. I explained everyone's role and went over the backup plan.

"Once in the city you," I looked at and pointed to Mindy, "will be given a throwaway cell phone. It will have three numbers stored in the contact list as M, R, and X. In case we are separated and you need help or direction call Rita or me. X is the field commander—call him only if you are faced with a dire emergency and cannot reach either Rita or me. You will be given more information later. Any questions thus far?"

They looked at each other, shook their heads and answered, "No sir."

"Good. You're going to need a passport and driver's license, so let's go face the camera."

Most of our flight time from Albany to New York was spent in the landing pattern at LaGuardia. Lester and Mindy had looked out the window the entire time. As we were deplaning Mindy turned to me with a frown and said "I thought it would be larger."

"Well, it's pretty big, but Moscow is probably three times larger and has a couple million more inhabitants. Moscow is a horizontal city while New York is a vertical city. However, Moscow has only dreamed about goods and services offered in New York. You'll be surprised.

The limo pulled up in front of the Battery Point Ritz Carlton. The driver opened the doors while a bellhop stood waiting. As Rita and I took a few steps toward the hotel entrance Mindy seemed unsure of what to do. I knew she was wondering about what to do with her suitcase.

"It's okay; they'll take care of it." She shrugged and walked with me to where a doorman ushered us inside. Rita paid an early-check-in fee and we then followed the bellhop to an elevator. When he opened the door and we entered our two-bedroom suite on an upper floor, Mindy walked to the middle of the drawing room and then looked inside one of the bedrooms. She reentered the sitting room, rubbed her hand across the bar as she walked to the glass doors consisting of two fixed panels and a slider.

She stood for a moment before turning to face me and said, "I see what you mean. Moscow has many fine old buildings with impressive ornate façades and elegant interiors reminiscent of Paris, France or so I've been told. Recently, American chains have built some fine hotels, but there's nothing like this anywhere in Russia, not even the new Intourist hotel."

"This is just part of the show. People frequenting hotels such as this and other places you will see are, to borrow your term, living a façade.

They write off their stay in the city against the companies they work for or they have government expense accounts and live like this on the back of taxpayers. New York has been a troubled city for the past seventy-five years. Murder, rape, mugging, rioting, and just about anything you can name happens daily. In the seventies it was unusually bad. The city ran out of money and credit. All services were shut down. There was no public transportation, garbage piled up to second-floor windows. The city fathers declared bankruptcy. A federal taxpayer bailout gave them new life in 1975. Now, not only do other big cities face the same ordeal, the federal government is on the verge of bankruptcy. My advice to both of you, if you decide to leave the Club once you have paid your dues, settle in a farming community as far away from big cities as you possibly can and never visit one ever again."

They were both staring at me as if I'd lost my mind. Their jaws had dropped and their eyes were blank. No doubt I sounded like a raving maniac to them. I figured I'd better get them back to the here and now. No sense burdening them with reality.

"Sorry, I get carried away sometimes. Let's continue with your introduction to the Big Apple. Freshen up and we'll be on our way. You girls get first choice of bedrooms. Mr. Hightower and I will take the one you don't want." When Lester looked at me it was easy to tell he'd had other ideas about sleeping arrangements. I could understand his disappointment. They were developing a relationship just as I'd intended when I had arranged for them to dine together at the Club. Where they would take it would have to happen on their own time and without an extra shove from me.

Rita had brought to my attention they could use new clothes. Lester wore the same jacket to dinner every evening. He alternated between two shirts, two pairs of pants, and two ties. Mindy's wardrobe was limited as well. She would have looked great in a flour-sack dress, but she'd grown up in a cultured society and it was easy to tell she considered her two dresses lacking in elegance and, in her mind, less than presentable when dining at the Club. Girls had this thing about their appearance. If they looked great, they felt great. When they thought their appearance was inadequate, they felt incomplete. Guys felt the same way, but to a lesser extent.

The limo was by the curb. The driver was standing outside—I'd asked him to wait while we checked into the Ritz Carlton. He opened the doors as we approached. When we were seated I gave him the address of

Bergdorf Goodman on Fifth Avenue in Midtown Manhattan. He nodded and closed the doors.

Our pilot had rotated at 6:32 AM—getting around in the city took time. I checked my watch as we exited the limo—in the three hours since we had arrived all we had accomplished was getting checked into our hotel. It was 11:24 a.m. I asked the driver to pick us up at 5:30 p.m. Shopping was going to take time—I hoped six hours would be enough. Even when women's clothes fit perfectly they were never quite right without alterations—a tuck here, a pinch there, and so on. I must admit, I was a little hard to please myself. The difference, of course, for me shopping was a chore, for women it was a fun day.

"Why don't we pop up to the fifth floor and have a bite before we hit the galleries. The restaurant should be open for lunch about now." Our young protégés had been wide eyed from the moment we entered the store to the time we were seated at a window table with a sweeping view of Central Park. Lester broke the silence.

"I have no idea where we are, but we're not in West Virginia."

"No, you are not. This can be a fun and exciting place to visit, but it won't take long before you will start wishing you were back in the hills and hollows of West Virginia. All the things you are seeing and will see serve to mask the criminal element controlling the city. These criminal elements can be found inside and outside government—they feed on and support one another. The assassination we are here to witness would receive no more than thirty seconds on the local news stations, if he were not a producer for late-night news on a major network—it's all too common an occurrence to rate more time. Miss Mindy can tell you about the hazards of big cities."

"I can indeed. Having grown up in Moscow I learned from an early age where it was safe to go and where I should never go. The city, as Mr. Scott says, is a fun place as long as you stay on the beaten path and never venture into unfamiliar areas.

"New York promises to be very exciting. Twenty years ago GUM, the most elite store in the Soviet Union, was restricted to members of the politburo, military officers, and other high-ranking officials. Now it is open to everyone, but it in no way compares to this store.

"I agree with you, sir. I know very little about all the things America has to offer, but after having seen the Catskills I can say without reservations, I will never consider moving to the city to live. As you say, they are fun places to visit. Having the opportunity to see the Big Apple, as you refer to it, has been one of my dreams. You reminded me of something I knew and subconsciously denied. In big cities, excitement and heartbreak along with good and evil reside side by side."

"Okay, no more downers for today. Let's enjoy doing what we came here to do—shop. While you girls are looking at the latest fashions, Mr. Hightower and I will see if we can find anything of interest."

"Rita winked at me as she said, "Well, just make sure you keep your mind on clothing and don't go hitting on any of the sexy little sales girls."

"We wouldn't dream of it." I looked at Lester and asked, "Would we?"

"No sir."

Mindy looked at me with sad eyes as she said, "It will be fun looking, but I can't buy anything."

"Don't worry about it. Miss Rita is rich and has a no-limit credit card."

Mindy looked at Rita with wide-eyed astonishment and blurted out, "You're rich?"

"Mr. Scott exaggerates from time to time, but I can afford to buy us some new clothes."

"I can't pay you back."

"You've been paying me back since the first day you joined the Club." She turned to Lester. "Mr. Scott tries to give the impression that he's cheap, but if you see something you like, buy it. He'll pay for it."

"Okay, let's get started. We'll meet in the bar at five o'clock."

Mindy gave me her little-girl smile again. "I don't drink."

"That's good. Order water, a soda, or whatever—they'll serve you anything you want. Try a Shirley Temple." She still had a puzzled look when Lester and I walked away.

You can put the best custom-made suit money can buy on some men and they will still look like bums. Fortunately, Lester was not one of those guys. He was a good-looking young man—he and Mindy made a handsome couple—but he needed a little tutoring in social expression. I had the solution, or so I thought—it was worth a try.

The girls were already seated when Lester and I arrived. Rita was sipping on a Piňa Colada while Mindy looked suspiciously at the Shirley Temple sitting on the table in front of her. Lester appeared apprehensive as the cocktail waitress approached our table. When she inquired as to our pleasure he looked at me as though waiting for instructions. I doubted he'd ever had anything other than beer and the wine we shared with him at dinner. To save him embarrassment I ordered Carolans Irish Cream on the rocks for both of us. When he tasted the low-alcohol drink he looked at me and said, "That's a long way from West Virginia moonshine."

"You drink moonshine?"

"I tasted it once. Once was enough, it burned all the way to my stomach."

"When I was a kid back in the hills of Tennessee my grandfather had a still set up back in a hollow. He'd run off a batch every couple of months. It smelled to high heaven when it was fermenting."

"Did you drink it?"

"Nope, never even tasted it, anytime I'd ask for a taste he'd always say, 'Son, moonshine is for selling, not drinking.' Mr. Hightower, since you're anxious to be involved in Chimney Sweep, I have a proposition for you if you are interested. Are you interested?"

"Yes sir. Who do I kill?"

"You are not ready to start pulling triggers yet. I was fortunate to have two professionals bring me along. I was a lot like you. I was angry and didn't care about living—I just wanted my ounce of revenge. My mentors taught me to care again, in time I got past my anger, and was able to focus on what is important. I would do this myself, but I'm a little too old to play the part. As a shady con man, I'm one of the best, but this calls for a young man polished enough to convince a reporter he's on the staff of a US senator. I was pretty rough around the edges when Miss Anna and Miss Rita began molding me into what passed for acceptability in most social situations. They were fourteen years old when they killed two men—like Miss Mindy, they had no choice. Also, like Miss Mindy, they were refined, proper young ladies. Genesis is stretched too thin with Chimney Sweep to help you develop the confidence you will need to pull off what I have in mind. I should have asked her before proposing this operation, but I'm hoping Miss Mindy will volunteer to be your tutor."

I looked at her for a moment before asking, "Is this something you could and would feel comfortable doing?"

"I can be his coach as long as he understands when I point to things he should or should not do I am trying to help him and he promises to not become defensive."

"Mr. Hightower, would you like to take on this project and are you agreeable to Miss Mindy's stipulations?"

"Yes sir. I am anxious to begin paying my debt—I owe the Club my life. I'll do whatever it takes. It will be my honor to have a teacher as pretty as Miss Mindy and I promise never to get upset or yell at her."

"Okay, great. You do understand the grooming must be on your free time. You both have jobs at the resort—they come first."

There was no hesitation by either of them when they answered, "Yes sir."

"Good, I'll lay out the plan for you when we get home—in the meantime we have a job to do. So, everybody grab an armload of bags and boxes and let's meet our driver. He should be arriving just about now."

Our purchases were all stacked together underneath our table and chairs. There was no reason to sort them out now, so I gathered up as many as I could carry comfortably. While Mindy and Lester were gathering up packages Rita leaned close and whispered, "You sly devil."

I whispered back. "Well I've been taught by two sly little devilettes—does this mean I've graduated?"

Still whispering, "You are going to pay for your little devilette remark."

With a grin I said, "I certainly hope so." Her eyes sparkled and a mischievous little grin I'd come to know so well touched her lips as she raised an eyebrow.

The Budding of Love and a New Team

"He who lives on hope will dine from an empty plate."
—Mindy Patterson

The New York chapter's field commander was sitting in the lobby reading a newspaper when we walked into the Ritz. An attaché case sat on the chair beside him. He gave no indication of having noticed us even though Rita and I had worked with him when we took the guy out in Central Park.

Ten minutes after we entered our suite I answered a knock at the door. Before either of us spoke, using a supersensitive open-ended receiver in the frequency band used by voice sensors to transmit data to nearby receivers, the commander swept the room for bugs. When he was satisfied there were no listening devices in the room, I turned on the television just in case there was something we'd missed. He then spent the next forty minutes briefing me on his operation. His primary plan was first-rate and well thought out. He had an equally good backup plan in case one was needed. Also, he was prepared to pack it in if something unexpected threatened exposure of his team or their security.

Posing as a potential deep-throat the commander had the producer of the local late-night news of a New York network believing he was going to get names of people engaged in a conspiracy to intimidate the mainstream media through murder and mayhem. It was understood he would receive more than just names. He'd been promised voice recordings, videos, and pictures of those involved. It was understood the guy selling information was a conspiracy insider. The producer would receive material in installments. The first exchange of money for material was too tempting to pass up. For a mere ten-thousand dollars he was to receive pictures and a recording of two conspirators plotting to execute the guy in Central Park. Since this had been a local assassination it served as sufficient bait to spring the trap. If, after the first exchange of information and money, the producer liked what he'd bought, he could, for one hundred thousand dollars, buy the name of the next target, who the hitters would be, when and where the next assassination would take place.

The fact that his name was on the list and had moved up and was now nearer the top of the revised list he'd received with the second letter, served to expose his lust, envy, hate, and stupidity—lust for power, envy of fame and fortune, hatred for American capitalism, and stupidity to the point he wouldn't be able to pass up the deal even if logic told him he should report everything to the authorities and let them handle it.

The commander had been given the name and location of a junkie mainlining heroin by a Club member on the police force—a detective in the Manhattan Narcotics Division. Once convinced the commander wasn't a nark, the druggie was anxious to do anything, other than honest work, for money to feed his habit. The junkie met the commander in a different location every day to receive money for his habit. He was given only enough cash to pay for his daily fix. If given too much money up front it was unlikely he'd show up to deliver the package. With access to a stockpile of heroin he most likely would have been zoned until his supply ran out or possibly he would have overdosed. Receiving just enough cash for a single fix every day until it was time to take down the target would guarantee he would be eagerly awaiting the day when he'd get his hands on the big money. Also, knowing he could come by his daily fix by simply showing up at a given place and time would keep him on the hook until it was time for the takedown.

All he had to do for ten grand was to swap briefcases with a guy sitting on a park bench. A guy he'd never seen before nor would ever see again. Neither of them would see anyone or anything ever again. The producer hadn't realized the person he'd had several very short telephone conversations with was not the person he would meet with at a time and date to be specified later. The only face-to-face meetings had been between the commander's designated hitter and the junkie. The producer and junkie would meet at Robert F. Wagner Jr. Park. The park was only a football field away from our hotel-room window. Using the two Barska 11-33x50

Tactical angled spotting scopes with Mil Dot Retice Side Focus Systems and tripods I had in my luggage, Rita and I could watch the takedown unfold from the comfort of our hotel suite.

The commander had incorporated some very interesting details involving the briefcase switch. He was taking out two birds with one stone and attempting to cripple two others. I liked his thinking. In addition to taking down the producer, known to have said at a recent CPUSA presidential convention, "I don't find anything wrong with communism—unfettered capitalism is the problem." He went on to say, "Some of my best friends are communists. I'll help you take the country down the road of communism as far as you want to go." He was taking out a junkie who'd beaten a murder rap. An elderly couple, unfamiliar with New York City, had made a wrong turn and ended up in an area where no one in their right mind would dare venture. While trying to turn around and backtrack they came to a dead-end alleyway. The druggie dragged them out of their car, beat them up, robbed them, and left them to die—and they did.

Liberal judges had set so many precedents by handing down decisions based on excuses for criminals' inability to know the difference between right and wrong that justice had become a joke. The courts surmised you were unable to determine the difference between right and wrong if you were too poor, too rich, uneducated, had been abused, were not of white European heritage, used drugs or alcohol, were confused about your sexual orientation, or insane at the time of the crime. It all boiled down to "Soft bigotry of low expectations."

The junkie didn't even face a trial. The judge sent him to a drug rehab hospital for three months and then he was released back onto the streets. If things went as planned, he would receive the sentence the judge should have handed down.

The third part of the briefcase swap was what set the commander apart from other members in the New York chapter. Most would be satisfied with taking down the producer. Taking out the druggie would be a bonus. The field commander was taking it to another dimension. It was apparent to me he had friends in high places. He was privy to information unavailable to 99 percent of the population—possibly because of his present or past job. I didn't inquire as to his sources.

He had collected copies of email and letters between two congressmen and presidents of companies applying for federal grants to assist them in the development of alternative energy. There were pictures of these congressmen with presidents of said companies, as well as pictures with call girls provided by the same company presidents. He'd collected copies of wire transfers of stock from these energy companies to the congressmen's personal portfolios—there were no records of payment, shares mysteriously appeared. When these shares sold two weeks after the companies received their grants the sales were recorded and money paid. The same scenario played out two months later when the congressmen received more shares without buying them, but pocketed huge profits when these shares sold. Some months later, both companies folded, but not before the company's presidents and chief executive officers dumped their stock and put the profits in offshore banks. There were deposits of hard cash as well; only about 20 percent of the grants had been invested in the companies. The commander was counting on investigators interest in photocopies showing wire transfers from brokers to the congressmen's bank accounts in the same banks to take precedent over the how and why the two dead men met their maker.

This evidence wasn't likely to convict anyone, but it would be retained as evidence from the crime scene and would make life difficult for these two congressmen. Also, questions of insider trading might be considered. The commander not only was a con man, he had picked a sleight-of-hand artist to deal with the drug addict. The junkie had no idea the briefcase he was to receive would have ten thousand dollars in it. He thought he was getting ten grand for delivering what was inside the one he would be carrying. Knowing the druggie could not be trusted to deliver the briefcase if he was given ten thousand dollars before the deed was done, the Club member handling the junkie would cut in half one hundred C-notes while the junkie watched. He would put the left half of the hundred dollar bills in an envelope, tape it shut, and then put it in an inside breast pocket of his jacket. The right halves of the hundred dollar bills would go into another taped-shut envelope and be placed in another pocket inside his jacket. This would take place inside the Club member's car a few minutes before the meeting. Actually the car used had been purchased in the name of the junkie a month earlier. This alone would raise questions and demand an investigation. Needless to say there would be additional information on the congressmen along with pictures of cabinet members and other government officials inside the car. The question of blackmail would be considered by investigators. This would serve to shine a brighter spotlight on the congressmen and possibly initiate FBI surveillance of others in and out of government. The conclusion might be: A long-term relationship existed between the producer and the junkie involving blackmail aimed at government officials. The question, of course, what went wrong at this meeting?

The handler would drive to a predetermined area to meet with the druggie. Originally, the commander had planned to use 10X50 Leica binoculars from an isolated area in the park to make sure the producer was waiting rather than a substitute. Leics, as they are known by those familiar with these very expensive binoculars, worked well in low light. He'd been in the producer's presence enough times to recognize his face and body structure under every possible condition. When satisfied the person waiting was the producer and not a stand-in, he would call Zack and give him the go-ahead. With the druggie still in the car, his handler would drive to the park, reach into his pocket, and hand over an envelope along with a locked briefcase to the druggie. The envelope would be identical to the two stuffed with halves of hundred dollar bills, but it would contain pictures and additional information on the congressmen. He would then exchange briefcases with the guy sitting on the bench and return the one he'd picked up to Zack and receive the envelope with the matching halves of hundred dollar bills, or so he thought.

The junkie was so whacked out, gullible, or just plain greedy—perhaps all three—he had never once asked his handler why he didn't deliver the briefcase himself and save ten grand. Oh well, such was the reality of stupid people on drugs—logic wasn't their forte.

"Thanks for the briefing."

"My pleasure, Mr. Scott." He removed three throwaway cell phones from his attaché case and explained the white strip coding before placing them on the bar.

"The only way you can get to the contact list of M, R, and X is to first punch in 'caper123' and then hit enter. I'll give you a call with the time and date as soon as I've finalized the deal."

"Is there any reason to suspect he may have police surrounding the drop?"

"In my opinion, only a very remote chance—it's a consideration, but I'm not concerned. He thinks he's going to scoop the entire media as well as the FBI. He will wait to see what he gets in the first drop. If it looks promising then he'll go for the who, when, where, and how. He, of course, knows he will be required to tell the FBI if he gets names and places. Armed with knowledge of the time, place, and intended victim he can break the story seconds after the FBI swoop in and make arrests. I'm not psychic, but my guess is he's thinking everyone will perceive him to be a hero. He can probably see himself as time's Man of the Year. No, he won't bring the feds in on this one."

I thanked him again. We shook hands and he left. I locked the door behind him.

"Okay, you heard the instructions for using the phones, so repeat it back." I pointed to each of them in turn. Everyone had it correct. "Okay, one more time." They repeated the code correctly a second time. Just to be safe I had them repeat it a third time as I passed out the phones.

I handed the single-stripped phone to Mindy. I kept the three-striper for myself, and handed the other one to Rita.

"Keep this with you at all times." The statement was for the benefit of Lester and Mindy. Rita didn't need a reminder.

"Okay gang, get your party duds on, we have a dinner engagement." Only Rita and I knew we were going to the Gershwin Theater before dinner—a surprise for Mindy and an introduction to culture for Lester.

Lester and I were almost finished dressing and about to enter the reception area of our suite. I said about finished because Lester needed to make an adjustment to his appearance. I was still standing in front of the mirror when I said, "Mr. Hightower, mirrors are your friend. There is a reason dressing areas have full-length mirrors. Don't ever pass up a friend and the opportunity to check your appearance. People judge you, in part, a large part I might add, by the way you present yourself. This will be especially true in the role you are going to adopt for the duration of your first project. You will find it the same throughout life. You never want to be an embarrassment to yourself or the person or people you are with—little things add up. So, let's begin. Come stand beside me." His expression didn't exactly convey appreciation. It was more of a "Who are you to tell me how to dress." Obviously, he needed clarification and encouragement rather than criticism. I nonchalantly added, "I didn't just walk out of the hills and hollows of Tennessee aware of the things I just mentioned. Without help from someone who cared I'd still be wearing white socks and black shoes with a brown suit. Don't know if you noticed but I don't wear white socks or brown suits."

"What's wrong with brown suits?"

"What do you associate with the color brown?"

He thought for a moment or two, grinned and then said, "I see what you're saying. Thanks for steering me in the right direction this afternoon."

"My pleasure. Now let's make sure the girls see us as confident and mature rather than mediocre and boring." He walked over and stood beside me. I had yet to don my jacket, so when I pointed to my shirt it was easy for Lester to see, even with the pleats, the way the edges where my shirt and fly buttoned were in line. He adjusted his shirt and then looked at me for approval. I gave him a thumbs up and a high-five.

"If you were wearing a belt rather than suspenders and a cummerbund, you'd make sure the edge of your belt buckle lined up with your shirt and fly."

"So, that's what you call this thing." he fingered the cummerbund. "If I went back to where I grew up wearing a cummerbund, this ruffled shirt, and pants without pockets and a strip down the leg people would think I was a girl."

I laughed. "If I went back to Moonshine Holler in Tennessee I suspect people would question and make snide remarks about my sexual preference."

I slipped on my jacket, and we walked into the sitting area where Rita and Mindy were dressed and waiting.

I took one look at Rita with her flaming-red hair swept up in a French twist dressed in a silk strapless emerald-green cocktail dress with matching high heels and no bra, and said, "You are not wearing that dress out in public."

"Oh and why not?"

"Well, for one reason, I say not. A second reason is because you are going to set off a riot the minute you remove your coat, and if you need a third reason, I don't want the public privileged to what I consider private property."

"I'm wearing this for you, not the public." She moved close against me, gave me a kiss, whispered, 'Later' and winked as she backed away. She knew what she was doing to me and she enjoyed it—so did I.

Lester might have glanced at Rita and might have heard the conversation, but his eyes were on Mindy—and why wouldn't they be. With long blonde hair and wearing a classic calf-length black cocktail dress with five-inch heels she was going to turn every head we encountered from the time we left our room until we returned. I imagined her as Anna when she was nineteen.

For Lester's benefit, the girls then went into a short and rehearsed one-act play directed by Rita. She pretended to have just noticed us. She looked at us back and forth a couple of times and said, "How handsome you gentlemen look this evening."

She then turned to Mindy and asked, "What do you think we should do? It's the dinner hour and no one has asked us out. Should we just sit around and hope for invitations or should we call an escort service?"

Mindy's eyes sparkled almost as much as her jewelry when she stepped forward and untied Lester's bow tie and retied it. When she finished it was perfect. She quickly backed away before he could muster up too much courage and attempt something he shouldn't. She gave us approving looks and then turned back to Rita. "Yes, they are indeed handsome, but I don't think we should sit around and hope for invitations to dinner. A girl who lives on hope will dine from an empty plate. Let's call an escort service."

When I looked at Lester, he was staring at me waiting, it appeared more like begging, for me to bail us out with flattering phrases to win the girl's approval and forgiveness—he had no idea it was a game to teach him to respect Mindy and to never take her for granted. I was distracted by Mindy's remark about hope resulting in an empty plate. Just as distracting was the momentary change in her voice and facial features. It took Rita to pull me away from my thoughts.

"I'll check with the concierge."

I looked at Lester. "Do we dare ask these beautiful women for a date and risk the embarrassment of having them turn us down or shall we take a chance?" I didn't wait for him to blurt out an inappropriate answer. They were standing together now.

Lester didn't see me wink when I asked, "Would you lovely ladies grant two undeserving scalawags the honor of dining with them and the privilege of your company this evening?"

Rita looked at Mindy. "What do you think? Should we give them a chance?"

"Well. I don't know. They are, as you say, quite handsome in a diamond-in-the-rough sort of way. Do you suppose we would be safe with them?"

"I don't know. They do appear a bit roguish. What do we do if they attempt uninvited advances?"

"We break their fingers one at a time until they get the message."

"Then I say we take a chance."

Mindy turned toward us, curtsied, and said, "We accept your invitation."

I looked at her, bowed, and said "We thank you."

Rita had arranged for a limo. When the phone rang I knew the driver was waiting. I punched the speaker button and answered, "We'll be down momentarily." And then turned to the trio and asked, "Shall we go?"

I walked toward the door, followed by Lester. When I reached the door and opened it for everyone to exit, the girls were still standing in the middle of the room. This was no surprise. Class was still in session. Lester had another lesson to learn.

"The driver is waiting." I could tell Rita was stifling a giggle when she said, "We ladies are waiting for you gentlemen to help us with our wraps." She emphasized ladies and gentlemen. I pretended to be embarrassed—Lester wasn't pretending.

I gave the Gershwin Theater's address to the driver and arranged to have him pick us up after the final curtain fell. Just before we turned onto West 51st Street I looked across at Mindy and asked, "Do you trust me?"

"You agreed to adopt me. So, yes Father, I trust you." I pondered for a moment another odd remark. There was something a little different about Mindy this evening. Something I couldn't put a finger on. I had a nervous feeling it was leading to someplace I wasn't prepared to go—but where?

"Will it be okay if I blindfold you for a few minutes?"

"I won't mind if you promise to stay with me while I'm blindfolded."

"I promise to never leave your side. First, I'd like to give your clutch to Mr. Hightower for safekeeping."

She handed it to me with a quizzical look. I passed the tiny clutch to Lester. "Keep this safe until Miss Mindy asks you for it." This was another lesson for Lester. He must have seen Rita give me her clutch after I draped the stole around her shoulders. Then again, maybe not; even though I'd made a show of putting it in my jacket pocket. He'd had eyes only for Mindy since we'd walked into room where the girls were dressed and stood waiting. Although she extended her hand holding the clutch toward him he didn't understand the gesture. Also, he was too captivated by the act of wrapping the cashmere stole around her shoulders to notice.

He took the clutch and looked at it and then at me. I opened my jacket enough to expose the end of Rita's clutch protruding from an inside pocket as I removed a sleep mask from my breast pocket and handed it to Mindy. Lester got the message and placed her clutch in his pocket while she placed the mask over her eyes and tied it in back.

Although I was attempting to second-guess Mindy and trying to find meaning where probably none existed, I thought it a nice gesture when she addressed me as "Father." For a moment I wondered what it would have been like had Emily and I married and had a bunch of kids. I would never know. It was a fleeting thought. I could not be happier with the way my life had unfolded and wouldn't want to change anything. Emily dying without ever knowing true happiness or realizing her dream was my only regret. Referencing my statement about adopting her in conjunction with referring to me as her father was, I thought, a bit odd. As we turned off Broadway my mind cleared out everything other than how to keep Mindy from figuring out her surprise.

Before we reached 222 West 51st Street the driver fell in line with other limos and taxis dropping off people at the theater. When it became our turn he opened the curbside doors for us to exit. I took Mindy's hand. As soon as she was clear of the car Rita took her other hand and we warned her of possible hazards as we walked her into the theater. Several theatergoers gave us quizzical looks as we led Mindy down the aisle to our seats. We'd reserved seats only two weeks in advance and were fortunate to get orchestra seating on such short notice.

By the time we were seated Mindy already knew she was in a theater. Since we had not picked up a program and since she could not have seen playbills as we passed through the lobby she had no clue as to what she was going to see. As the lights dimmed I told Mindy she could remove her mask. Minutes later, as the curtain was lifted and she saw cottages in a peaceful little village with the rolling hills of a vineyard in the background; she hugged Rita, and whispered "Thank you." She then put her fingers to her lips, reached across, touched them to my cheek, and again whispered "Thank you."

When the curtain fell for intermission Rita brushed her lips against mine as she whispered, "We are going to freshen up," reached inside my jacket, removed her clutch from my pocket, and gave me another chance to appreciate her dress or lack thereof. The interaction wasn't lost on Lester. He had Mindy's clutch in hand when she turned toward him. She gave him a smile and a "Thank you."

We watched them blend into and then disappear amongst the throng filling the aisles. I stepped into the aisle and motioned for Lester to step in front of me—another lesson. As we made our way to the lobby, he asked, "What do they carry in those little-bitty purses?"

"Not much, lipstick, eye makeup, comb, emergency funds in case we ditch them, perhaps lip-gloss and a couple of lozenges, and in our case, a very special cell phone. They will likely have a small hanky, but normally they depend on the gentleman to supply the handkerchief in case one is needed."

We were standing next to our seats when the girls returned. Lester was a quick study. When Mindy offered her clutch he took it and placed it in his pocket. She gave him another smile and another "Thank you."

The driver dropped us at 56 Beaver Street ten minutes prior to our reservation. Just as I predicted, all eyes were on Rita and Mindy as we followed the hostess to our table.

Lester helped Mindy with her chair while I assisted Rita. When she was seated I removed the stole from her shoulders and draped it over the back of the chair. She thanked me. I leaned forward and whispered, "It wasn't my intent to be chivalrous. I just wanted to look down your dress again."

She turned and whispered, "You dirty old man." and then gave me a smile and a peck on the cheek.

I'm sure Lester would have enjoyed taking a peek down Mindy's dress, but he feared the consequences—a broken finger.

Delmonico's was jam-packed with after-theater diners. When we removed the girls' stoles, eyes bulged. Several wives and girlfriends spoke with their escorts. These gentlemen promptly returned their attention to the appropriate tables. Much to the displeasure of their dates, they continued to glance in our direction. I was waiting for the sound of an open hand contacting with a face followed by a quick departure.

"Miss Mindy. Miss Rita and I planned the ballet as a surprise for you. We remembered you telling us you were schooled in ballet by the Vaganova Ballet Academy. We had no idea you would know from the opening curtain you were going to see Gisele. How did you know?"

"I recognized the setting. I danced the part of a jilted virgin in our recital my last year at boarding school."

"Really, you continue to amaze me. Perhaps you will dance for us sometime."

She smiled and shrugged ever so slightly. "Perhaps."

Dinner went well—no riots. At the hotel I checked in with Anna. She had nothing new for us, so I passed the phone to Rita. In between giggles they talked in sister-speak—a language only they understood. Ten minutes later they disconnected. Rita's eyes sparkled and she was all smiles when she looked at me.

I had the spotting scopes focus in on the bench where the news producer would be instructed to sit and wait for what I'm sure he considered the twenty-first-century deep-throat he was grooming to be more beneficial to him than Mark Felt of 1972-73 Watergate scandal had been to Woodward and Bernstein. He probably expected his contact would provide him fame far eclipsing the attention Felt had brought Woodward and Bernstein. Greed and vanity had been the undoing of men since the beginning of time and it wasn't likely to change—at least not for this low-life newsman.

After turning down the lights I used Leica binoculars identical to the ones the commander would have been using in his original plan, to scan and become familiar with Robert F. Wagner Jr. Park and adjacent streets and areas. It was a small park, but very impressive the way it was laid out using the Statue of Liberty as a focal point.

"Okay gang, according to the field commander, tomorrow night is likely going to be a rehearsal to the Fourth of July fireworks show. I'll go over everything with you tomorrow. The commander will join us tomorrow night and further enlighten us as to what we can expect to see. It's getting late. We had a very busy day. So, I suggest we get some rest and be refreshed for whatever tomorrow may bring."

Lester was surprised, and said as much when he found our beds had been turned down and our pillows fluffed. I reminded him we were not staying at Motel 6. I was almost asleep when I heard our bedroom door open. Lester walked into the drawing room and pulled the door closed behind him. He was back in a couple of minutes. I gave him time to settle in and then looked across at his bed and asked. "She wasn't there, huh?"

After a few short moments of silence he answered, "I figured she might be. I guess I was hoping for too much." Another brief period of silence before he asked, "Do you think she likes me?"

"She likes you, but she's not the girl you see in 'R' rated movies. She requires courting. Women want to be taken, but not until they decide. Scarlet didn't carry Rhett up the grand staircase. It may take a long time before you can take that trip with Miss Mindy. I suggest you be patient. Learn the meaning of signals she sends you. She'll tell you when she wants you to take the next step."

There was a longer silence. Finally he said, "Thanks."

Lester wouldn't get much sleep tonight. Sweet dreams can keep you awake same as nightmares.

It was ten thirty by the time I showered, shaved, finished dressing, and entered the drawing room. Lester and the girls were dressed, waiting, and looking a bit put out. They weren't smiling. I looked at Rita. "What?"

"We're hungry. We were considering going to breakfast without you. Our reservations were for thirty minutes ago. Breakfast service ends in half an hour."

"What are we waiting for?"

Our timing was good. The run on breakfast had ended. The lunch crowd hadn't shown up yet. We were seated at a window table with a view of the park, the Statue of Liberty, and Ellis Island—pretty much the same view as from our suite.

With nothing to do before midnight we ate unhurriedly while engaging in small talk unrelated to the reason we were in New York—it was very pleasant. With a blue-sky day—as blue-a-sky day as you're likely to experience in NYC—I suggested an afternoon carriage ride in Central Park, dinner at the Boathouse, followed by an evening carriage ride. With everyone in agreement, Rita was on the phone immediately making reservations and arranging transportation. I showed our keycard and signed the bill. Rita and I were using the names we'd used in DC five years earlier—Warren Taylor and Jennifer Settle. When projects were finalized all identification used was returned to Miss Rebecca in records and accounting. She renewed these documents as required, thus keeping them current in case they were needed later. Lester and Mindy had chosen Ralph Climer and Brigitte West.

Our limo driver dropped us near the New York Carriage Company station at four forty. Our afternoon ride was to begin at five and end at seven. I figured two hours might be a bit long without a break. While Lester assisted the girls into the carriage, I told our driver I'd like to stop about halfway through the ride for ice cream and a comfort station. Also, I arranged for two pedi-cabs to take us to the Loeb lakeside restaurant when our afternoon ride ended. They would return for us in time for our nighttime ride. I then instructed our coachman to have flowers to include jasmine or plumeria, something with a spring-time aroma, and truffles waiting for each of the girls when we arrived for our nighttime ride.

The day was perfect. The warm afternoon sun was a bonus. The ride was smooth and pleasant. The big Clydesdale didn't appear to know he was pulling a carriage. He walked along effortlessly as though he was out for a stroll in a pasture. My thoughts took me back to the Tennessee farm I'd given to Ben and Mary Lou when I thought I was going to be executed for a crime I didn't commit. Actually, I was executed. I just didn't die, although everyone thought I did. Anna, whom I barely knew back then, had begged the Club to intervene. They did. She saved my life. In the Club I found a new home, camaraderie I hadn't known before, and love one finds only in a dream. I put an arm around Rita's shoulders and pulled her close. She looked into my eyes and read my thoughts—she knew not to ask. She kissed my cheek and laid her head on my shoulder.

Everyone was ready for a break when we stopped for ice cream. The horse didn't seem to care one way or the other although he didn't refuse his grain and water buckets.

The sun was just about to drop out of sight when we were seated at a lakeside table. In Manhattan the sun didn't set. There was no horizon. There were only skyscrapers. Lights strategically located around the boathouse cast shadows about and reflected in the lake. Fish, feeding on insects drawn to the lights, occasionally disturbed the surface.

Rita had looked intently at the lake for several minutes. When finally she looked at me and managed a smile, I nodded toward the lake. "What kind of fish do you think are surface-feeding?"

"Probably minnows or stickleback; I doubt there are trout or other top-feeding fish in this lake."

"I thought stickleback lived in brackish and salt water."

"Mostly they do, but as the ice age receded some were trapped in what became freshwater lakes. Watching the dimples takes me back to the time when Anna and I fished the meandering stream running through my parents' farm. I was just trying to remember the feel of a sixteen-inch rainbow on a two-weight Sage fly rod with a 1X tippet."

"Do you miss those days? Do you think of them often?"

"Not often, only when something reminds me, even then only for a minute or two. The terror I experienced when my parents were murdered, the uprooting of life when Anna and I were forced to run for our lives, and the hardships following those events override all the fun memories. I wouldn't trade what I have now for my childhood." A tear glistened in her eye and began to pearl down her cheek. I wiped it away with my finger and put it to my lips. She smiled and said, "thank you" as she gripped my forearm.

She knew I'd always be there to kiss away her tears and said so. Flashbacks can be triggered by things seeming insignificant to others. Some mind trips into the past can be pleasant—some not pleasant at all.

Dinner went as expected with one exception. The question came out of the blue and I was unprepared. She was looking directly at me when she asked, "Father, may I have a glass of wine with dinner?" Her having addressed me as "Father" for the second time in the last two days was momentarily disarming. It took me a moment to organize my thoughts. It was out of respect to those signing the Declaration of Independence, the Founding Fathers, the revolutionists, and their families that we addressed Club members formally. I answered as though she had addressed me as Mr. Scott.

"Miss Mindy, I appreciate you asking me. However, you are no longer a little girl. You are one of the most responsible young women I've ever met. You do not need anyone's permission; however, you may want to ask Miss Anna about her first drinking experience before sampling a glass of wine."

"I know, I just wanted my father's permission."

""You flatter me. Although I'm not worthy, it will be my honor to serve you in the role of your father anytime you need help or clarity. Unfortunately, or perhaps fortunately, you do need approval from the State of New York. You must celebrate two more birthdays before they will give you their permission."

"I know, but if ever the time comes I decide to take my first taste of wine or champagne, I wanted to know I had your permission." She hesitated for a moment before continuing. "I grew up in one day at age fifteen. Before then I had my parents and the boarding school to choose for me and direct my life. I wasn't required to make decisions. I can identify with Miss Rita and Miss Anna. They also grew up in one day. They had the good fortune of having Mr. Elmore adopt them, perhaps not legally, but they could count on him to guide them in their decisions. The Club rescued me and has taken care of me, but I am still scared. In many ways, I'm still a little girl. I need a father.

"You said you would be proud to have me as your daughter. You said you would adopt me anytime I asked. I'm asking. Would you adopt me legally with papers and whatever is required, so I'll know I will always have someone to help me with decisions and take care of me?"

Having finished her question she began to cry. Lester was quick on the draw. He offered her a handkerchief. She took it, whispered, "Thank you," dabbed her eyes and managed a smile. I stood up, pulled her chair back, and took her hand.

"Would you give your father a hug?" She stood and we spent several seconds in a father-daughter embrace. When I helped her back into her chair she sighed as though a great burden had been lifted from her shoulders. Her eyes were bright and her smile back to beautiful when she said, "Thank you."

I sat down and looked into her eyes. "I'll have Miss Rebecca start the paperwork as soon as we get home." I received another "Thank you" and another smile. Suddenly, I was scared. What if I couldn't live up to her expectations? Was I capable of being a father? I had no way of knowing. Neither did I have a choice. I'd just made the most serious decision of my entire life.

We were finishing dinner when I remembered the statement she'd made the prior evening. I was still looking at Mindy when I said, "I'm not sure how to address my daughter. I think until we make the adoption legal I should keep it formal, perhaps later Mindy will be acceptable for the Club. I can even call you Lidiya if you like."

"Please don't. I am no longer Russian."

"Last night you made a very interesting statement. You said 'A girl who lives on hope will dine from an empty plate.' What did you mean?"

"The statement defines the reason I want to forget my Russian name and my birth country. Hope was the reason I foolishly chose to believe something I knew was nothing more than a dream. I do not regret my decision or what happened to me. It brought me to the Club and you." She took in a deep breath and then exhaled slowly before taking a normal second breath and continuing. "For as long as I can remember, Russians have placed their faith in hope, it was all they had. Even after the wall came down, it was still their only choice. I came to believe hope was nothing more than an excuse for not doing something yourself to improve your life. In fairness, there was nothing most Russians could do except hope things would change for the better. Hope life would get easier. Hope they wouldn't be cold or hungry during the coming winter. Russians have been living on hope and eating from an empty plate for so long, it has come to be expected. Even with the Soviet Union dissolved very little has changed. Those in charge back then are, for the most part, still in control today."

I have no idea how long her monologue would have continued had she not looked at our faces. "I'm sorry; I didn't mean to bring you down.

Please forgive me and thanks for letting me vent." She started to cry again. Lester was Johnny-on-the-spot with his handkerchief.

"I think it's time for another father-daughter hug." The tears were gone when I helped her back into her chair.

Rita reached across the table and touched her hand. "If you need a mother to go along with your new father, I'm available. I know I speak for Miss Anna as well."

"Thank you." Mindy paused just long enough to show respect before adding, "While on Aeroflot I dreamt of fame and fortune without realizing there are things far more important. I pray I don't wake to find this is just a dream."

"Mr. Hightower, would you pinch Miss Mindy so she'll know she's awake and not dreaming."

"Sir, it would be my pleasure, but I don't want a broken finger." After the laughter died away, Mindy smiled at him and said, "I'll be gentle. It will only hurt for a little while." They were too involved smiling at each other to notice when I winked at Rita and said, "We may have to get married to make the adoption legal."

She leaned toward me, looked into my eyes, and accented every word as she mouthed them slowly. "We're already married and don't you forget it."

Playfully, I removed the knife from her plate and moved it out of reach, "I wouldn't dare." Her eyes were sparkling when she smiled and gave me a quick kiss on the cheek.

Our pedi-cabs were on time and returned us to our waiting carriage. The flowers and candy got me a hug and a kiss from Rita. Lester received a "Thank you" and a peck on the cheek. *Lost and found* was simmering. A nighttime carriage ride along lamp-lighted lanes in the park can be nice, but will never compare to a horseback ride on a moonlight night in the country. Nevertheless it was having the desired effect on Lester and Mindy. Rita snuggled up when I slipped my arm around her shoulders. A few minutes later she whispered, "They're holding hands."

"How much do you think we should charge the director for our matchmaking skills?" She giggled and then gave me a long passionate kiss. I pulled her closer as we continued to whisper and embrace. Halfway through the ride Lester found enough courage to move beyond holding hands and put his arm around Mindy. She didn't shy away or remove his arm. We pretended to pay them no mind and near the end of the ride as we came out of a rather dark section of the lane they were kissing.

We pretended to be unaware of their romantic display as Rita whispered. "It appears *Lost and found* is destined for success."

"No doubt a spark has landed in the tinder and is growing brighter with every passing second. I hope it burns slowly. I'll have a talk with Lester. You should probably have a girl-to-girl talk with Mindy." Then with a touch of sarcasm, added, "And perhaps throw in a little motherly counseling." Which got me a poke in the ribs.

"Oh, so you don't think I'm capable of being a mother?"

"I think you're capable of being anything you want to be." She gave me a little squeeze and whispered "Now you're fishing." I just smiled. Did I mention I smile a lot?

At the hotel Rita and I prepared for possible physical streetside involvement in the upcoming event. I changed into black sweats and running shoes. The commander had phoned confirming the exchange was going down at 1 a.m.—just two hours away.

Lester had changed into black sweats and running shoes as well. I suspected he was hoping to go with us if we were called on to assist. Rita was wearing black tights and a bulky sweater. We were standing at the window when Mindy came out of the bedroom without shoes and dressed in a baby-doll nightgown. My head snapped around and then back to Rita and in a whisper asked, "Is this your idea?" With her eyes opened wide in a surprised and disapproving gesture, she shrugged and shook her head. Still whispering I suggested she have a mini conference with her "I think it's time for your first mother-daughter talk."

Before either of us moved or found our voice, Mindy said, "Last evening you asked if I would dance for you." She continued before we could speak. "I don't have toe shoes so I can't go on point, and my nightgown is the closest thing I have to an appropriate dress. The carpet and room size will limit me from actually dancing. I can show you only a few movements. Perhaps one day I can actually perform for you. In the meantime I just want you to know, I really can dance."

She began without waiting for our response. She explained positions as she moved from on to another. After ten minutes she explained, "The *pirouette* is performed flatfooted and can be done continuously"—she did a half dozen without stopping. "This is preparation for the *tour en l'air*. If you can't perform a single *tour en l'air,* you can't dance." She leapt into the air and made one complete turn. "To become a dancer you must master a double *tour en l'air*. A really good dancer can do a triple. Once every hundred years or so comes a dancer capable of performing a quadruple *tour en l'air*." Without further explanation she leapt into the air again and made four complete revolutions before gracefully touching down. We were astounded. She continued before we were able to comment.

"I will attempt one difficult movement for you. I think the room is large enough for me to squeeze in a *grand jeté* without bouncing off the wall." She moved near the window, so as to have the entire room to work with, and after two steps took to the air. Her grand jump was graceful and beautiful. She floated five feet above the floor, her toes pointed, legs perfectly horizontal and split 180 degrees fore and aft. Her head was tilted as though looking into space at a distant star. She held her arms in a position so as to have her face appear as a portrait in an oval frame. Upon touching down she gave us a *fondu* and disappeared into the bedroom. We applauded long after she'd closed the door. Lester was still trying to get his eyeballs back into their sockets.

Minutes later she returned wearing her little-girl look and an outfit matching Rita's. We had encouraged Mindy and Lester to buy these outfits at Bergdorf Goodman, just in case.

"I didn't know I had such a talented daughter. Would you like to take school with a company here in New York?"

"Thank you, no." I love to dance, but dancing is hard work and totally consuming—you must run through your exercises every day. As tempting as your generous offer might be, I want to stay with the Club and my new family." She hesitated for a moment and then added, "A ballet bar and a mirror in the gym would be nice."

"I'll see what I can do."

My striped cell phone chimed. When I connected the message was simple, "On my way up." Since our suite had an excellent view of the park I suggested he use it for command central. He accepted. Two minutes later I answered a knock at the door. The field commander and a lady entered. Each carried a piece of soft-sided luggage. Both were dressed as though returning from a night out. I would later learn they had attended the Gerald Schoenfeld Theater. At 1 a.m. a couple with similar features and dressed identically would be seated at Coogan's, an after-hours restaurant on Broadway in upper Manhattan. Should there ever be a question as to his whereabouts when the briefcase exchange went down, he would have the theater ticket stubs as well as the bill and credit card receipt from

Coogan's. Also, along with the hostess and servers, there would be a dozen people willing to testify they were in the restaurant.

"May we use your bedrooms to change?"

"Certainly." Rita pointed the commander to the bedroom Lester and I used as she escorted the lady to the bedroom she shared with Mindy. I surmised she was anxious to change clothes quickly and the reason she removed her wrap before entering the bedroom. Lester and I did double takes. No one would forget the lady was at the theater or in the restaurant. The lady's jewelry was eye-catching and her dress, what there was of it, made the one Rita wore the previous night appropriate for church.

Minutes later they returned dressed as a couple on their way home after working late at the office. Their IDs would check out, but were phony. Each chapter had created a number of fictitious individuals with addresses, driver's licenses, and so on to be used during events involving assassination.

The commander checked his watch and made a brief phone call. Shortly thereafter I answered another knock at the door. Two men entered, one in his forties with the other ten to fifteen years older. The older man set two pieces of hard-sided luggage on the floor and picked up the two pieces of soft-sided luggage brought up by the field commander and the lady and then departed without saying a word.

Rita and I knew and had worked with the field commander when we took out the guy in Central Park. We didn't know the lady or the other two men. There were no introductions. This was Club policy. Identities of Club members were known to only a few outside individual chapters. Even when introductions were made, names were likely to be bogus. A custom started when General George Washington used spies, known as The Six (officers' wives posing as loose women), to hang out in taverns. British officers and regulars eager to impress these women divulged their secret plans to capture and destroy the militia's supplies and weapons stored at Concord and to capture the rebellion leaders Samuel Adams and John Hancock. Warned of the plot, General Washington had the supplies relocated and his Minute Men waiting when the British showed up.

The shot, from North Bridge, heard round the world and the success of the American Revolution were due to these women's dedicated efforts and the foresight of General Washington to use spies. Even today the names of The Six were unknown, and so it had been with the Club.

The younger man placed a hard-sided suitcase on the bar and opened it to expose a built-in device with wires, cables, gauges, switches, and potentiometers. The lady took charge of the suitcase while he set a larger and bulkier second suitcase in front of the three glass panels providing us with a panoramic view of the park. The center panel was a slider that opened up to a narrow balcony. He removed the cover to reveal an eighteen-inch satellite dish, slid open the glass panel, and placed it on the balcony. The lady had three cables connected to the suitcase on the bar ready to hook into the satellite dish. She made the connections, returned to the suitcase and began playing with the switches and potentiometers while watching the gauges. The dish began moving up and down and back and forth searching for a satellite. The dish's computer found and locked onto the satellite.

The commander checked his watch again and announced, "Time to get the show on the road." Using a cable provided him by the lady he plugged his cell phone into the electronic gear inside suitcase and made a call. It rang a couple of times and then a voice answered,

"This is Zack." His voice was clear, without the telltale sound of a speakerphone.

"You set? How far are you from your destination?"

"I'm five minutes away, sitting on dead ready, and getting anxious." We knew he was referring to the druggie sitting beside him. We also knew the man referring to himself as Zack could hear the commander but the doper could not. Zack was pretending the call was coming from the person the druggie was to meet.

"Okay, let him snort a line of blow, or whatever it takes to get him through the next hour and we'll be home free. I'll get back to you as soon as we're set."

"Roger that."

While the commander was on the phone with Zack, the younger man removed a big ear from a third piece of luggage and focused it on the bench. The final item he set up was a narrow beam transmitter. It too was focused on the bench. As he set up each piece of equipment the lady connected them with various wires and cables to the suitcase on the bar and powered them up.

Upon disconnecting his call to Zack the commander asked if we could turn off all the lights, and then made another call. I pointed to Lester and Mindy. Within fifteen seconds all lights in our suite had been extinguished.

A man answered, "Hello."

"This is Baxter, you ready?"

"I've been waiting for your call."

"How long will it take you to get to the park?"

"Five minutes, ten at most. I have a room at the Ritz. I'll leave my room soon as we finish this call and walk across the street." Our mouths fell open as we looked at each other with wide and disbelieving eyes. He was in our hotel.

The commander showed no emotion as he continued. "Okay, that's good. You remember the deal? Ten thousand dollars in small bills. No escort and no cops."

"Yeah, I got it. I'm not stupid you know." It was all we could do to not laugh.

"Okay, here's the deal. When you arrive at the park, walk across the grass to the point jutting out into the river. As you face the Statute of Liberty, look to your right. You will see three groups of three benches each. Sit on the middle bench of the center group. When it's clear I'll walk across the lawn and we will exchange briefcases. Once I see you are positioned I will call and give you a single-digit number. When I approach I will verbalize a different single-digit number. You add the two together and tell me the answer. If you give me the correct number we will exchange briefcases and I'll leave as quickly as I came. After you've had a chance to examine the contents of the briefcase I will give you a call and we can discuss the next drop. Any questions?"

"Only two, what's the number and what's the purpose of this little game?"

"Once you are on the bench you'll get the number. I'm not going to meet with a cop pretending to be you. I want to make sure you're there in person. I know your phone voice, but people sometimes sound different in person. Any funny stuff and the deal is off. Understood?"

"Yeah, I got it. I'll give you fifteen minutes from the time you give me the number, if you're not there by then, you can color me gone. Capisce?"

"Listen up and pay attention, tough guy. I don't need you. You need me. There are lots of people willing to pay for what I'm selling, so don't get cocky. I'm doing this because I'm a little down on my luck. I chose you because you aren't doing so hot yourself. As a matter of fact, you're a nobody. You produce a nothing half-hour news cast no one watches. You're just one in thousands doing the same thing all across the country and around the world. You're looking for fame. I'm looking for fortune. I'm offering you a chance to move above the also-runs. I have access to a lot of information. It can be yours if you're willing to pay. We can be a team as long as you keep in mind who's in charge. You wait on that bench until I tell you to leave. Capisce?" The commander waited through a couple seconds of silence and then added. "I'll call you as soon as you park your sorry rearend on the bench. I'll show up when I determine it's safe to do the deal." He hesitated and then left no doubt as to who was in charge when he hammered the question again, "Capisce?"

"Yeah, okay, I'm on my way." The producer knew he was out of his league, but made one more effort to play the tough guy. "You'd better not be wasting my time." He disconnected before the commander could respond.

We'd held it as long as we could. We all burst out laughing. There was enough light shining through the glass panels for us to move around without tripping or bumping into furniture. The commander had suggested I leave the area in front of the center glass panel free from clutter. I'd set up my spotting scopes to either side. I checked to make sure they were still focused on the bench where the soon-to-be ex-producer of late-night news would sit. The commander was already peering through his Leica binoculars watching the street. I picked up my Leics and began watching Battery Place between the hotel and Robert F. Wagner Jr. Park.

Traffic was sparse to nonexistent. When a man crossed the street I asked, "Is that your guy?"

"That's him." The commander was on the phone immediately. The man calling himself Zack answered after the first ring. "He's on his way. How's your client?"

"We're cool. We can handle the unexpected."

"Okay, Move up to the bus stop and wait for my call. It probably won't hurt to review the doper on his part in the drama, just in case."

"Roger that."

We continued to watch the low-life producer as he headed toward the bench. Obviously this wasn't his first visit to the park. Probably, since he'd been given the option of choosing the place for exchanging money for information, he had chosen a familiar location. From the Club's perspective, it had been a good choice.

Again the phone was answered on the first ring, "This is Zack."

"You in position?"

"Affirmative."

"Our target is in the park. Everybody clear on what to do?"

"Affirmative."

"I'll get back to you with the number. Stand by."

The guy appeared only remotely concerned with his safety. He walked around the three benches and then peered underneath before he sat down. Although the park was not well lit, I didn't have any problem eliminating the possibility of someone sitting, lounging, or walking around. Conditions were right. Without something unexpected turning up it would all be over in five minutes.

I watched though my spotting scope. The guy had his cell phone in hand, but still trying to put up a tough-guy façade, didn't answer until the fifth ring. "Okay, I'm here. What's the number?"

"I'll leave the number up to you. What's your favorite number?"

"Thirty-six, it's my mistress's breast size." The producer was trying to be cute, but the commander didn't miss a beat.

"Sounds like an easy number for you to remember. So, we'll add the three and the six. Your number is nine. Can you remember nine?"

"Yeah, I can remember nine. I told you I'm not stupid."

"Well, neither am I, and going to prison is not high on my wish list. If I see anything specious, we'll delay until I consider it safe to proceed. I'm headed in your direction as we speak. So, hang tight."

Within five seconds he was on the phone with Zack. "The magic number is nine. Our boy can give him any single-digit number he wants. You know the plan—the guy's response will be the sum of the two numbers. The only other thing our druggie needs to remember, in case the producer tries to get cute and gives him a bogus sum, is the number thirty-six—his girlfriend's bra size. Have him make an off-handed remark about her. Tell him to not let the guy bully him, and to make sure it's a hand-to-hand exchange."

The druggie still believed Zack was talking with the guy he was going to swap briefcases with. "Got it. My representative understands. He's on his way."

The line, "He's on his way" was a prearranged code to let the commander know Zack had put his phone on speaker so we could hear his instructions to the druggie.

"Here's the briefcase you'll be giving to the guy you're meeting. Don't fall for the old con where you put yours on one bench while he puts the one he's giving you on another bench and then each of you walk to the opposite bench. Too much can go wrong for such a swap. Tell him he can hand you his as you hand him yours. Tell him it's your way or no way. Also, make sure no one is sneaking up on you from behind. I haven't dealt with this guy before and I don't trust him. Okay?"

"Don't worry; I'm used to dealing with people you can't trust. Say, man. This thing is sure heavy, what's in it?"

"He's a slick guy. All the more reason not to trust him. He wants to be paid in hard currency. There's twenty pounds of silver coins in there. In case you're having trouble with the math, I'm paying you twice as much as I'm paying him." Zack threw in the silver story to cover the weight of the explosives, batteries, and the electronics. Also to make sure he knew it would be more profitable to bring back the other briefcase than to take off with the one he was going to deliver.

"What's the lock combination?"

"If he asks, tell him I'll phone it to him after the swap is made." All this was BS to make the druggie think we were all going to profit from the deal. Zack threw in one more sweetener. "If the document this guy gives you turns a profit for me, what's the chance you and I could become partners in future exchanges?"

"Works for me, man."

"We'd better not keep him waiting too long. You're on your own. Can you handle it?"

"Don't worry about me, partner. I'll be back in a sec."

"Be careful." We heard the car door open and then slam shut. A few second later Zack said "Okay, as soon as he's out of sight I'll exit the vehicle and disappear. I'll be standing by if you need me."

"Thanks, we'll take it from here."

We watched the druggie walk across the grass. The guy on the bench stood up as he approached. "You sure took your sweet time. Where've you been?"

The big ear worked perfectly. The lady adjusted the volume and the audio came in clear. It was as though they were standing in the room with us.

"Cool it, man. Let's do this and get outa here."

"Okay, give me the case."

They were standing within two feet of each other, when the commander instructed the lady to arm the two electronic detonators. She complied and reported, "Done."

"Stand by, detonate on my signal."

The druggie continued, although we'd have been happy to have him hand it over then and there.

"Not so fast, I want to make sure you're who you say you are. You add the number six to your number and give me the sum."

"Okay wise guy, the sum is twelve."

"What happened, man? Your girlfriend's boobs shrink?" I motioned for Lester to take over my spotting scope. As he peered through the Barska I whispered, "Pay attention to the druggie. This is not his first rodeo. When it comes to running a con, I'd say he's a pro."

"You're a regular little wiseass aren't you?"

"Okay, I'm outa here."

"Alright, alright, the sum is fifteen."

"Why did you waste our time pretending to be a tough guy? Here's mine, let's have yours."

The commander flipped the power switch on the big ear to the off position and uttered a one word instruction. "Now!"

The lady pushed two buttons simultaneously. A flash lit up the benches and surrounding area, followed a quarter-second later by the report of an explosion.

The commander shrugged, "My demolitions expert told me a block and a half of C-4 was more than enough. Guess I shouldn't have insisted on two blocks. Cleaning up is going take a while."

"Yeah, I'd say the yellow tape is going to stay up for several days. I like your style, Commander. I think you can take care of business in New York without further supervision."

"Thank you, Mr. Scott. We've come a long way since you started organizing local chapters. We are on the edge of a paradigm shift clubwide and nationwide. *Genesis* and *Chimney Sweep* are foremost on members' minds these days. There's a new energy throughout the Club and growing rapidly. We've been waiting for a leader—thanks again, Mr. Scott."

"You're welcome, sir. I'm serving my country the only way I know how—the Club is my calling." A knock at the door broke the mood. I was glad. I've never been comfortable responding to flattering remarks.

The same older man, who'd earlier taken away luggage for the commander and the lady, entered wearing coveralls with a janitorial logo when I opened the door. He wheeled a service cart with a broom and mop, along with a five-gallon bucket and several towels and a couple of overfilled black-plastic trash bags into the room. The younger man was already busy packing up the equipment, including the spotting scopes I'd brought and the cell phones we'd been given. Within three minutes the equipment had been loaded into the service cart and covered with towels and the trash bags. The younger man had donned coveralls, pulled from one of the trash bags, sporting the same janitorial logo as on the older man's coveralls. They left without speaking or looking back. Our suite had been sterilized.

I shook hands with the commander. As he and the lady departed a siren wailed in the distance. It grew closer and was soon joined by the ominous sound of other sirens approaching from different directions.

"Mr. Hightower, how about we let the girls go to bed while you and I watch the local news channel and discuss what we observed during the last hour?"

"Yes, sir." I turned on the television, touched the mute button on the remote, and switched to NY1.

"Today's news is going to be very interesting. You'll see how news releases differ from what really happened. The police have their reasons for withholding information and the media have their reasons for exploiting events. The police don't want to divulge leads they might have while assuring the public there's no reason to be concerned about their safety. On the flip side, the media want to panic as many as possible while alluding to nonexistent leads and motives.

"Before we get into tonight's events I have a short speech concerning Mindy—circumstances being what they are, I believe we can be less formal than is normally required by the Club."

"Yes, sir."

"I have a dilemma. Mindy has asked me to be her father. I am honored. I intend to be the best father I can be."

"Yes, sir."

"Like you, I found the girl of my dreams and then, before we could get married, someone killed her. My life fell apart. With the help of Anna and Rita I put all the anger behind me. Mindy can do the same for you—she has scars that need healing as well. This may become problematic in your relationship. Just let her direct your actions and everything will work out the way you both want. I know there's a mutual attraction, a budding romance if you prefer. One thing you need to keep in mind above all else—I am her father and if you abuse her in any way or break her heart, I'll break your legs. Understand?"

"Yes, sir."

"Good. Now we come to another of my problems. The director has charged me with helping you with your first project. Before I can help you it is imperative you put aside your anger and the past—in this I believe

Mindy will help you if you let her. To complete a project, discipline is crucial. It cannot be taught; it must be achieved through observation, logic, patience, and experience. We'll begin if you're ready. Are you up to it?"

"Yes, sir."

"Okay, what did you see happen tonight?"

"I saw two bad guys get blown away."

"Yeah, that's what I figured. What you should have seen was a plan coming to a successful conclusion. A plan that began with the choice of a target, and continued in a logical order of reconnaissance, rehearsals, baiting the trap, setting the hook, and concluding with the desired results. All without leaving a single clue connecting the action to the Club—the only clues were left deliberately to mislead the investigators."

"I hadn't thought about all the work and planning, I was just focusing on the end result. You made your point well. From now on I'll keep the overall picture in mind."

"Tonight you witnessed an event resulting from a concerted effort of an unknown number of Club members and the work of countless hours. For your first project you won't have a supporting cast. Genesis will help you with planning and direction, but for the most part, you'll be on your own. Will that work for you?"

"Yes sir. When do I start?"

"Tomorrow."

School Days

"The illiterate of the 21st century will not be those who cannot read and write, but those who cannot learn, unlearn, and relearn"

—Alvin Toffler

Someone once said, "No one leaves Washington (DC) a better person than when they arrived." This cannot be said of Lester. Back home in the Catskills he completed whatever work Miss Rebecca assigned him and then spent the rest of his time with his teachers. Mr. Bartow helped him expand his general education. Mr. Ainge introduced him to the down-and-dirty side of politics. Mr. Wilson schooled him in the art of self-defense and hand-to-hand combat. Miss Marie taught him civil and constitutional law. My daughter, Mindy—Anna, Rita, and I had adopted her as she'd requested—taught him grace and grammar. What else she taught him, we didn't know and didn't want to know.

He was a quick study and ten months later he was ready for his first field adventure. He'd begged for the opportunity. Now we'd find out if his capability to perform was equal to his loyalty and desire to contribute. The next month was spent with Miss Karla, in charge of planning. Genesis assisted and advised him when he had questions—there were many.

We determined he was as ready as he'd ever be for his first time in the field—there was no substitute for experience. With a plan in place and sanctioned by the board, Rita, pretending to still be in France, called Frank—he now considered us to be friends. He answered on the third ring, "Hi Frank, this is Jennifer. I hope my call has found you well and enjoying life."

"Thanks, Miss Jennifer. I am well and hearing your voice is a cheerful addition to my morning. How are Warren and Miss Rachel?"

"We're all well, Frank. Thanks for asking. If it's not too much of a problem, I have a favor to ask of you."

"For you Miss Jennifer, it's never a problem. How may I help?"

"Frank, you are such a dear. I have a couple of friends, Ralph Climer and Brigitte West in need of a place to live for six months, perhaps longer"—we couldn't see a problem with them using the names they'd used in New York City—"Could you please give me a call when you have something available?"

"I'll have a one-bedroom and a two-bedroom unit available at the end of next month, if that's okay."

"The two bedrooms will be perfect. Thank you, Frank." The conversation continued for a minute or so longer. I felt more and more guilt each time we used Frank's friendship for what some would consider devious and unlawful motives—if the truth were known and faces could be connected to our "assassinations for liberation," we'd head the FBI's most wanted list. On the flipside, a majority of Americans would approve our actions and we'd be on their prayer list.

We kept the same seating arrangement for dinner the director had set up when he asked Genesis to help Lester. The grief he carried for the loss of his young wife and the hate he had for those who had raped and killed her dominated his thinking. He would not be an asset to the Club until he could put it all behind him and think rationally under pressure. Mindy had problems of her own. She was a victim of rape and deceit. She kept her emotions in check, on the outside they didn't show—not until she broke down, cried, and asked Genesis to adopt her. Inside she was unsure of her worth as a young woman. Not only had the school she attended in Moscow taught her to be a proper young lady, she had learned to remain calm in the face of danger and how to kill if necessary. The one thing the school could not teach her was how to be young, far from home, and not be lonely. It seemed logical to put them together and let nature—a boy-girl relationship—heal them. The plan was more successful than we'd anticipated.

We'd asked the director to keep the seating arrangement in place—it now served as the family dinner table. We'd ask questions of Lester and

Mindy relating to their project and situations they might encounter during the execution of their plan. Also, we answered their questions and salted our answers with advice whenever we felt the need. We had tried to trip them up when they presented their cover stories to questions we asked. Anna, Rita, and I agreed—they were as ready as they could be without experience. It was time for them to get their feet wet. All we needed was for Frank to call. They would need to expand their wardrobe and buy a car. We would help with shopping once we had them settled in Georgetown.

I had no intention of putting Lester and my daughter in a situation involving violence. Although they had been victims of violence and had killed their attackers, they weren't ready to initiate an offensive of aggression—they were capable and willing, but, in the opinion of Genesis, not mentally ready.

It is next to impossible to hack into a government computer. Not only will security programs detect and thwart the intrusion, it will identify the source—something we couldn't afford. All computers have a weakness. Whether a computer is designed for home or corporate use, national defense or super-secret spying, security programs are designed to prevent external infiltration. If you have physical control of the computer you can program it to follow instructions from programs you install at the terminal. All you need are access codes. Normally, this is not a problem. People authorized to use government computers gain access by inserting a keycard containing their encoded information. Then by physically entering a personal code they are granted access. With a minimum understanding of programming, once given the right to enter the computer, they can set up their own folders and create codes to protect any program they install against detection. We needed a special program capable of hiding from firewalls and security sweeps of outgoing email that Lester could install on government computers. Anna could create the required program, but she was up to her ears encoding and managing the flow of data for the Club. So she decided to farm out the writing of a program to a club member she believed capable and loyal. She sent a handwritten note via the concierge: "Mr. Hughes, Miss Anna Borden requests you join her for dinner this evening, table two, ten o'clock."

An extra chair had been added to accommodate Mr. Hughes—originally there were seven chairs at the table. Two had been removed to provide privacy when Genesis took on the chore of matchmaking.

He arrived precisely at 10 p.m. Anna thanked him for honoring her request and graciously presented him to her other four guests. Although aware he was a club member, we had not been formally introduced. She waited until we'd made our selections for dinner and then offered a toast to his good health and longevity.

"Mr. Hughes, do you remember when, almost two years ago, I was setting up security for the Club's communication tree and the flow of information using a series of laptops controlled by my computer? Do you remember questioning my security system?"

"I do. I apologized and will do so again if it offended you."

"I wasn't offended, Mr. Hughes, to the contrary. I was flattered you were concerned. Also to have someone as knowledgeable as you overlook the bombs I'd left on your computer was a bonus in flattery."

"I must admit, Miss Anna, it was an embarrassing moment."

"Do you remember me saying: I considered melting your hard drive, but I thought I'd wait to find out if you were a friend or foe?"

"Yes, I remember."

"Do you remember your reply when I asked: Which are you, sir, friend or foe?"

"Yes I said: 'It may be difficult for you to trust me after you caught me trying to hack into your computer, but I swear to you, I am a friend.'"

"Do you recall my answer?"

"You said: you believed me and then asked if I would be willing to assist you if ever you should ask."

"And your answer was?"

"I would be honored."

"Well, Mr. Hughes, the time has come when I need your help. There are no members more suited for the job I have in mind, than a former officer of the National Security Administration, an expert in code breaking and computer programming. Does your offer still hold?"

"Absolutely, what do you need?"

"I suspect it is more difficult to hack into some government computers than others. I surmise different agencies rate a higher level of security than others. Am I correct?"

"You are indeed correct; hacking into the FBI's counter-intelligence database would be considerably more difficult and riskier than, let's say, the Treasure Department's computers."

"What about computers used by members of congress and their staff?"

"Compared to the ones mentioned it would be child's play."

"How about computers used by cabinet members?"

"Considerably more difficult than the ones used by congress. Your line of questioning leads me to conclude you already know there are different levels of security for computers throughout government."

"I supposed as much, but I needed you to verify my suspicions. It is my understanding all government computers are backed up offsite every twenty-four hours."

"Yes, you are correct. Some are backed up more often than others. But the data are backed up at least once every twenty-four hours."

"If I had someone inside, could you write a program this person could install to instruct the computer to back up to an additional offsite location undetected by the computer's security program?"

"No problem. The first thing I'd do is give this person a program to copy and extract all elements of the security system. With the extracted data I can determine how to get past their security and write a program to send back up information to your computer, my computer, any computer you designate. However, this will require a computer with superfast random-access memory (RAM). I can build a computer to provide everything you need, except for the hard drive. What you have in mind would require a petabyte or possibly an exabyte of storage. I'm sure you know already, an exabyte hard drive could store all words spoken by humans since the beginning of mankind. You could step down to a petabyte. A petabyte hard drive filled with music would take two thousand years to play. However, to maintain and sort through collected data the government stores every day would require more personnel than we could provide. Also, when you purchase a hard drive in the petabyte or higher range you attract attention.

"I suggest you cascade a series of newly released ten-terabyte helium-filled hard drives—two of these hard drives could store all written material in the Library of Congress."

"You are indeed a genius Mr. Hughes. I'm also interested in email; will email be in the backed-up data we receive?"

"Miss Anna, I thought you were going to challenge me. I can write a program on a thumb drive your inside person can install in ten seconds with instructions to add a blind copy, without it showing in the Bcc address box, to every outgoing email and forward all incoming email to whatever address you choose—without anyone the wiser. Since most people in government use laptops and other portable devices to work on projects when they are away from the office it has become very easy. Enter the program, with instructions to mutate—this will allow the program to stay hidden—and it will spread as email is sent, received and forwarded.

"Before you mentioned email, I was waiting for the right moment to suggest you forget about capturing data and concentrate on email. This is where all the underhanded back-door deals are made and where people are most likely to incriminate themselves."

"You have made excellent points, and I thank you. Self-incrimination is what we want to isolate and store. Concentrating on email only would require less time and effort. So, let's forget everything but email. Do you have other suggestions?"

"You already know once we begin hacking into government computers we become vulnerable. Should we be discovered it would be relatively easy to track our meddling back to our location—as you so aptly demonstrated when I attempted to elude and bypass your firewalls.

"Remember when several years ago an alleged suicide left the White House staff facing investigators and answering questions about missing records, how a computer hard drive, supposedly, had been damaged to the point data could not be recovered, and a flurry of phone calls could not be traced—everyone had conveniently forgotten who they called immediately after learning of the suicide. These calls were untraceable because the numbers called had bounced the call to another number.

"We can use a variation of the same system to avoid having someone trace the pirated emails to us. By setting up a network connection at an unrelated location anywhere in the country—or the world for that matter—and bounce it to another terminal. We can then use laptops with software to let us sort through emails sent to the second terminal and store anything of interest in a third location.

"We can place acid bombs in the second terminal, as you have done in the computer you use for committee communications. Should anyone start a trace we will be alerted in time to set off the acid bombs and cut access to the final link.

"Fantastic, I thank you, sir. One other question—can you add a program to allow us to put email on selected computers without anyone suspecting it resides on their hard drive?"

"No problem—we did it all the time at NSA. I can instruct the computer to accept and hide data from any outside source you designate. I can have the computer accept data randomly rather than at specific times to make the program more difficult to detect. I can have it startup immediately or delay any action for years.

"For example, several months before the Gulf War we, at NSA, infected an industrial printer we knew Iraq needed for its national air defense system. We sold it to them via an unsuspecting third party. Once the printer was installed and powered up the virus spread throughout the system and awaited our command.

"After Saddam annexed Kuwait and before General Schwarzkopf launched his offensive to drive the Iraqis out of Kuwait, we activated the virus using an F-15 with a special code in its IFF. When the Iraqi radar painted the F-15, their defense program automatically attempted to squawk the Eagle's parrot IFF (Identify, friend or foe). The especially coded message sent back to their defense-system computers, disguised as IFF codes, released the virus. Within minutes the virus had wiped out Iraq's entire defense-system's computers, leaving them without radar surveillance and communications."

"Was that a one-time action?"

"Of course not, we have viruses lying dormant in hundreds of computers around the world. We know one or more of these countries will give us cause to intervene within the next ten years—the question is when and where.

"I will add a caveat, if I may?"

"Please do."

"No matter how knowledgeable you are or how smart you think you are: there is always someone more knowledgeable and smarter."

"You are indeed a master of your trade and an asset to the Club beyond what is known or suspected. I sincerely thank you for your contribution toward our first effort to enlighten our countrymen as to the dishonesty and deceitfulness of our government officials. We believe by showing the public how devious those in power are and what they are willing do to stay in power, they will reform rather than risk prison. Also, I thank you for your wise counsel."

"My pleasure, Miss Anna, I can start right away on the security extraction program. It would be easier if I could meet with whoever will be using the programs. Hopefully, this person is computer literate."

"Thanks again, Mr. Hughes, I knew I could count on you." Nodding towards Lester and Mindy, "Mister Hightower will be the man inside. His computer knowledge is limited. Miss Mindy has been working with him to elevate his computer skills. She will be receiving, categorizing, and saving the data. She is more at home with a computer than the average person, but they can both learn from you. If you would be so kind as to work with them for the next month I know they will be forever grateful, as will I."

He looked over his new pupils, smiled and asked, "Are you two serious about your education?"

They answered simultaneously, "Yes, sir."

He smiled again and asked, "Is tomorrow too soon to get started?"

Again, they answered in unison, "No, sir."

"Good, I'll see you tomorrow after breakfast."

Anna thanked him again and added, "I have taken on more responsibility than time permits. Once you finish working with our protégées, would you be available to assist and perhaps advise me with other programs?"

"I was hoping you would ask. I would be delighted to work with you."

Six weeks had passed quickly—the result of hard work, long hours, and the excitement of the coming adventure. Lester and Mindy studied with Mr. Hughes in the mornings and worked their regular jobs, for the Club, in the afternoon and sometimes into the night. When they had spare time in the evenings, they spent it with Genesis, asking questions and practicing the roles they would play in their initiation project. I feared they were too eager and counseled Lester routinely to keep his eyes and ears open, to suggest actions when the time was right, but otherwise let things flow naturally. The most difficult part was convincing him that slow and easy was the ticket to experience. With experience he would know when the time was right to instill ideas into the minds of his targets simply by asking questions and making statements.

We were expecting a call from Frank any day and decided a few days of relaxing in an out-of-the-way place were in order before we turned Lester and Mindy loose on politicians in the District of Columbia. An even better reason—Anna hadn't taken a day off in more than six months. Rita and I'd had a day or two to kick back when we were observing the New York City operation. Since then we'd been tied up with preparing Lester and Mindy for working a project on their own.

Mr. Hughes had been bored with technical research for the Club—for him it wasn't challenging. He welcomed the opportunity to relieve Anna and get back to something he enjoyed—a black-ops-type operation. Two days' working with her and he had routing and her formula for decoding and encoding memorized—the rest he considered routine. If a problem came up he could check with her by satellite phone, the scramblers would eliminate eavesdropping.

Rita leased a villa, complete with servants and chef, on Spain's Costa del Sol, for two weeks. The following evening we boarded an executive jet at Albany International for Malaga. Time lost traveling west to east added to flight time and clearing customs, plus the van ride, put us in our *casa de playa* just in time for the traditional siesta. This suited Anna, Rita, and me just fine. Lester and Mindy wanted to explore—this too was fine with me. I gave each of them a handful of large—denomination euros and asked the driver to make sure they stayed safe—for extra incentive I unceremoniously slipped him five one-hundred euro notes. Once they were on their way, we unwound from our trip in our customary fashion and were relaxed and sleeping when they returned.

Shortly after we were up and dressed, Chef Alonso announced tapas would be served by the pool in twenty minutes. November temperatures in the northern Mediterranean can be chilly. Although Spain's Sun Coast was a bit warmer, one finds shorts and a tank top a little light for late afternoons—we dressed accordingly. Warm tapas and sangria, a rosé wine infused with the fresh flavors of raspberry and strawberry served up by Anso were perfect for a cool afternoon as the temperature dipped into the sixties.

Lester, looking a bit disappointed, asked, "Is this dinner?"

"No, these are snacks to get you through 'till dinner. No self-respecting Spaniards would consider having their evening meal earlier than eight or nine o'clock. Dinner is a social event, and is taken slowly with conversation and gaiety. It normally lasts for two hours or longer and often well past midnight on special occasions."

When the first small plate was placed in front of us, Lester looked at the small portion, consisting of no more than four bites, apprehensively and asked "What is this?"

"I've learned its best, when in foreign countries, to never ask what you are eating. If it tastes good, eat it, if not, don't eat it. When a guest in someone's home, you eat it and smack your lips even if it doesn't taste good."

Using his fork he scraped away some of the vegetable sauce to expose a snail, "What's that, it looks like a snail?"

"The French are known for escargot, but Spaniards have a way with snails as well—try it, you'll like it."

I'd already finished mine when he mustered up enough courage to try one. Anso was already serving a second round of tapas when Lester smiled, looked around the table, and announced, "That's good. I like it."

Mindy had not yet touched her sangria and asked, "Father, may I taste the wine?"

"Sweetheart, have you had your talk with Anna about alcoholic beverages?" Now that we were a family we'd dropped the formalities except when in the presence of other club members.

"Yes Father, I have."

"This is as good a time as any. Just keep in mind it's not a replacement for tea, water, fruit juice, or sodas."

"I will, I promise." She took a sip, wrinkled her nose, shrugged and said, "It's okay, but not as exciting as I expected."

I smiled, she smiled, "You'll be okay, sweetheart."

It was nine o'clock when Chef Alonso called us to *comida*. It took only a day for us to adopt the ways of our host country—it was after eleven when we pushed back from the table. We had not mentioned anything from the past or discussed the future. We had taken the holiday to rest our minds and renew our energy—we came as tourists, intent on doing touristy things.

We slept late. Everyone stumbled in for *desayuno* at about the same time. Anso had set out hard rolls, jam, butter, cheese, muesli, yogurt, and blood oranges. He brought coffee as we arrived. I was spreading butter on my second roll when the girls filed in—Lester was last to show. When Anso placed coffee in front of him he looked at me, "Why did he bring me a soup bowl full of coffee?"

"Bienvenidos a España." He gave me a quizzical look.

Mindy leaned over and whispered, "Welcome to Spain."

I'd informed the driver earlier that we'd need his services every day unless he was told otherwise. He opened the doors on the van as we approached. First on the list was shopping—the girls wanted to shop for beachwear—so he dropped us on Calle Larios in Málaga, a centrally located street with a mixture of well-known chain stores, independent boutiques, and numerous street vendors. Málaga, one of Spain's more modern cities had cafeterias and ice cream parlours competing with tapa bars, *ventas*, and the more formal *restaurantes*.

While the girls shopped, Lester and I strolled and talked while feeding street entertainers' kitties when we'd stop to watch and listen. Eventually, as we shared a bottle of valdepeñas at a sidewalk table outside the *venta* where we'd agreed to meet the girls for lunch, he broached the subject I'd most wanted to discuss.

"Mindy and I want to get married after we finish our initiation project, but she won't commit to it unless you approve. I've wanted to ask you, but I've been too afraid."

"Why have you been concerned about asking me?"

"Because if you disapprove I fear I would go crazy."

"Can you make my daughter happy?"

"Making her happy will be my number one priority as long as I'm alive."

"Will you protect her?"

"With my life."

"Do you remember the conversation we had about abusing her and busted kneecaps?"

"Like it was yesterday."

"I would like to talk with the two of you at the same time, so once you've finished your project come see me and ask properly. Until then, keep your mind clear and focused on your project."

The girls arrived at just the right time to facilitate a subject change. We shared a couple of classic *tortillas espanolas* and another bottle of valdepeñas *vino* before returning to our villa.

I was all set for my siesta. The girls had other ideas. They wanted to show off their new beachwear and dip their toes in the Mediterranean. I knew this time of year the water temperature, even on the Sun Coast would be in the sixties. I had an excuse—no bathing suit. When Anna and Rita came out sporting their new bikinis I was tempted to go sit on the beach and watch. It was then I noticed Mindy's bikini and whispered to Anna, "Why did you let her buy such a tiny bathing suit?"

She whispered back, "There's nothing wrong with her bikini. When girls have it they want to show it."

"Maybe so, but does she have to show so much?"

"What would you have her wear; a 1930s' style bathing suit?"

Before I could answer she continued, "You haven't complained about my bikini and I'm showing more than she's showing. Stop being so protective of her—she'll grow up just fine. She wants you to be proud of her—she won't disappoint you."

What could I say? I shrugged and smiled. She rewarded me with a kiss on the cheek and teased me with a bump of her hip. She was right; there wasn't enough material in her entire suit to make a handkerchief. They slipped on their outer beachwear, headed for the patio and descended half-a-dozen steps to the beach. Lester, wearing cargo shorts and a tank top, joined them. I watched as they crossed the sand to the water's edge, and then kicked off my shoes, and stretched out for my nap.

I was awakened by Rita dangling her wet hair in my face. "It's tapa time. Everyone is waiting for you."

I stumbled into the bathroom, washed the sleep from my eyes, combed my hair, and joined them on the patio by the pool. Anso commenced serving the moment I sat down. Rita was on the phone with Frank. His call had come a minute or so before I arrived. I missed the first part of the conversation and couldn't hear Frank.

Rita was saying, "I'll post a cashier's check to you tomorrow morning for the security deposit and six months' rent." A few moments of silence—we could only guess at what Frank might be saying—and then Rita responded, "Ralph and Brigitte will move in by the end of the month. More silence. "No, we're in Spain—we won't be back in Nice for another week." A brief pause, "We're fine, thanks for asking." Another pause, "You're a sweetheart, Frank. We'll see you the next time we're in the District. Thanks for everything."

One reason we had chosen Spain for our vacation was to be able to send Frank a check drawn on a bank in Europe with European postmarks on the envelope. Deceiving honest people didn't sit well with me—sometimes, when involved in chancy games it becomes necessary.

We really did need a vacation and I knew there would be few tourists on the Sun Coast in November. I wanted to give Lester a view of the world outside West Virginia and his brief stay in New York City. Apparently it was working as planned. According to Anna and Rita, after I responded to his question at breakfast about coffee served in large bowl-like cups with *"Bienvenidos a España,"* he had asked Mindy to teach him the languages she spoke.

While we were on holiday we did not mention or discuss club business. We became tourists for the entire two weeks. Our driver took us on a different tour every day. It ended too soon.

If you can do it, it's not bragging

> We hang the petty thieves and appoint the great ones to public office.
>
> —Aesop

On the night I first met the director, he said to me, "There is no segment of society or government we cannot reach into and extract information from."

I was skeptical. What he said was powerful; I considered the possibility he might be bragging in order to impress me—he did. Or scare me—he did. I quickly learned he was not bragging—as Broadway Joe said, "If you can do it, it's not bragging."

"We know you did not commit the crime you were sentenced to death for—the murder of your girlfriend."

He dispelled any lingering doubts as to whether or not he was bragging when he said, "We also know about the unarmed drug lord you shot to death on a roof in East St. Louis."

He could have only retrieved this information from the Treasury Department—the Drug Enforcement Agency has only recently been moved to the Justice Department. This assassination occurred twelve years ago when I was known by my birth name, Geoff Jepson.

At the time of our conversation, I was unaware of the Club members' job history, education, intelligence, and dedication. They could see the future if left to socialists and their fellow travelers in media, Hollywood, unions, and their progressive myopic-low-information base—they didn't like the vision unfolding before them. Most political leaders are puppets and do their masters' bidding as long as they are permitted to fill their own pockets.

Some are controlled by big business, some by Marxist/socialists of the sixties who continued the cause of the twenties' and thirties' communist-controlled unions, parlor pinks, and those in government—the Alger Hiss type. Very few had an interest in preserving the Constitution or the liberties our founding document guaranteed.

With this knowledge it was easy to understand why receptionists, secretaries, file clerks, and others of the same ilk, are the only ones required to turn in résumés when applying for a position with the establishment in the District of Columbia. Other positions were filled at the suggestion-or insistence-of puppet masters. Department heads were appointed; friends of Cabinet members became assistants, this method of growing the establishment continued all the way down to the lowest rungs. In time, those having proved themselves loyal to their benefactor, who understood and played the game, move up the ladder—all others were dismissed and forgotten.

Aware, as I was, that several of our club members had retired from powerful government positions, it came as no surprise when Lester received a letter addressed to his Georgetown address informing him that he'd been accepted as aide to a staff assistant in the Justice Department. Neither was it a surprise to learn, the birth certificate, issued to (one) Ralph Climer, proclaimed him twenty-six years old—he looked his age, twenty-two. Records at a prestigious school showed him to have a degree in social science, majoring in social engineering.

Genesis spent $40,000 for a new BMW 328 to promote Lester's new image—Ralph, a youngster with an eye on a career in the political arena. Fifty thousand dollars went to Bergdorf Goodman for his and her wardrobes—Mindy had to look, as well as play the part of Brigitte, the socially acceptable wife of a young man destined to become a political star. To make sure they would not be caught short of cash, Genesis provided them with individual bank accounts and platinum credit cards—total amounts charged to their credit cards would be deducted from their bank accounts at the end of each pay period.

Rita had booked a suite in the Four Seasons at 2800 Pennsylvania Avenue NW for two weeks. Rita and I spent the time introducing Lester and Mindy to the District, making sure we stayed away from Georgetown—

we didn't want to run into Frank by accident. We wanted him to believe we were still in France. We also stayed away from eateries we'd frequented prior to taking down El and his Middle Eastern friends.

With Mr. Hughes taking care of the Club's communications, Anna was able to join us for the second week. Anna brought a request from the director—it is understood, a request from the director is a direct order. He suggested we visit and meet with the owner of Club Holly, a newly opened resort in Potomac, Maryland. I didn't know the specific connections between Holly Voorhees and the Club. Various groups, unknown to one another, work on their own within the Club. By ordering us to meet with Miss Voorhees the director had signified that she could be an asset to Genesis—if not now, sometime in the future. When or how—I hadn't a clue.

Anna had limited information on Club Holly: it was expensive and geared toward elected officials, movers and shakers of "The District", (thus the nation), as well as wannabe VIPs. Considering the possible advantages of being a part of such an organization, I determined it would fit into Lester's new role as an up-and-coming member of this elite group of scoundrels. With this in mind, the five of us called on Miss Holly Voorhees.

The doorman passed us into a large foyer, consisting of a colorful terrazzo floor, accented with American-walnut wainscot—walls above the wainscot were sectioned into vertical frames of walnut matching the wainscot. Although not appearing as lighting, the overhead glowed softly, illuminating the foyer. Hidden spots accented nude paintings of the Romantic and Renaissance periods. Each painting, in a gilded frame, had been perfectly centered in each of the wall frames. The walls inside the frames had been painted in different Williamsburg colors to highlight the nude's background hues.

The room, sparsely furnished with upholstered benches along either wall, had been designed to ensure all eyes entering the room would focus on the two desks of elegant design, opposite the entrance. They would look past the display of freshly-cut flowers covering the top of a ten-foot oval table with gilded trim matching the frames containing the nudes. The table, strategically centered in the foyer with six wingback chairs, matching the upholstered benches, would go unnoticed except as a hazard to be avoided as they walked toward the two incredibly striking, seductively-dressed young ladies behind the desks.

The desks were on either side of heavy double-doors made of the same polished walnut as the wainscot. A rather large tuxedoed gentleman stood in front of the doors. I surmised he was there to make sure everyone remained cordial. I gave my name to the smiling young lady seated behind the desk to the right side of the doors. She touched the desktop in front of her. In response to her touch, a light, appearing as a mist, fanned out from the top of a narrow, ten-inch column, standing between a monitor of the same height and a membership card scanner The light mist projected a keyboard onto the desktop in front of her. She touched a few light spots on her desk, checked a message on the monitor and announced, "Miss Voorhees is expecting you."

A moment later one of the double doors opened and a tuxedoed young man appeared at her elbow. She glanced at him momentarily, then returned her attention and smile to me, and said, "Please, show Mr. Scott and his guests to Miss Voorhees's office."

We followed our escort through the door, held open for us by the man I surmised to be the bouncer, passed a counter with ten check-in stations—since only two stations were staffed, I suspected the others were manned only during conventions, golf tournaments, and other such events, or as needed. The room, decorated in the same terrazzo floor, American-walnut wainscot, and Williamsburg colors opened into a four-story atrium the size of a football field.

Pathways wound around and underneath full-grown trees with colorful blossoms. Hidden fans filtered and moved air, without so much as a whisper, through the trees and along the walkways—one could imagine a soft summer breeze. We walked past waterfalls with fragrant flowers cascading on either side of the tumbling water. Flowers and ferns grew beside little streams flowing into small pools where koi swam in circles or scavenged for food where branches of plants growing around the edges, drooped out over the water.

Nearly invisible pastel-psychedelic hues played across the overhead, suggesting clouds and streaks of sunlight. Hidden spots illuminated the flowers and trees. Indirect underwater lighting added iridescent glows to the colored fish. Malibu lights lined the walkways.

Boutiques with names of recognizable designers shared the perimeter with dinner clubs, gift shops, and restaurants. Patrons wandered about or sat at tables, in open-air cafes, nestled in amongst the trees and flowers, accessible only by stone steps and footbridges. Elegant young ladies, each in a different designer dress, short with an eye-catching décolletage, delivered colorful drinks to couples and groups sitting at tables in the small cafes. Young men in white jackets served salads, pupus, tapas, and hors d'oeuvre on seven inch plates.

Above the shops, bars, and restaurants glass doors of French design, opened onto balconies, permitting non-member guests occupying these suites, the opportunity to look out over the rainforest like atmosphere below—these guests were not permitted to visit sections of the club reserved for members. Visitors desirous of membership in Club Holly were restricted to this area of the resort until reports from investigators had been completed and they were approved. Nonmembers booking special events were similarly restricted.

At the opposite end of the atrium our escort entered several numbers on a keypad, waited to be asked for an authenticator and then entered another series of numbers. We entered one of a half dozen glass elevators and were whisked to the top floor. The door opened and we stepped out of the elevator into a small, although well-appointed, foyer. The young man remained in the elevator. The door closed and we were alone.

Holly appeared from out of nowhere wearing a belted, two-piece Dior cocktail dress with a 100th Anniversary Commemorative Special Edition Set of Mikimoto pearls. She was beautiful beyond description. Her movements were as graceful as those of a ballerina. When she spoke, her words were melodious.

After the introductions I thanked her for receiving us, she thanked us for coming. We followed her into her personal conference room—plush chairs strategically surrounded a twenty-foot oval table.

Tuxedoed young men held our chairs and then left the room. An attractive young lady placed individual bottles of cold water and chilled glasses in front us. A second, equally striking young lady, using silver tongs, offered steamed towels. I took one, refreshed my face and hands, and then dropped the towel onto a silver tray carried by a third young lady.

The girls disappeared and conversation began. Holly gave us a rundown on her resort, including some of the amenities, and the membership structure—there were different levels of membership.

When asked what perks came with her seven-figure membership fees. She smiled and answered, "With the exception of street pharmaceuticals, Club Holly is not unlike Alice's Restaurant."

It wasn't spoken, but the meaning was made clear in the first line of the song, "You can get anything you want at Alice's Restaurant."

As our conversation ensued, it became obvious she already knew we were interested in unscrupulous federal legislators and other government officials. How she knew, we didn't know. Neither did we know her connection to the Club. Apparently our goals were the same. She chose to approach them from a different direction.

When I informed her how Lester would be involved in politics, she suggested he make use of her records. Holly had kept voice recordings, videos, and financial records on hundreds of clients at her Georgetown brokerage firm. Now, with Club Holly having been open two years, she had records on perhaps thousands of people either in or connected with government. These records were kept in a vault at a private storage company, with copies in her bank in Geneva. She gave Genesis the passwords required to get into the vault and the codes necessary to decipher her records.

She would share these records with the understanding we could not use anything traceable back to her—on this she was absolutely clear. To make sure we understood, she touched on a couple of specifics known only to certain members of the Club—specifics, if made available to the FBI would mean execution for Genesis.

She made Ralph Climer (Lester) an honorary tier-one member. Tier-one, she said, would permit him to associate with and gain the confidence of morally bankrupt members of government. It would give the impression he was a high roller and aid him in convincing these people he was a fellow traveler—he could be bought and sold. His studies in social engineering would serve him well dealing with the likes of government con-artists—it's easier to con a con than an honest person.

"As an honorary member, not all privileges available to paying members will be extended to you, Mr. Climer. Considering your beautiful fiancée, Miss Bridgette West, sitting beside you, I can't imagine why you would be interested even if they were."

Miss Voorhees suggested we stay for dinner and assigned a charming and exquisitely dressed young woman of about twenty-five to show us Club Holly. From Miss Voorhees's personal quarters, we followed the woman back into the foyer where we'd waited to meet Holly. She then opened a door into a common area equally as impressive as others we'd seen. All elevators, except the one we rode to reach Holly's private quarters, opened into this area—corridors led away in several directions.

Our tour guide informed us, "Most staff members live in this wing. The beauty salon, exercise equipment, Jacuzzis, swimming pool, and all other amenities are for their use only. The other two wings contain suites for our tier-one members and their guests. The floors below are for tier-two and tier-three members—access requires members to enter their personal membership numbers on a keypad and then respond with another set of numbers to satisfy the requested authenticator code. Every effort is made to prevent anyone from entering an unauthorized area—an area beyond their tier level."

We took an elevator to the lower level and another open area with a twenty-foot overhead. Twinkling chandeliers and wall fixtures of Swarovski crystal were for aesthetics only. Again, hidden spots accented expensive art and elegant furnishings. Indirect sources of soft lighting painted the entire room. From this imposing common area, members could enter into clubs, restaurants, and the pro-shop with access to the golf course, along with areas providing other amenities and conveniences not available to non-member guests staying in suites off the atrium.

Similar to the entry foyer, less the bouncer, two desks and two young women graced an area in front of three sets of double doors. Our tour guide volunteered, "Behind these doors is our investment and financial center."

The young woman had no sooner spoke then a former White House spokesman approached the smiling young ladies, he was promptly escorted through one of the doors—she returned a few seconds later.

"Is this the only way in and out of the financial center?" I asked.

"It's not the only way out, but it's the only way in. The doors correspond to membership; the amenities on the other side of the doors depend on your tier. The design is more elaborate than our Georgetown Financial Center, but it operates the same."

"Our Georgetown Financial Center?"

"Yes, Georgetown is where Miss Voorhees first opened her business."

She didn't elaborate further. We didn't ask.

Dinner was served on Spode china atop linen tablecloths; napkins of identical design were placed in our laps. We ate using International sterling-silver flatware and our libations were poured from Baccarat crystal decanters into matching stemware.

As we satiated our appetites on scrumptious cuisine and took pleasure in the captivating ambiance, our escort pointed out several elected officials—some I recognized—along with cabinet members and other principal beltway players. She did the same during the lounge show.

When the entertainers took a break the young lady led us back to the entrance. We thanked her and departed.

As we waited for the valet to bring our car—I'd leased a Maybach 62 for our two-week stay at the Four Seasons—Rita asked in a whisper, "Did you notice all the pretty young women mixing it up with middle-aged men?"

Anna whispered back, "There were also more than a few young studs in the company of several, shall we say, women in their prime."

I joined in the whispering, "I think they are models. If not they certainly could be."

Still whispering, Rita replied, "Looks and smells like a cathouse to me."

Our car arrived. Once inside and buckled up, I engaged the powertrain and said, "Rita, I think you are spot-on, and from what I see, a very successful cathouse. It seems like a natural fit—the world's oldest profession and the second-oldest profession working the same side of the street. When you think about it, there are more similarities than differences between the two—it's just a question of who's paying and who's getting screwed."

I would later learn Holly's support of certain charities had caught the eye of the Club's recruiting team. With the director's approval, the team made an effort to find out who she was, what she did, and her personal history—their endeavor hit a dead-end. Beyond discovering she was a successful investment counselor favored by politicians and other influential members within the District, and had recently opened an exclusive resort, no history on Miss Voorhees existed. Out of the blue, she'd opened an investment brokerage in Georgetown and had become an overnight success.

Two years after Club Holly opened, the committee discovered that on her eighteenth birthday, she'd petitioned the court for a name change. To their surprise, the judge granting her request had retired and become a member of the Club.

Without revealing her birth name he recounted her desire to rise above the squalor of a third-generation welfare family and fight the political system that enslaved people to life in the ghettoes. There had been only one way out and up for her—she took it.

The judge believed she would be an asset and volunteered to approach and hopefully recruit her. Having recognized the judge, Holly had been a bit apprehensive, but upon learning why he had contacted her and after given a brief history of the Club's origin and underlying principle, she eagerly pledged her support.

After divulging more insight into her success than the judge cared to know, she swore an oath of loyalty to the Club. She volunteered to assist in any way she could, but declined to become a member.

The judge still lived in Foggy Bottom and hardly ever visited the Club's resort in the Catskills—home to Genesis. It was several months after our visit to Club Holly and on one of the rare occasions the judge visited the director. The reason for his visit went undisclosed—everyone's knowledge of Club operations was on a need to know basis. It was on this visit I met with the judge and inquired after Holly Voorhees. According to his memory, the following exchange had transpired after he'd unveil the Club's *raison d'être*:

> ". . . I thought I was alone in my quest; it is very comforting to learn otherwise. I prefer to continue moving forward with my plan to re-instill integrity to government. Integrity in government is an oxymoron, but it is my dream—probably an impossible dream never to be achieved. Even so, I will not be deterred . . . ."
>
> "Miss Voorhees, when you stood in front of me asking for a name change I recognized a determination in you that would not be denied. I had no way of knowing what direction you would choose, but I had no doubt you would achieve your goal."
>
> "It is gratifying to learn you had faith in me and to know you approve of my success. I will support you any way I can, but I prefer to not become a member of your club. My reason is this: if ever I'm required to respond in court to accusations concerning my operations I do not want such proceedings to taint your organization."
>
> "Miss Voorhees, the connection could only be made through your own volition since I have, as have all other club members, sworn a blood oath to take all knowledge of the Club to the grave.

> "For the more than two hundred years since the Club's inception, no one has ever failed to honor their oath. I assure you, your secrets are safe with us. If you change your mind we would be honored to have you as a member. In the meantime, I am authorized to extend the full resources of the Club to you if ever the need should arise."

"Judge, I'm curious as to how Holly came by the information she referenced so accurately, regarding me and my team?"

"When I met with Holly, at the behest of our director, to offer her membership and request her help in our quest to prevent the central government from completely taking control of our lives, she was reluctant to discuss her operation.

"I'm of the opinion the director knows more about Holly then he had been willing to disclose to me. Nevertheless he recited a couple of interesting facts about Genesis. I was authorized to make these particulars known to Holly should she require an incentive to help us.

"She mulled over the information I'd disclosed regarding the Club. A few moments of silence passed before she asked,

'How do I know you won't betray me?'

"It was then I passed on the information, authorized by the director, to make known to her—the unsubstantiated illicit behavior she quoted you. I further informed her, other than me, you and your team would be the only club members authorized to contact her.

"She gazed into my eyes for several seconds. Her facial expression gave no hint of her emotion or her thoughts. Finally she said, 'Have Genesis visit me. I will make my decision after talking with them.'"

"Judge, I have no doubt you are correct when you say, 'I'm of the opinion the director knows more about Holly then he had been willing to disclose to me.'

"The director would never put Genesis at risk beyond the necessary danger we face in actions against America's enemies—even then, it is our choice. We are free to decline the challenge should we decide it too hazardous. I'd say he trusts her implicitly."

"Mr. Scott, I'm inclined to agree with you. However, outside of providing us with a list of politicians willing to sell influence to the highest bidder, I don't see how she is going to be an asset to the Club."

"I've turned this over in my mind several times and I'm with you, judge—we already know most of the influence peddlers in congress, as well as their puppet masters and their lapdogs. Holly has thousands of video and voice recording of government officials in questionable situations we could use, but she made it clear we can't use anything traceable to her. So how does she fit in?"

"Mr. Scott, I'm only guessing, but the director may have volunteered our services as the strong-arm side of her blackmail scheme when she decides to put her plan into action."

"Well, it could be fun watching them squirm. Government officials have come to believe they are untouchable. I, for one, would enjoy attaching the thumbscrews and listening to their songs."

"As a retired judge, I can assure you they have a lot to sing about. I guess we have but one choice—wait and see."

"Guess not." Little did I know, two years would pass before Holly would contribute to the Club's most elaborate undertaking since I had become a member, and in a way I never expected.

After considerable planning and long hours of discussing raid array and pinwheel backup, multiservers, servers backing up servers, and the like—things were coming together. Anna agreed with Mr. Hughes on the three major points—cascading ten-terabyte helium-filled hard drives, forgetting about collecting and storing backed-up data, and concentrating on email. Using keywords we'd filter out the majority of messages. We would keep only those with potential value—routine traffic did not interest us.

Bouncing the signal off satellites was not a problem and would eliminate the possibility of a trace. Our internet service would require a physical address. This would not be a problem since we'd use a fake name and automatic payments from a bank account set up with the same fake name. Should someone become inquisitive we would be alerted and could abort the operation. A few months later we could start up again using a different name and different service.

While discussing possible locations, Jake's name came up. Jake had unknowingly been instrumental in our most successful operation to date. It had been our last action before Anna, Rita, and I took a three-year hiatus. If he still owned the motel, gas station, and restaurant in Maryland it would be perfect for what we had in mind. Jake's business had been a gold mine in the forties and fifties when his father owned it. Business remained good after he inherited it until the new highway bypass was built. The stream of vehicles driving through the small town and past his place disappeared overnight. With a pump-your-own-gas station and two fast-food restaurants on the bypass, travelers had no reason to drive through town. He was losing money keeping it open. What little business that came his way didn't pay the bills. He had boarded it up, put a For Sale sign in the window and moved to the District—he hated living in the city. He was living in subsidized housing when we found him. Anna was the only one he met. She was pretending to be an attorney representing Mohammad El. She wore a wig to hide her pretty blonde hair and tinted glasses to obscure the color of her blue eyes, so it wasn't likely he'd make the connection should they ever meet. Even if they did she'd deny having ever met him.

We did a quick investigation and located Jake, just as we'd hoped, back at his property in Maryland. After the feds had removed the bodies and what little evidence they could find, Jake was told he could move back in. He'd used part of the money Anna had given him to convert three of the motel's ten units into a nine hundred foot living space for his personal use. With all the amenities of a condominium—a living room, kitchen, laundry room, and a nice sized bedroom, Jake was quite comfortable. He'd sold all the old vehicles stored in the truck-repair building as scrap, cleaned it up, converted it to a car repair facility, and was eking out a living as a mechanic. He'd converted the two gas pumps to twenty-four hour self-service—swipe a credit card; pump your own. With the money left, he partitioned off the kitchen from the café, installed a few vending machines, and converted the café to a waiting room for his customers. The area behind the lunch counter he used for his office.

Lester was still a bit too eager, but sooner or later he had to get his feet wet. I knew Jake would need to collect information on his new boarders, including make of automobile and license number. I gave him a list of questions he might be expected to answer. We rehearsed a conversation he was likely to have with Jake. Lester was a quick study and with Mindy there to bail him out if he stumbled, I didn't see a problem. So I'd rented a car similar enough to Lester's BMW that Jake wouldn't notice it was a different car the next time he saw it—I should say, the first time he saw Lester's BMW. When renting the car I'd used the name Melvin Hollister.

A light rain had been falling since midmorning and turned into a downpour as Lester drove their rented Beamer into the parking lot and pulled alongside an older Ford pickup parked in front of a sign that read *Manager*.

Lester and Mindy opened a door with a sign that read *Office* and hurried inside—they could have just as well taken their time, they were soaking wet before they reached the door.

Lester was about to push the button, countersunk into a sign that read *Buzz For Manager*, a second time when Jake walked in through a backdoor.

"Hi, what can I do for you folks?"

"Sir, I work up in Baltimore. I'm looking for an out-of-the-way place where I can get away from the city on weekends."

"I can empathize with you on that one—never liked the city myself. What's your line of work?"

"I work for a distribution center. Shipments come in from places all across the country. I have to figure out who gets what and make sure everything is loaded onto the proper delivery van. It can be a bit nerve-racking sometimes, but the main reason I want to get away is to find a quiet place to write."

"You an author?"

"No sir, I haven't sold anything yet, but I'm working on it."

"What do you write about?"

"I'm a mystery writer."

"Well you came to the right place if you're looking for mysteries. Five years ago something bizarre happened here in this complex. Nobody ever figured out what it was all about. Some say it was a dope deal gone bad, but I don't think so. There were five Arabs and a black guy found in different locations on the property—all dead. I think my place was used to import and hide out Middle Easterners, Muslim terrorists probably, entering the country illegally.

"A limousine from the Iranian embassy was the only vehicle on the premises. I'm guessing the limo driver had delivered their forged passports and travel visas. I suspect he intended to deliver them to a location set up for dispersing middle easterners entering the country illegally into the general population—probably through a church or some-other do-gooder organization. I think there were more than five Arabs on the premises. I'm guessing there was a second limo and those surviving the shoot out escaped in it.

"Nobody could figure out what went wrong, a disagreement, probably. I suspect it had to do with money. Money, one way or another, is always the problem."

"Were you here at the time it happened?"

“No, I was living up in DC. I'd rented out the entire complex to the black guy found knifed to death here on the premises.”

“What'd he look like?”

“Don't know, never saw him. Some lady lawyer brought me the deal and paid me in cash. After it happened the FBI asked me all sorts of questions. But I couldn't help them. I told them what I just told you. They kept after me for months. Finally they said I could move back in if I wanted. Since I still had the money the lady lawyer gave me, I fixed things up a bit and I've been living here ever since.”

“Sounds mysterious for sure; might be something I can use as basis for a novel.”

“So what do you have in mind, would you like to reserve a unit for weekends?”

“No sir, I want to lease one of your units for a year. I'd like to move a few things in including a computer for research—I'll have a professional deliver and set it up—will that be a problem?”

“Not at all, would you like to look at one of the units?”

“Absolutely.”

Lester and Mindy followed Jake to the unit furthest from the service station; incidentally, it was the unit where Rita had stabbed Mohammad El and slit his throat by the back door. Jake lived in the three units he'd renovated and redesigned closest to the service station. He unlocked the door and they entered a musty smelling room with flaking paint and the standard furnishings of a sixty-year-old motel. The small bathroom had probably been updated thirty years ago, but nothing since except, perhaps, a couple of coats of paint. When Lester saw Mindy's nose wrinkle, he knew what she was thinking.

“Sir, this is fairly small, and needs a lot of work. If I pay for all the work, would you authorize me to open up the wall to include the room next door and along with this room create a single unit? By including the extra room I could renovate and modernize the entire unit and make it comfortable enough to serve my purpose. I'll have a professional builder do the work at no expense to you.”

“I don't have a problem if you're going to pay for the work.”

“I'll pay for the work, my fiancée will choose the furnishings, carpet, paint color and all the little things to make it comfortable, but I'll need your written authorization and a signed lease for one year, with the option to renew the lease.”

"You haven't asked me how much the rent will be, so I figure you must have an amount in mind. What are you willing to pay? I had $750 a month in mind for one room, but since you are going to spend a lot of money to fix up everything, how about I give you the two room unit for $900 a month?"

"What if I give you $1,000 a month and you provide someone to have it clean, fresh, and bug-free when we arrive on Friday evenings?"

"It works for me. I'll need the first and last month's rent plus $5,000 in case you tear up everything and don't come back to finish the job and I never see you again."

"Shall we draw up a contract?"

Lester and Mindy were all smiles when we met at the Bourbon Steak, a restaurant at our hotel. They were anxious to tell us of their successful meeting with Jake.

"Goebbels was right. If you tell a lie big enough and keep repeating it, people will eventually come to believe it. Jake was an easy sell—I should be a politician.

How does Senator Ralph Climer sound?" Looking around the table and realizing all eyes were on him, he probably thought we were laughing at him.

When he added, "Why not?" I realized he was serious.

He continued, "I could hang out at Club Holly, rub elbows with the movers and shakers, lie to them just like they lie to everyone else. I think it's doable. You said you need me to be able to con a reporter into believing I worked for a senator. How about we give them the real thing."

I was impressed with Lester. He'd come a long way since the day when he didn't know what road to take to get out of West Virginia. He'd probably never heard of Joseph Goebbels back then. I glanced at Mindy. Her gaze was fixed on Lester. She was beaming as she listened to him relate the encounter with Jake and his statements about becoming an elected member of congress.

I didn't know if he was looking for support, but encouragement was in order. "I believe it's doable too, son."

He was grinning from ear to ear when his head snapped around and his eyes met mine. "You've set yourself a worthy goal. I believe you are up to the challenge."

Mindy's head snapped in sync with Lester's, she was still beaming when she looked at me and smiled. When I smiled and winked, her smile broadened as she looked at me for another moment or two before turning her attention back to Lester. It was with mixed emotions I realized I would soon have a son-in-law—my use of "son" when I addressed him was meant to convey I had accepted the obvious.

I turned my attention back to Lester and said, "Just don't let the establishment corrupt you once you get there."

"It would never happen, sir. My family, all of you, will always come first—I would never betray you or the Club.

"When I first mentioned the politician bit, I was only kidding, but now, after considering the possibility, I'm inclined to believe it can be done."

Lester was confident but anxious when he met his benefactor at the Department of Justice on Pennsylvania Avenue. His security badge and ID declared him to be Ralph Climer, aide assistant. He needn't have been concerned. He was just one of hundreds of people with the same clearance badge in a bloated government agency. No one took note of or questioned his being there. In a few days he'd learned his way around and knew what was expected of him. He and a couple of other young people were glorified secretaries for an aide to one of the numerous staff members. He had a workstation with a computer, printer, telephone, desk, and filing cabinets. His job consisted mostly of research for whatever the aide was working on for the staff member.

A month later, following Mindy's instruction, contractors finished renovating the motel room and had it livable. When the workers cleaned up and pulled out, Mr. Hughes, wearing coveralls sporting a well-known Internet-service logo moved in and began setting up a computer terminal—three days later everything was set for accepting and storing email. Lester had already extracted the security information from his office computer—only two more steps and they would be in business. Mr. Hughes needed a couple more days to complete the program Lester would download to his computer at the Justice Department. He would then send an email to the aide he worked for, thus initializing the program. Incoming email to the motel terminal would be slow at first, but as the virus mutated, traffic would swell until there would be a steady flow. Once the program had infiltrated all computers in the department, Mr. Hughes would give Lester another program to kill the virus in all but staff members' computers, including his, thus severing any obtainable links showing the virus entered through his computer. This would reduce the number of emails received at the motel room terminal, but the amount would still be unmanageable. To make sure all the targeted computers were infected would take the better part of a month. Then our work of deleting emails of no value and storing those with potential would begin.

Mr. Hughes's handiwork was well hidden from the casual observer. It wasn't likely even Jake would notice the room was a wee bit smaller than before renovation began. On a desk near the door stood an all-in-one desk-top computer designed for home use. Entering a code on this computer would unlock a section of wall opposite the bathroom. The wall could then be opened manually to reveal two monitors, keyboards, and printer. All associated hardware, although hidden from view but easily accessed, had been installed behind the same false wall. With this setup Lester and Mindy could sort email simultaneously.

The all-in-one served another function as well as providing a key to the main terminals. The camera remained on when they were away. Triggered by a motion sensor it recorded everything anyone did upon entering the room. Should there be evidence of tampering with or trying to open the wall, the all-in-one would identify the intruder.

Six months had passed since we received the first email from a Justice Department computer. Mr. Hughes was indeed a genius. From the very beginning he'd written improvements into the programs we used at our terminal as well as at the one Lester kept updating at his workstation. By using keywords, 90 percent of email generated at the DOJ would not be sent to our computer. Of the 10 percent transmitted, our local program directed 95 percent to our junk-mail folder—this folder was automatically deleted every eight hours. We could search with keywords anytime we desired. Translated: of every one thousand email messages generated at the DOJ we kept five. Even so, this was no small number. The Department of Justice employed 125,000 people; if every employee sent only one email a day, using our formula we would receive almost 1,600 in a five-day workweek. These would be filed in three different folders cross-referenced to sender, receiver, and subject—some would have multiple addresses, thus requiring additional folders.

However, not everyone in the department sent email, but those of interest sent numerous messages every day. Also, of interest was email passing between departments.

Four months after we'd streamlined our system, Miss Laura of *Alpha* committee brought an interesting bit of information to the attention of Genesis. As our media reaction expert she'd noticed several citizens were upset at a letter they'd received from the Treasury Department stating they had underpaid taxes for several years and demanded to see their tax returns for the past seven years. The letters listed the amount of tax owed as well as penalties and interest on the unpaid balance. These citizens were spread out over several states and different areas within those states. The only connection was their involvement in soliciting names for a petition opposing a bill submitted to congress by the Executive Branch. They believed the investigation was payback for their contribution toward the bill's failure to pass in the House and was meant to dissuade them from continuing their quest when the bill was reintroduced—it had already been announced the bill was in the process of a bipartisan rewrite and would be reintroduced at a later date. These citizens were demanding an investigation. A spokesman for the Treasury Department denied the charges, stating there had been no wrongdoing by anyone in his department. He attributed the fact that only people involved in soliciting names for the petition had received identical letters with the same date to nothing more than coincidence. He claimed identical letters had been sent to thousands of other citizens. However, no one had come forward to substantiate his claim.

Miss Laura continued to monitor what little coverage the networks allocate these citizens' accusations. The media were quick to back the IRS labeling the group as disgruntled tax cheats. They were said to be not only greedy capitalists, but unpatriotic for not wanting to pay their fair share of taxes.

Genesis inquired of "Turnkey," the name given to Lester's and Mindy's operation—turnkey is the name attached to the jailer responsible for opening the gate to people entering and leaving prison—if email had passed between DOJ and IRS prior to when letters were sent out by the Treasury Department.

Mr. Hughes drove to Maryland to deliver the request and assist in the search. To say he was there to assist was a bit of a stretch. He was there to conduct the search and teach Turnkey how to perform a similar search of their stored data for specific messages. He instructed Lester and Mindy on keystroke entries and basic procedure when conducting such a search.

In fewer than eight hours the program had copied more than 600 messages to their search folder. These were messages between the DOJ, IRS, and the Executive Branch during the time frame stipulated. More than 100 referred to this group of citizens in question, with several mentioning them openly. One email from the Executive Branch to the Department of Justice asked, "What can be done to discourage this and similar interference?"

The reply suggested "This could be accomplished most efficiently and with greater impact by the IRS than any other department. These messages had been forwarded to the Treasury Department." A reply from the IRS had requested names, addresses, and social security numbers. Three days later the DOJ supplied the requested information. The names and numbers had been sent, by email, to DOJ from the FBI.

This incident, alone, justified the expense of setting up and maintaining Turnkey. These departments of government considered themselves untouchable and no longer tried to hide their illegal activities. Now we had irrefutable evidence showing how the Executive Branch had involved other departments in the harassment of ordinary citizens. The question: how to use the smoking gun we held?

Genesis, Turnkey, and Alpha met with the director to decide on a plan of action. Miss Laura suggested, since the citizens group had obtained legal representation, we should let things cook for a few more days. Things were heating up with new accusations and denials occurring daily. This generated considerable interest amongst viewers; therefore the networks were staying with the story. Even while trying to keep viewership high the media continued to denigrate the citizens who were claiming harassment, thus lending credibility to the government's denials.

A week later, the networks were giving little airtime to the story—it appeared a dead issue. Another two days passed before a copy of an email from the Executive Branch to the DOJ suggesting a particular group of citizens should be discouraged from interfering with a certain bill before congress was forwarded to several newspapers and major networks. Neither the press nor the mainstream media mentioned receiving the email—not one story appeared in any of the nation's newspapers or the evening news. The following day, a copy of the response from the DOJ to the Executive Branch was forwarded to the same newspapers and television stations. In addition, copies of both emails were sent to the group's counsel. While the media remained silent the plaintiff's attorney went public with the email and again asked congress for an investigation. The media could no longer sit on the story.

Reluctantly, a special prosecutor was appointed who immediately moved to summon email from the three department heads in question. After reams of useless data were delivered it was discovered there had been a glitch in the backup systems in all departments accused by the people's counsel, of wrong doing. Email from the time frame requested had been lost due to the systems breakdown and failure to back up data.

Genesis met with the director and it was decided we should release all email we had linking different departments to the case including the one sent by the Treasury Department, addressed to the FBI requesting names of the "troublemakers" and the FBI's reply, which included the list of names requested—both had copied the DOJ and the Executive Branch. None of the individuals involved had to be told what had been requested and what was desirous of the Executive Branch—the department heads had been appointed because they were all of the same mind as the president, and did not need instructions. They knew what he wanted done and they did it. Postmarks on the letters declaring thousands of citizens to be tax cheats had been sent out by the IRS ten days after the list had been sent to the Internal Review Service by the FBI.

Genesis and Turnkey met to celebrate our success—since Mr. Hughes had made our operation not only successful, but possible, we now considered him a member of Turnkey. We'd reserved two adjoining two-bedroom suites at the Four Seasons for the weekend—one for the girls and one for the guys. Anna had been preparing Miss Susanne and Mr. Aireandale for more than a year to assist with the Club's communications terminal. The terminal served to link all club chapters via the committees and required monitoring daily. Anna's system of communications had been deployed when the Club voted to adopt the original plan to reclaim America for the people set forth by Genesis. When Mr. Hughes came on board with the project, training was accelerated. Now she was confident enough with Miss Susanne and Mr. Aireandale watching the store to take a mini-vacation.

Interesting was the only term that came to mind when I recalled Bourbon Steak's approach to food preparation and the way dishes were presented. Their menu appealed to the bold and daring. The rest of my party appeared to be in an adventurous mood, even Lester—his holiday in Spain had awakened an exploratory epicurean spirit. A porterhouse steak from their charcoal grill appealed to my mood—serious. I was excited about Turnkey's success, but uneasy about the question I knew would be put to me before the evening ended.

There was nothing to justify my anxiety. Lester had vowed to protect Mindy and to provide for her every need and pleasure—every need and pleasure he was capable of giving her. She obviously adored him. Not only were they devoted to each other, but dedicated to the Club and its cause as well. Wasn't this precisely the outcome Genesis had intended when we placed them at the same dinner table? So, why was giving my blessing troubling for me? The answer was simple. Before she confessed her need for a father and expressed her desire to have me adopt her, she was just a beautiful and talented young lady. Now she was my daughter and little girl—someone needing my protection. When I first met Lester he was awkward, insecure, and filled with hate. Over the past two years I'd watched him grow into a handsome and personable young man, filled with confidence and promise. I couldn't ask for a better son-in-law, but it was difficult to relinquish responsibility for my daughter. Even to someone as capable as Lester.

The *sommelier* had finished with the customary rituals wannabe wine connoisseurs had come to expect. We held our glasses high and said nice things about one another—toasting and sipping—until our glasses were empty.

There was no denying Turnkey had been successful in exposing collusion between government officials in different departments. When charges of harassment surfaced, department heads circled the wagons and claimed to be clean as wind-driven snow. Even with release of the first two emails these officials and their spokesmen denied any wrongdoing—their only shortcomings, they said, had been in not realizing their backup systems had malfunctioned. Then, with the flood of incriminating emails in the hands of the special prosecutor these same officials had suddenly developed a bad case of amnesia. Under examination by the prosecutor, everyone involved in this act of collusion had trouble remembering anything other than their name. More than a few took the fifth, invoking their right to refuse testifying when their answers might incriminate them—one cannot be forced to testify against themselves in a court of law. Others resigned, while several went to prison.

Through it all, the media supported the administration and gave cover whenever it could. The investigation would get only a few seconds of coverage each day. The mainstream media were in agreement—it was impossible for the president to know the actions of everyone in his administration. Maybe so, but people he appointed to these posts knew what he wanted. They didn't need to ask or obtain approval or permission. Department heads knew, by the mere fact they had been appointed, they and the president were of the same mindset. They also knew their actions of support, legal or otherwise, had been preapproved—they didn't need to ask. I was thinking a letter to the networks reminding them of what had happened and continued to happen to a number of their socialist comrades would be in order.

As we watched the pastry chef create desserts of our choice, our table was refreshed with a clean tablecloth, napkins, wine glasses, and silver. After I tasted and nodded my approval, the wine steward poured two inches of tawny port in each of our glasses while the waiter served our freshly prepared desserts. They left our table when the pastry chef bade us bon appétit. With one last toast, dinner wound to a close. We finished our dessert and returned to our suites. Sliding doors, serving as a wall between the adjoining suites, had been slipped to either end making for one large common area.

As everyone retired to their respective bedrooms, I chose a comfortable chair and waited for what I knew was coming. I didn't have long to wait. Mindy held Lester's hand as they approached and then took his arm and stood very close to him when they stopped in front of me.

"Sir, you know why we are here. You know the question I am going to ask. While waiting for Anna and Rita at a table outside the *vina* where we had lunch in Málaga, you and I shared a bottle of Valdepeñas and talked. When I expressed my desire to marry Mindy, you asked several questions which I answered honestly and from the heart. You told me to wait until we completed our initiation project and then ask properly. Sir, I stand before you asking for your daughter's hand in marriage. Sir, I beg you, please do not deny me permission to marry her."

"I believe your answers were honest and heartfelt—I have only one more question for you. But first, Mindy, is it your desire to marry Lester?"

"Yes, Father."

"The ship of matrimony doesn't always sail on calm seas. Keep in mind, Anna, Rita, and I will always be here to help you trim the sails on your little boat when it hits rough waters.

"Back to the one last question, Lester, do you think it necessary to mention our conversation about broken legs and busted kneecaps again?"

"No, sir, I remember it well." I extended my hand to Lester.

"Then I give you my daughter to love, keep, and protect. From this moment on I will consider you to be husband and wife. We will do the paperwork and get a magistrate's signature when time permits."

He pumped my hand enthusiastically and repeated several times. "Thank you, sir."

Mindy hugged me, kissed me on the check, and whispered, "Thank you, father." She kissed my cheek again before letting go.

"Go on, get out of here." I didn't watch to see where they disappeared to, but I heard only one door open and close. I envied them their youth and their dreams and their visions for tomorrow.

I turned out the lights and sat in the dark for a while. My mind wandered randomly through the last ten years of my life as my subconscious chose film clips and displayed them on the backsides of my eyelids—some beautiful and exciting, some sad and hurtful.

I was considering filling a rock glass from the bar with twenty-five year old Glenmorangie—included in a list of extras I'd given the concierge—and getting drunk when Anna's lips touched mine. I hadn't heard her cat-like stealth approach—ninjas could learn from her. She sat in my lap for awhile reminding me, without speaking, of how much better life was when sober than when drunk—a life I'd known, as Geoff Jepson. Thirty minutes, perhaps an hour passed before she led me to her room, removed my clothes, and then tucked me into bed with Rita. I no longer envied the newlyweds their youth or their dreams—I was living a dream.

The end

Epilogue

Genesis, a title conferred on Anna, Rita, and me by the director declaring the three of us a single unit, now has the attention of bureaucrats and the media. The Club's monitoring team has determined we are making inroads.

Several news anchors appear nervous when discussing political policy and when interviewing politicians. A few were bringing up stories and facts they would have omitted and kept hidden in times past. A small number are serving up fewer softball questions for the political left and at the same time showing more respect toward those on the right. They appear to be backing away from their hard-line liberal bias. Some are now softening their tone toward conservative causes, although we still hear their favorite term, "Rightwing Conspiracy" for too often. The changes are subtle and may not be noticeable to the public, but The Club's monitoring team continues to point out changes at our monthly meetings.

Due to operation *Chimney Sweep* combined with efforts by *The Apprentice*—a title bestowed by the director on my adopted daughter and her fiancé, now her husband—several public servants retired and a few are serving prison terms.

With the help of Holly Voorhees, Genesis is preparing to take on education and Hollywood. At the same time we will increase pressure on corrupt government officials and the media.

More assassinations are likely. All too often there is no other solution. The Club does not hesitate to hand down the proper sentence to traitors when the courts refuse to do their duty.